KING PENGUIN

BIRTHSTONE

D. M. Thomas was born in Cornwall in 1935. He was educated there, in Australia and at New College, Oxford, where he gained a first in English. He has been a teacher and lecturer, and is now a full-time writer. His first novel, *The Flute-Player*, won the Gollancz/Pan/Picador Fantasy Award. His most recent novel, *The White Hotel* (Penguin, 1981), which received the 1981 Cheltenham Prize, is an international bestseller. He has published five volumes of verse, including *The Honeymoon Voyage* and *Dreaming in Bronze*, and is also well known for his translations of Russian poetry, including *The Bronze Horseman and Other Poems* by Alexander Pushkin (Penguin, 1982). He has also won a Cholmondeley Award for Poetry, an Arts Council Award for Literature and the *Los Angeles Times* Fiction Prize. He has three children and lives in Hereford.

D. M. THOMAS

Birthstone

A KING PENGUIN

PUBLISHED BY PENGUIN BOOKS

Penguin Books Ltd, Harmondsworth, Middlesex, England
Penguin Books, 625 Madison Avenue, New York, New York 10022, U.S.A.
Penguin Books Australia Ltd, Ringwood, Victoria, Australia
Penguin Books Canada Ltd, 2801 John Street, Markham, Ontario, Canada L3R 1B4
Penguin Books (N.Z.) Ltd, 182–190 Wairau Road, Auckland 10, New Zealand

First published by Victor Gollancz Ltd 1980
This revised edition first published in Penguin Books 1982

Made and printed in Great Britain by
Richard Clay (The Chaucer Press) Ltd, Bungay, Suffolk
Set in VIP Imprint

AUTHOR'S NOTE AND DEDICATION

This novel is dedicated to Elizabeth Ashworth, friend and fellow poet, who collaborated with me in the first stages of composition, until pressure of other work compelled her to withdraw. I gladly take this opportunity to thank her for her creative contribution to the embryonic stages of *Birthstone*.

D.M.T.

1

My elderly companion was in some distress, and I offered her my *Daily Mail* to fan herself with. We had joined a slow line of caravans and heavy lorries, and the sun poured down oppressively through the glass top. On a reverberating haul uphill, west of Exeter, under tall and stifling trees, one of the old ladies almost died. Her son gave a strongly American yelp, and had picked his mother up in his arms and was bounding with her towards the door. At first I thought he was carrying a child, it was such a frail bundle he held so lightly and tenderly.

The lanky American leapt out as the coach halted, and laid his mother on a grassy patch under the trees. I joined the driver and a couple of young couples outside, to see if I could help. The lizard-face stared lifelessly up at her middle-aged son. 'I think she's gone,' he said to us, with a kind of owlishly embarrassed smile, as if not wanting totally to destroy the holiday mood. I crouched beside him, suggesting he moisten her lips from my Cola can. 'She so much wanted to see Cornwall,' he said. The old lady was coming round; gasping for breath, lifted up to accept the Cola. A little pink came into her yellow cheeks. 'Gee, I'm sorry to be so much trouble,' she said. A transporter driver on our tail honked, and our young driver gave him a V-sign. The old lady was being helped to her feet and soon, with her son's assistance, she was able to climb shakily back into the coach.

Our slow progress resumed. The driver turned on some light music, which seemed to cool and soothe the old people a little. An hour or so later we stopped for tea and a small waterfall, somewhere on Dartmoor. I hung behind in the queue moving up the aisle. I had noticed Andy looking at me in his driving mirror. His V-sign to the impatient lorry driver had taken my fancy, and since he would be standing at the steps helping down the moribunds, I was hoping I could share a table with him.

I felt my wrist being tugged. I looked down to find the sick old lady gazing up at me with rheumy eyes glistening with tears. 'Can you help me, honey?' Her turkey-throat wobbled and gave me a vision of my old age. 'What's the matter?' I asked. 'I've lost one of the stones out of my eternity ring,' she said, holding up her left hand. I slid from the plain gold wedding ring and the diamond

7

engagement ring, deeply entrenched in her puffy finger, to the ring of sapphires on her middle finger. Her son – jack-knifed and groping – straightened and met my eyes. 'My father gave it to her just before he died,' he explained. 'It means a lot to her.' This remark brought on more crying from the old woman and I offered her a tissue from my handbag. 'Don't worry,' I said, 'we'll find it.' 'It could be anywhere with all these people tramping past,' the old lady snuffled. 'It could have stuck to one of their shoes.' I soothed her, saying I didn't see how it could have dropped into the aisle.

The coach was clear, and I scrambled round on my hands and knees among the sweet papers and cigarette stubs and other detritus. One or two people started drifting back. 'Now you go and get some tea,' said the old lady. 'You've been an angel. We won't find it.' 'I don't want any tea,' I said. 'I just hope you didn't lose it back there on the roadside.'

'Eureka!' said her lanky son, grinning, holding up the sapphire between finger and thumb. 'It was in my pants cuff!' His mother cried a bit more, for joy; wrapped it carefully in my tissue and put it in her handbag. I flew out of the coach as the driver jumped back in, and had time only to join the line for the toilet. It disturbed me that I felt bad-tempered.

Boscastle was a nightmare of bodies. The Tibetan screaming skull in the Witches' Museum was nothing compared to mine. I wanted to flit into the ghost-house, a glorified birdcage made of black thread and wire, a kind of rest room for perturbed spirits. And at our next stop, St Nectan's Glen, a gloomy damp defile under oppressive trees and rocks, I developed a bad headache. Where a shimmering cascade fell into a rock basin – St Nectan's Kieve – I saw the ghost-house again, suspended in the misty water. There was a small boy in the birdcage. The guidebook said two old ladies had lived in a cottage near this kieve. One had died and the other had sat by her corpse until she, too, was dead. Their corpses were found months later. I wondered who would find my body, when I died alone in some bedsit.

At the mock-Arthurian hotel in mock-Arthurian Tintagel, I didn't eat dinner. But after, in the bar, Hector, the lanky American, bought me a drink. He talked, somewhat tediously, about the College in California where he worked. I gathered that his field was astronomy. I told him I worked in a school, but I didn't go into details. He simply nodded, without interest. I inquired after his mother. 'She's at rest,' he sighed, glancing up. I noted, like rest room, another strange Americanism. I asked him if she'd be well enough to travel tomorrow. He looked gloomy, uncomfortable. 'I guess so. She's terribly stubborn. I guess she hasn't got long to go and she's determined to make the most of every minute.' I said I was sorry, and glanced around to see if Andy had come out from dinner. I guessed Hector to be in his late forties, and staid with it. His serious, prim manner did little for me. Crewcut and gangling, he stared down at me as though at a stellar photograph that showed puzzling discrepancies.

When I went out early on the sabbath, with a vague thought of finding a church, to say a thankful prayer for being alive, I was surprised to see Hector on the tennis court, playing against Andy the driver. Hector was bounding around with boyish enthusiasm and amazing energy, a cross between Bjorn Borg and Jacques Tati. In shining whites, against Andy's everyday jeans, he looked much younger than I had taken him for. Clearly he knew how to play, and was thrashing his opponent off the court. Back home he played every day, he told me later, as he liked to keep in shape.

I visited the Camelot Snackbar, the Merlin Craftshop, the Mordred Bookshop, the Tristan and Isolde Boutique, the black contorted cliffs nothing could despoil. The massed clouds had covered the sun for good, but suddenly it blazed through, blinding me, enchanting the dull sea. It half created, half fitted in with, my awed sense of the randomness of experience. Not in my flawed life alone, but in all brief lives. I thought of the eternally winsome smallest child, Gretel, in *The Sound of Music*, killed in a car accident days after finishing the film. 'The sun has gone to sleep,' she lisped prophetically, 'and so must I.' Random and meaningless though it was, we hungered for it. I was glad it was my spirit and body taking the hot sun.

Craving a cigarette, I took the half-full packet out of my handbag and threw it over the cliff. This need for nicotine, continually suppressed and reawakened, was not the least of the miseries I had to endure. I hated the woman who was killing me by slow degrees.

I wondered what had made her choose such a holiday. A coach tour was bound to appeal mostly to the old. She had made a terrible mistake, and I wondered if I should break off. But it was paid for; that was a blessing, as well as an incentive to continue. I should take what I could from it. Relaxing, I lay back on the grass, shut my eyes, and enjoyed the bursts of warmth between shadows.

I must have stayed out there too long. I'm not good with watches. When I got back to the hotel the British Heritage moribunds were gazing wrathfully at me through the coach windows. Cheekily I sat in the empty seat by Andy. I asked him who had won the ladies' crown at Wimbledon, explaining that I'd been camping in Connemara all summer. Actually I wasn't sure where I'd been. I was pleased to find Virginia Wade had pulled her game together at last – mountainous Miss Stove's crushing of her in the first set was fresh in my memory – and took it as a good omen. Andy said that he was a student earning some holiday cash. I said he handled the coach like a professional, and also that I liked men with beards, especially if they had blue eyes. 'I go for younger men,' I said. 'That's a coincidence,' he said. 'I go for younger women.'

I returned to my proper seat. Bodmin Moor hurtling by was bleak and ugly. We blew a tyre on some broken glass and I enjoyed sitting on a wall and watching the driver sweat for an hour. But then I felt sorry for him and gave him my can of lager. It was not his fault if I had laid myself wide open. Unfortunately his insult had interested me in him even more, as so often happened. I still had romantic dreams about the car salesman who had called me an arsehole and pissed in my mouth. I felt my loins stir for the goodlooking rude young driver, and kept my eyes on his mirror to try to catch his glance. With the delay and the holiday queues, we were hours late reaching St Ives, and missed dinner. I didn't want to eat anyway. I climbed early into bed and wondered what I was doing and where I was going.

By morning a thick drizzle had set in. The great tourist mass drifted miserably from one cheap souvenir shop to the next, looking for something to remember. I visited the Barbara Hepworth house and garden museum, and felt more moved by the rough blocks still waiting for her dead hands than by the smooth finished sculptures. The uncouth granite seemed to be saying, What's keeping her?

When I trailed bedraggled into the hotel dining room, Hector genially summoned me to join them. Mrs Bolitho said they'd had a nice walk along the sea front and wasn't it nice that it was cooler? Hector said why didn't we hire a taxi and go look at some of the Bronze Age monuments for which this part of Cornwall was famous. We had a whole rest day in this place and there was little we could do in the rain. 'Are you interested in ley lines?' he asked. 'It depends what the line is,' I said brightly, lifting an eyebrow, and Hector said, 'There are supposed to be some especially good ones around here.' You couldn't expect a middle-aged American who goes on a touring-holiday with his white-haired mother to be attentive to puns.

In the taxi Mrs Bolitho explained that their forebears were Cornish emigrants who had moved to California in the last century, and their little community did Cornish things still, like baking saffron cake and singing Cornish carols from the bottom of mines. So she and Hector were fascinated at actually being in their home away from home. It was the high spot of their tour. In her Bermuda shorts and sallow skin she looked a true representative of American senior citizenship, ready for any new experience except the grave, any new country except old Tir nan Og. Hector, in his neat brown suit and yellow roll-neck sweater, an umbrella hanging from his arm (the drizzle had ceased), had to carry his mother over the stile that led from a bumpy lane to the heart of the moorland where something called the Men-an-Tol awaited us.

We stood around it, Hector breathing heavily from helping his mother. It was a granite ring with a neat hole drilled through it, just big enough to crawl through. Like the handle of a trapdoor, but set in short grass dotted with clumps of sheep droppings. Facing the hole, one on each side, were two granite posts about four feet high. There was nothing around except patches of heather and furze, and one or two boulders. On the raised horizon, like a closed fist with the index finger lifted, was the outline of one of the old tin-mining engine houses. There was a sense of wind blowing over the grass, as there always is on a moor even on the stillest day. Full of hotel cabbage, I added to it, silently.

And here was this granite ring, sitting quietly in the silence every hour and every minute for the last four thousand years. 'What was it *for*?' I wailed; because I always want to know what things are for. Hector consulted his guidebook again. 'Sun disc. Or birthstone. And later, people used to crawl through to cure their ills.'

Mrs Bolitho got up from where she had been resting against one of the posts, and thumped her palm down on the Men-an-Tol. 'Old stone cunt,' she said, and chuckled. Swiftly and childishly, she apologized for her bad language. I said, 'It doesn't bother me.' Flushed, Hector started an earnest lecture on Bronze Age astronomy. I felt sorry for him, and warmed to his dryness up on these moors. I hoped a nice view of my snug-jeaned arse would cheer him as I scrambled through the stone. Then we had a vision of Bronze Age stocking-tops, peeping from under Bermudas, as the old lady got down on her hands and knees and Hector, cackling, pushed her through. She reminded me a little of Gagool, the ancient bald crone in *King Solomon's Mines*, trying to wriggle under the rock before it crushed her.

I snapped them with my old box camera; and then Mrs Bolitho, struggling with a light meter, had difficulty fitting people and stone in. 'Give Jo a big hug, honey,' she said. Genially he did as she asked, and squeezed my shoulder, as though the sight of my

11

wriggling bum had touched something in him. Weak sun made us squint. She kept us waiting so long, I giggled, grew coy, tried to run away. Grinning, Hector wrestled me into staying. The trouble with having lost so many years is that I *do* so often feel and behave like a teenager. I suppose I was giggly because I felt something momentous in the moment. Mrs Bolitho's arthritic hand trembled and squeezed.

'That finishes the reel,' said Hector, inspecting the camera. 'I guess we took a lot in Bath and Glastonbury. Maybe we can get them developed some place along the way – if we stop anywhere long enough to sneeze, that is.' He added in rather a sarcastic tone, though still with a pleasant smile: 'At least you'll have some *up-to-date* pictures of yourself, Jo.' As I had no idea what he was talking about, I kept quiet, though I felt my cheeks redden. His mother said, 'Hec!' admonishingly. I tried desperately to work it out. Could Joanne have got talking to them earlier in the trip, and maybe shown them – what? The twenty-year-old 'bathing beauty' snaps I'd found in my bag? It was alarming, the thought that she might have talked to the Bolithos. And shown them snaps that could only have emphasized the effects of the passing years. Hector squeezed my arm and said he only meant I'd have some nice colour photos to remind me of the vacation. I felt weak with relief, and had to rest against one of the upright stones.

'We don't have anything like this back home,' the old lady sighed. 'Do we, Hec?' We agreed there was something moving and mysterious about the stones, and it would be a nice idea to drop in at a village pub for a chat with the locals. They'd be able to tell us more. Our young taxi driver surely wouldn't object to a couple of quick Scotches. Thirsty for knowledge and a bourbon, in Hector's lumbering phrase, we moved back through the furze clumps, over the short grass. At the stile, Hector again did his reverse-pietà bit, scooping her up with 'Come along, Momma! Upsadaisy!' as though lifting a tired child. Patiently he helped her down the stony lane to the grass verge.

Our taxi was no longer there. The old-fashioned black limousine had turned into a green Viva from which a man and woman were climbing. Since we owed the driver several pounds by this time, it was inexplicable where or why he had gone. We stayed around a while, thinking he might be filling up with petrol or something. Carelessly the couple in the Viva had left their keys in the ignition, and I had an impulse to leap in and drive away. I like the freedom of cars; the thing I most regretted about poverty was that I couldn't have one. We remembered passing through a village a mile or so up the road, called Madron according to Hector's map, on our way from the Merry Maidens and Pipers of Lamorna. We headed back for it.

I had to admire the old girl's pluck. She, so frail before, was now 'springing' along – I had to stride out to keep up with her – in a way that it would be footling to ascribe entirely to the vision of Scotch on the rocks.

It was drizzling again and seemed more like a winter dusk as we reached Madron, though it was just opening time. There were a couple of working men chatting to the stout barmaid in the little pub. We perched on stools; Hector ordered our drinks. We said we'd lost our cab, and were met by a kind of joyful compassion. I was tremendously impressed by the lurid erotic imaginations of these Cornish folk. Practically every remark, however innocent, was climaxed with sexual innuendo. It did not matter whether they were addressing Hector, or Mrs Bolitho, or me. 'There's *somethin'* funny there, my handsome' (of the mysterious hole). 'I'll 'ave the same as you, my lover.' 'Whereabouts in Cornwall did they come from, my sweetheart?' It was the same among themselves. 'Missus'll give me stick when I get home. See 'ee 'gain, my cock.' 'All right, my bird, see 'ee 'gain.' And it was the barmaid who was 'my cock'; as though she wore a dildo under her broad floral dress. It was all done without flickering their eyes, even. Yet the endearments kept dropping luridly in the smoky air. Mrs Bolitho was flushed, laughed excitedly at their dry humour, and responded with an aged flirtatiousness that delighted them. She was thrilled, she said, at how easily they understood what she and Hector were saying – better than most *Americans* did. Hector nodded agreement, saying he guessed they spoke a kind of American Cornish; his students thought he spoke a very strange dialect.

There was a bad moment when I went to the toilet and found myself in a kiosk, putting a phone down. Not knowing where I was, I was frightened, wondering if twenty years or something had gone by. But I saw a pub sign and was reassured.

We caught a bus into Penzance, where we could make a connection to St Ives. Terrifying hairpin bends in the dark didn't curb Mrs Bolitho's excited chatter. Hector, his close-cropped nape in front of us, seemed lost in his own dreamworld. Waiting at the bus station in Penzance and eating fish and chips from a paper, Hector said he felt like opting out of the tour and staying on in St Ives for a week or so. There was so much that was beautiful. 'I guess we'd be missing a few nice spots, but this is what we really came west for.' Mrs Bolitho was quick to show her enthusiasm. 'That's a wonderful idea, honey. Oh, I'd love it!' The hotel rooms in St Ives were nice – hers even had colour TV. It probably wouldn't be expensive; and even if it was – it was likely to be the last real holiday she'd ever have. Hector and I looked at our shoes.

Hector lifted his gaze and met mine. 'Will you go along with that?' he demanded. I was startled; it hadn't occurred to me I was in on the deal. I said I didn't know. 'Naturally I'll pick up the check,' said Hector. His mother placed her knotted old hand on my arm. 'You'd be doing us a very great favour.' She looked me coyly in the eye and whispered, for him to hear, 'Hector thinks you're a real English rose!' I was about to say I was an Irish rose, but stopped; I don't quite know what I am. I said they ought to think twice before inviting a strange lady to share their holiday. Hector choked on a fishbone. 'I guess we've already made that decision, honey,' said Mrs Bolitho. I was touched by the implied compliment. I'd have to think about it, I said; I really wanted to see Dorchester and Stonehenge. In truth I wasn't sure if I could keep up appearances. The incident of the phone kiosk had shaken my confidence.

While his mother was herself in a phone box, trying to ring some distant Cornish relatives, Hector put his fish and chip packet down on the bench and took my hands in his. 'I wish you would,' he said earnestly, looking into my eyes. 'Well,' I said, smiling, 'it looks like Fate, Hector!' 'At the end of the day it would be less tiring,' he said. 'It means a lot to her I should have some fun.'

I was a little stung by the way he put it; but I said, okay, if they were sure. His mother had come up beside us. 'That's wonderful, isn't it, Hec? I couldn't get them, honey, I'll try again tomorrow.' 'Wonderful, it really is,' he said, gulping the last bit of cod, and looking, in the dark shelter, curiously fishlike himself with his thrown-back head, open mouth and unblinking eyes.

Back at the hotel – Hector lingering at the reception-desk – I found myself accompanying the old lady to her room, at the rate of about three feet an hour. She was very tired. It was like unlocking Cheops' Tomb, I sat among the embalming fluids while she went to the toilet, in case she broke a hip or something. Through the open door I heard her groaning and grunting. 'We'll be wonderful company for each other, honey,' she gasped.

2

I did my usual morning inspection in the mirror; consoling myself with 'laughter lines', 'Rubens', 'puppy fat'. I found another grey hair among the red, and pulled it out. I sighed, thinking I was probably doing the right thing. Probably nobody but an ageing henpecked academic like Mr Bolitho could find me worth a second glance.

The American couple were on to their toast when I came in to breakfast. Hector greeted me with the news that we could not stay on at the hotel; as we might have expected, it was fully booked. But there'd been a stroke of luck. The hotel manager owned a holiday cottage near some place called St Just, not far from Land's End. The young couple staying there had had news, last night, of a family tragedy, and had driven home through the night. The cottage could be ours for the next week and a half. Hector said he'd clinched it there and then, and he hoped I approved. We could eat out, to save us slaving over a cooker; and he'd got them to ring a car-hire firm and there might be a chance of hiring one at the end of the week. Meantime there were buses.

I felt a shade uneasy about this rapid progress. From a coach party, to a threesome at a hotel, to a cottage all to ourselves, maybe miles from anywhere. And unease shot up to hysterical alarm when Hector added that there were two bedrooms, one with a double bed and one with twins, and he assumed (with a genial smile) we ladies would like to share. I stirred my coffee in silence, and his mother said hastily, 'Jo might want a little privacy, honey.' 'Oh sure!' said Hector; well, in that case, they could share a room. He stood, flourished his furled umbrella with that look of boyish embarrassment, and went off to fix transport and tell the driver of our changed plans. Lola (I had gone too far to refuse the intimacy) squeezed my arm and said I was looking radiant. She squeezed it again, and whispered, 'That was a really beautiful experience last night.' I concurred, burying myself in the bacon and egg.

We could go, said Hector, in the coach. It was setting off in a couple of hours, round the coast road to Land's End, and on back up the southern coast. It went through Pendeen (the little village where our cottage was). He'd seen Andy and explained that we'd lost our hearts – 'and an old taxicab, sweetheart!' Lola said,

15

grinning – and Andy was fine about it. He had even said he'd try to get us a rebate. He probably couldn't care a fuck, I thought, after shacking up on the beach with a little hippie girlfriend.

They went off to do some shopping, while I packed. It was going to be difficult carrying the Douanier Rousseau wall print I had bought: I admired it again – a beautiful sinister scene of a pine forest with a house islanded in snow in the foreground, from which a man and a woman, in harlequin costume, were emerging. They were dwarfed by immense black trees. The scene was bathed in the light of a full moon edged by a tiny black cloud in a clear sky. The image of a Clown reminded me of Dr Salmon, and I phoned through a telegram to him: AM STAYING WITH CORNWALL. LOVE, LEAR. He might not know about the holiday, and would need reassurance. It would also tell him it was me, since he knows I'm the Shakespeare fanatic. I pictured his crestfallen face: he was in love with Joanne.

I carried my case down and found Hector and Lola saying cheerio to our fellow travellers. Lola had fitted in a quick hair appointment. She'd had gold tints put into the grey, and looked awful. Imagining waking up to it every morning, I thought of backing out. Hector, carrying a string bag full of food packets and jars of orange juice, honey, etc., looked tired, and a little blue round the lips. I wondered about his heart. A man in his late forties shouldn't have to carry a Ph.D. and his mother across a stile and then a bag full of shopping. I wouldn't let him take my heavy case. I'm very strong though I try to disguise it in the interests of femininity. It was as much as he could do to heave their own luggage, and his mother, on board.

Lola was puffing and red in the face. She leaned back in her seat and talked to me over her shoulder. 'I think I overdid it yesterday. It's my blood pressure. Not good. I'm glad we don't have far to go, if it's going to be as hot as the trip down. I think we've made the right decision, don't you, Jo?'

Today was beautiful. Even the rocky brown hills, to our left as we travelled down the quiet coast, carried no cloud; and the sea was visible most of the time to our right, beyond the gently sloping, mild green fields, small and hedged with clean white stones – and stones too, 'growing' as it were, in the fields. The sea was a deeper blue than I can ever remember seeing, as tangible as the fields and hedges, bluer than the sea of Connemara. 'It's beautiful,' sighed Lola. 'I can see now why my great-grandpa loved it so.' 'What I love is the light,' chimed Hector. We were strolling around the village of Zennor, where the coach had stopped to let people have a drink at the Tinners' Arms and see the mermaid combing her hair on the pew of the church. And Hector was right, the light was really strange, clear – unbelievably lucid – and pearly at the same time. The light that never was on sea or land, but haunted this border between the two, like a changeling. 'It reminds me of Ethiopia,' I said. Lola's eyes stretched wide at the mention of a country she had never seen. 'You've been *there*?' 'Only on the astral plane.' Hector gave me an appreciative grin, and winked.

We consulted his wonderful guidebook on the mermaid in the church. It said that a mermaid had heard a village tenor, Matthew Trewella, singing in the choir. With her own song she had lured him down to the sea, where he dived in and drowned. And now they live together for ever. I saw him eating cod, like Hector. 'That's a beautiful story,' Lola sighed. 'We don't have old legends like that back home.' She was finding it hard going moving around in the heat, and she dragged on my arm. 'Sweetheart, do you know what the most wonderful word in the English language is? It's *love*. I read that in the *Digest* some time back and I thought, how true. Yes, the most wonderful word in the English language is love.'

I said I didn't think I knew what love was. Lola looked shocked. 'Gee, do you mean that? That's terrible, Jo. Don't you love your dear father and mother?'

I said they were dead.

'But you love them still, I should hope?'

I said I loved my father but my mother had been mad. 'I once held my hand out to be given a sweet and she gave me a spider instead.'

'Well, honey, she was giving you one of God's creatures, and it was probably better for your teeth. You must still love her. Even if she was unkind to you, you must still love her. "Honour thy father and mother all the days of thy life." I think the world of mine. I forgive my father his little weaknesses. We're none of us perfect, honey.' I walked on, bearing her dragging weight in silence. She asked me what my father had been, and I replied, a struck-off gynaecologist. I said it to get her off the subject of parents, and it worked, in so far as she started to talk about her prolapse, her blood pressure, her arthritis and her varicose veins. How boring other people's illnesses are.

I remarked how proud she must be of Hector. We were at the coach door and I pulled her up while Hector helped from behind. We sat together. 'I *am* proud of him,' she said, fanning her flushed face with her hand. He was wonderful to her, and deserved this vacation. 'How I wish his father could have come on this trip,' she

17

said, her eyes misting. 'He killed himself, you know.' It was my turn to look startled. 'How did it happen?' I asked. I had a quick vision of a gun at a temple. 'He worked himself to death. For thirty years that man never took a day off. Of course, he left a lot of money. But what can you do with money? Not a fucking thing. It was his heart, Jo. The day he died, I didn't want to live any more. Yet I wouldn't let the doctor give me a sleeping-pill, in case I didn't wake up. Now isn't that strange?

'Well, it taught me a lesson,' she continued. 'What's important is having a good time while we're here. I love this beautiful earth.' She smiled briskly and filled her chest and came out with 'Oh, what a beautiful morning', a cracked, shaking little musical phrase which brought heads turning to look at us. Mercifully she stopped, running out of breath.

We were dropped off at a bleak spot, opposite a terrace of granite cottages at right angles to the road. Parked on the grass-verge was the same green Viva we had seen near the Men-an-Tol. Crouching over the open bonnet, the thirtyish driver we had glimpsed getting out, and an A.A. man. The former stood up as we came across with our cases and bags. He had the look of someone who had run round a corner and crashed straight into a brick wall.

He led us – another appalling inconvenience to his sorrow – into the last cottage of the terrace. Slumped over a table, his wife was crying. He all but cried too, under his clipped cultured voice. They had left their year-old child, Cordelia – how I regretted my joke – at home with her gran, to get away on their own and because Mrs Johnson's mother loved having her. After their return from the Men-an-Tol and a supper out, they had found a telegram on the mat, telling them to ring urgently. From a box in the village they learned that the child had drowned in the bath while her grandmother was answering a phone call.

I imagined their state, last evening while we were having such a good time; but it was too painful to contemplate. The weeping woman would hate her mother till the day she died. They had wished, said Mr Johnson, to set off immediately, but by a crowning agony their car wouldn't start. The bored A.A. man who had taken his distracted call had assumed they were in St Just in Roseland – thirty miles away – not St Just in Penwith, and it had taken all night to sort out the mistake and send someone round. And now the man was not sure what was wrong; it wasn't just a flat battery, it was something electrical. He could start them, but how far would they get?

I felt so sorry for them, and so helpless, that I changed the course of events, retrospectively. I had not got talking with the Bolithos, or I had not asked the driver to stop at the Men-an-Tol sign. The whole trip had been an absurd attempt to solve, or escape from, the insoluble. If Joanne had not booked the tour, if she had not got on the coach at Victoria, the little girl would still be alive, for I firmly believe we are all a part of each other. If we had not gaped at holes, the grandmother would not have heard the phone ringing while she bathed Cordelia; she would not have had to search for the words to tell her daughter, when she rang, that the child was no more.

But we had done these things. Perhaps Mrs Johnson thought that, since we had in a trivial way benefited from their catastrophe, we were glad – or, greater horror still, had in some sense 'caused' it. I am prone to these absurd crises of conscience. I stood helpless and guilty before their grief. The half-bottle of brandy I'd bought in St Ives was open on the table and I was filling glasses.

The A.A. man walked in. It was as bad as he had feared. They would never reach Birmingham. The best he could suggest was to start them, drive behind them to the Penzance garage, and possibly they could fix it by late afternoon.

Mr and Mrs Johnson looked ready to break, incapable of taking a decision. Hector stepped in. 'Why don't I go with you, see you to the railroad station – there *is* one, I guess? – and you can get on the first possible train? I'll take your car to the garage and pick it up when it's fixed. We'll look after it for you. Maybe we can ship it back by rail, or you can come and pick it up later. At least you'd be on your way. The important thing' – putting his arm round Mr Johnson's shoulders – 'is to get you back to your daughter.'

'That's right, honey,' said Lola, caressing Mrs Johnson's hair; 'to your dear little girl.' There were tears in Lola's throat. Mrs Johnson clutched at Lola's hand, and nodded blindly. 'Use the car,' she said through her sobs. 'You need a car around here.' 'Of course, of course,' her husband added, distractedly circling the table. We packed the couple and their luggage in their car, and Lola said she'd go along too to keep Hector company while he was waiting around. I waved them off. Hector had his tennis whites with him and his racket, hoping he'd be able to strike up a game at the public courts he'd noticed while we waited for the bus. When they had gone, I unpacked, made a cup of coffee and cried into it.

All children are our own children. I couldn't help thinking of the little boy I'd had to pass into other people's hands. I found a vein,

19

and injected. My body had more holes than St Sebastian. But the pentathol was a miracle-worker. Since Dr Salmon had first tried us on it, two years ago, it had become much easier to survive from moment to moment. It had even brought us a little closer.

I decided to get some fresh air. On the way into Pendeen village I passed three fellows who grinned and winked. They were chalk-faced and overalled and had helmets with bicycle lamps. Potholers, I thought lyrically; then glimpsed above the slate roofs the headgear and smoke of a tin mine. I felt stupid. I turned right, past the mine, past grey, poor houses, down a road marked *To the lighthouse*. A short walk brought me to it. A sea mist was piling in – how quickly the weather could change – and as I reached the lighthouse its fog horn boomed, blasting my ears; and its glass turret of light began turning. I wished I'd brought my coat. I walked through a gate on to grass leading down to the cliff. Only a few yards down, I froze. Just a couple of steps to my right was the cliff edge and a sheer drop of a hundred feet: the cliff eaten away as if a slice of cake had been removed. As I turned back towards the safety of the booming, flashing lighthouse the shapes of disused mine stacks and engine houses lining the cliff were beginning to vanish in the mist.

'Are you *Cornish*, my lover?' said the lady in the village post office, after we'd chatted about inflation and the weather. She said she thought she could hear a trace of Cornish in my voice. I said it was probably a slight Irish lilt picked up from my parents. Her friendliness, following the potholers' winks, cheered me. I bought the last *Mail* in the rack, and an air-mail letter card.

I lay on my bed meditating on my horoscope. Then I tried to start a letter to Seamus. He's our brother, but we've never met him. He's a lot older, and having served in the war as a young pilot he settled in Rhodesia. Over the years we've exchanged Christmas cards but nothing else. His cards have changed from Seamus, to Seamus and Eileen, to Seamus, Eileen and Ian, to Seamus, Eileen, Ian and Hilary, and back to Seamus and Eileen. That's all I know about him. I'm always buying letter cards with the intention of making contact before it's too late, but I never get round to writing. Today, again, nothing would come. Instead, my thoughts turned into a poem:

> A child is dead.
> Sister, what does our horoscope tell us?
> The day is striped like my bathroom curtains.
> We have been to the lighthouse,

20

and three miners walking on a road
have told us with their smiles
that we are beautiful.

I trembled with pleasure when I read it through. It was the first poem I had written for over a year, and I could still do it. I especially liked the image of the bathroom curtains. Creative power seemed a compensation given to all disintegrated personalities (those drawings by Sybil that always made me shiver). We were like waste tips of rock, giving off rays. I was radiant, as Lola had said. As my wound was great, so was my bow strong. It was my day for holiday romance, and I'd do something with Hector, my bird, my cock.

3

'Not if you don't happen to have any balls.'

'It's okay,' I said. 'I don't mind.' I hugged him. He looked sick, as if I had unearthed a terrible secret.

'Really. It's all right.' We must talk it through later, I suggested; if he cared to trust me. Meanwhile I was going to have a bath.

'But you've *had* a bath,' he said. I felt confused, and explained that I love baths, because they were good for meditation, and I wanted to think quietly about what he'd told me. 'Don't worry,' I added. 'It doesn't upset me. I find it interesting – exciting.'

I put on my royal-blue trouser-suit with the gold belt and made myself up nicely.

Lola wasn't going to eat. She'd eaten a pasty at a Penzance pub that would see her through a week. Also she didn't want to miss the Waltons. 'I'm a great fan of the Waltons. I never miss them if I can help it – do I, honey? You wouldn't believe it but I passed up a show at your National Theatre last week so I could watch them! I'd seen the episode before, back home, but I still loved it. I think they're a wonderful family. Very genuine people. Do you watch it, dear?' I said I tried to avoid serials as I tended to get easily hooked and I never knew where I'd be. We left her settled in front of the set, a bag of peanuts beside her. I was pleased she was being sensitive to our feelings.

I had adolescent shivers on this our first night out alone together. Hector said he felt tired and I offered to drive. I felt guilty taking the wheel: so much had been stripped from the Johnsons in one

21

day. That was silly, though. Their thoughts would not be on their car left behind in Cornwall. I crawled through Pendeen; the mist, which had grown quite thick, was beginning to fall back again, but the dusk made driving difficult. I told Hector about the lighthouse and the sliced cliff. 'That must be the zawn,' he said. 'It's in the guide.'

We spoke of the Johnsons' tragedy, and I confessed my irrational guilt, my feeling that I'd somehow caused it because in a way it had been good luck for us. Hector said I wasn't alone in such feelings. There were still moments, he said, when he half believed he had caused his father's death.

He had gone to an observatory in Southern California, to research the data relating to colliding galaxies. (I didn't know such things existed.) Word of his father's death came through, and he had returned home. Three days after the funeral, he had watched the Northern State Baseball League championship: just to dull the edge of his grief. His local team, Grass Valley, had won the pennant; and the whimsical thought crept up on him that *thanks* to his father's death he had been able to watch the game. Every cloud had a silver lining. 'I knew it wasn't a *real* thought,' he said, 'but it keeps coming back and giving me the creeps.'

It was by far the longest speech I had yet wrested from Hector. I glanced at him from time to time as he spoke, slowly and earnestly: the dark profile against the clearing sky above the sea; one star coming through and the lighthouse flashing. I liked what I saw. I saw how such a man could be loved deeply.

In a little place called Trewellard we hesitated between a licensed restaurant and a 'Cornish Meadery' offering chicken in the basket. I rather liked the – through the window – quiet, lamplit atmosphere of the Tinminers' Tavern; but when we looked at the menu on the door, Hector commented that the price of a prawn cocktail was more than his forefathers earned, no doubt, for a whole week's slavery in the mines. 'I'd rather not eat here,' he said. 'Put it down to an innate puritanism.' The Meadery next door was noisier, and looked suitably puritanical: a square hulk, like a chapel.

The whole sky was now clear and brightly lit. Prolonging this moment of solitude, I slipped my arm through his, and exclaimed at the night sky. 'Do you know *all* the stars?' I asked; and he nodded. 'I know nothing, nothing.' I said. He pointed out Sirius, and then the constellation Orion. 'That's my favourite,' he said, 'The belted hunter.' It was an oddly wistful, lyrical phrase, for him, and spoken with the soft, tremulous twang I was beginning to

22

love. Then he indicated Capella, the Pleiades and Gemini. I was fascinated by this last group, because the myth held meaning for me: the stronger twin and the weaker, like Joe and me; for when we split off, he survived by standing firm like an oak, and I survived by bending like a reed.

We went in, to be hit by the noise. We found an empty pew – literally a pew – and rested our elbows on a barrel top. Clearly it didn't merely look like a chapel, it had been a chapel.

'Can you imagine, Hector,' I said, 'the effort it must take to convert a chapel? The kneelings, the cries of hallelujah, the threats of hellfire?' And now it was truly saved, and the pagan tourists, ourselves among them, were summoning chicken breasts, drinking mead 'the honeymoon drink' – I had felt it tactless to order it – and enjoying the attractions of waitresses dressed in long flowing robes coming round with wooden bowls of ice cream and chocolate sauce, and refilled carafes. I was aware of talking too much, too nervously. Hector was smiling wanly, playing with his wine glass, but brightening when the chicken arrived.

It was tender, and the wine (local apricot) was warming and heady, the atmosphere cheerful. It was a place you could bring children to, yet still have a drink and a good time. Hector spoke little between his munching, till I drew him out about stars and planets and things. He talked eagerly then. It had broken the ice. My hand rested on his as I drank in his knowledge. 'Teach me about the heavens, Hector,' I said. 'I love to be taught.' He said my enthusiasm was wonderful; he sure would. A flowing skirt served us more wine. Hector grinned up at her. 'Do you think she's pretty?' I smiled. 'Not so pretty as you,' he said. 'You must have been beautiful when you were young.'

I digested that in silence. When I looked up his aura had darkened. I asked him if he was well. 'Tired,' he said.

I returned to his 'wound'. I skirted round it gently and with lowered eyes, saying it made him more intriguing. As with Arthur's manly knights pricking over the plain, the last thing one needed to know was whether they had huge sexual organs, or even any at all (I was full of the paperback *Morte Arthur* I had bought). When I glanced up, Hector was holding his chest, and grimacing. 'I'm perfectly normal,' he whispered – or hissed. He winced, gave a kind of gasp. I recalled my fears about his heart.

'We'd better go,' he said, 'I'm sorry. I don't feel so well.'

His aura was grey. I was alarmed for him. He insisted he could walk without my arm, but he leaned on the counter while I paid the bill. 'I'll settle with you later,' he said, finding even these few words an effort. I thought of all the times my men had forgotten their wallets. This, though, was real, I got him outside and into the car. His tall frame, awkward in the small car, was jackknifed foetally, his head pressed to his raised knees as though this relieved the pain in his chest. I was glad the mist had cleared. I drove fast back along the zigzagging narrow road. Was he going to die on me in the car?

He leaned on me, his arm round my shoulder, and I got him inside. It was dark except for a lamp glowing in the living room. 'Brandy,' I said. 'No, no,' said Hector. 'Just help me upstairs and I'll be okay.' Gently I eased him up the stairs. He rested against me as I knocked on their bedroom door but it was already being opened from inside. Mrs Bolitho's startled face appeared, and the rest of her – looking, in her underwear, dumpier than I remembered from St Ives. Her heavily built bra flopped with a weight of breasts as they helped to take Hector's weight. I offered to run out and ring for a doctor, but the Americans thought rest was what he needed. They'd see how he felt in the morning.

I made some coffee, and added the last of the brandy. I thought I'd go for a stroll down to the lighthouse. I felt tense and alive with wine and – maybe – a vague sense of disappointment. The night was still clear, all his stars shining. I kept puzzling what Hector had meant by 'I'm perfectly normal'. Was he regretting his frankness to a stranger? Was he embarrassed? I could sympathize, but it was a pity. Truly I believed that sex without testicles, even without a penis too, could be more exciting. It would be up to me to prove it to him. I tried to work out what wars we'd had in the last twenty or thirty years. Perhaps he'd been wounded in Korea.

The great light flashed, the fog horn was silent. I looked out to sea. In the darkness I caught an echoing light flashing simultaneously, and a suggestion – it was no more – of the outlines of mine stacks and engine houses, out there on the water. Some trick of the faded light was mirroring the coast. 'It must be a fata morgana,' I said to myself, pleased with the phrase. It was one for my record of synchronicities. I'd been reading of Morgan le Fay, Arthur's half-sister, the enchantress.

I felt drawn to the zawn, but fearing to go in the dark, turned back. There was no light in Hector's and Lola's bedroom, and silence. I assumed he must be all right. I went upstairs very quietly and did my evening countdown. I had beautiful hair and eyes, still. And my breasts were youthful. I felt them draw taut as I stretched out in bed, and thought of the Johnsons, after their ghastly journey, lying together like effigies. True, I had terrible problems;

24

but I wasn't alone. Personalities split off because one person alone couldn't cope with an intolerable reality; yet was any reality tolerable?

I tried to say a prayer for Hector and me. The thought of the possibility of happiness brought on the night-terror, the zawn-terror, that I might go to sleep and never wake up, and never know that I had not woken up.

I was standing with Hector on a hotel balcony overlooking a lake. Through binoculars he was looking for colliding galaxies. Idiots, he said, they've gone through a red light. That meant he could marry me, but only morganatically.

I heard the lavatory flush, and met Lola in her housecoat. Her hair hung fresh – that's the only word – and glistening: she had washed it and brought out the gold highlights she had had put in at St Ives. It, and her cotton housecoat, pale blue, made her look almost girlish. We pecked a kiss. Hector, she said, wasn't up yet but felt better.

When I hadn't come down to breakfast, about an hour later, she came up to see if anything was wrong, and found me sitting on the bed in tears. 'What's the matter, honey?' she asked anxiously, sitting and putting her arm round me. I told her I was depressed because I felt fat and horrible, and she said why didn't I go with her to the beauty parlour and get my hair done and my chin lifted; that when one was no longer a spring chicken one needed a little morale boost from time to time. Her words weren't a great comfort. I think she sensed it; she went to the window, saying it was a beautiful day and the sun would cheer me up. She hoped Hector would be okay; she was a great burden to him, but it would not be for much longer. Her chin trembled and she gazed out. I pulled myself together for her sake, gave her a big hug, and said she'd be good for years yet. 'You're only as old as you feel,' I told her brightly. But suddenly she was a very frail old lady with breakable bones and transparent skin, and nothing to look forward to.

She hobbled off downstairs; I dressed slowly, trying to compose myself. What actually had made me burst into tears was a message from Joanne. It was there when I opened my notebook to jot down my dream about Hector. I was used to my sister's snide malicious notes, as I was to her other gifts – the nicotine craving, the two pregnancies, the four doses of clap (the first at fifteen and the latest announced on my fortieth birthday). Most of this message was taken up, as usual lately, with complaints about our childhood. She even had the gall to claim she had voluntarily copped out because she couldn't take the flood of memories. Father came in for most of her insults ('Our farter will have much to answer for when he slumps at the bar of judgement'). I was tired of it. I knew, of course, that our kind of problem is supposed to be grounded in dreadful childhood events. I'd eagerly read all the popularized case-histories. Hattie, Sybil's mother, had stuck flashlights and buttonhooks up her little girl's vagina. ('Makes Sybil's home life seem like the von Trapps'.') But whatever shit was there, I couldn't see any advantage in dredging it up; nor did I believe it was that much shittier than most children have to contend with. All ponds would appear as deep as hell if their filth were cast, including Jesus Christ's. If we had caused irreparable harm – and we had – it was no good passing the buck. We're all murky, and so by definition were our parents.

If she had limited her attacks to Mother, I could have sympathized. Mother's pond *was* so filthy there was no bright water, just green scum and schizophrenic crocodiles. But her barbs against Father were unfair. For someone of his remote and cerebral nature, it must have been dreadful to have to cope with her replicating psychosis, and with us. No wonder he 'burst out' occasionally. Joe and Joanne's rebellion I left to their own conscience; I was happy that I had been able to show him some affection and bring him a little happiness.

I was used to these arrowheads, dipped in the poison of her own guilt. More immediately upsetting was her attack on Hector: 'I don't object to a fuck, if that's what you want, but if you plan on getting emotionally involved with this guy I won't answer for the consequences. I've already made my feelings clear, to *him*, by deeds not words. Shit! Taking his tennis whites when they'd lost their daughter! And they say *we're* crazy!' She justified her interference (the possibilities of which were blood-chilling) as a return for my throwing away her cigarettes: she had woken in the night, following our arrival at St Ives, to find a half-smoked joint but nothing else, and had spent an agonizing hour. Somehow she'd guessed, rightly, it was *I* who'd thrown the packet away, not Joe.

The other fearful novelty in my sister's screed was her claim that a new sister had resurrected under analysis: Joan. Joan had died around VJ day. Joanna announced the resurrection in her usual teasing, crossword-puzzle style. 'The Maid has appeared to the Dolphin, and she's his new blue-eyed doll. Time is short. You better catch up, kid, in the dark wood, nel mezzo del cammin. So we can perish together bravely. Enjoy your gloria swansong, your virginia lupine strolls.' She finished with abuse of my poem, all the

26

more vicious because, in addressing it to her, I had tried to be friendly. She had scribbled a poem of her own –

> The holed stone
> thinks no evil, speaks no evil,
> cures nothing, gives nothing birth.
> Let them come to me,
> walking across the moors.
> I have holes of deep magic.

Considering it as I put on my make-up, I felt consoled. If anything was 'pathetically self-deceiving' it was this. (It should have been, holes of deep gonorrhea.)

Hector was finishing his coffee in the sunny 'breakfast nook', as Lola called it. He greeted my descent enthusiastically: 'Boy! You look swell!' Feeling myself flush, I said it was only an old skirt and sweater; but I knew the straight black skirt and V-necked sweater had a slimming effect, and I was pleased he liked the result. Whatever Joanne had done, it had clearly not put him off me. He thanked me, rather bashfully, for helping him home. All that mattered, I said, was that he felt better. 'The pain's gone,' he said, touching his chest. 'I guess I still feel tired.' He looked drawn. I told him he should rest, in the cottage, but he insisted the Cornish air would do him far more good.

We swore off Cornish pasties. Not that they hadn't been warned, said Hector. A guy at the pub had told them they'd been invented because they were the only food women could drop down a mine shaft for their menfolk and it wouldn't break. No wonder he'd had heartburn. 'You stick to mine, honey, huh?' said Lola, ruffling his hair. I said it would be better for all of us to eat in, generally. If we bought some beef and stuff somewhere, I could make Boeuf Stroganoff for us tonight. They didn't hear me; Hector was buried in his guidebook, and Lola was bustling around cutting sandwiches and filling thermoses. Her American energy, careless of the years, pleased and depressed me.

We decided we would visit the Logan Rock. It was so delicately balanced, said the guidebook, that the huge granite boulder could be made to tremble at a finger's touch. Or rather, that's what *used* to happen. Some crass naval lieutenant a hundred years ago had shifted the rock with pulleys, and destroyed the balance. But it was still a beauty spot, and you could pretend.

A chink of bottles and a rap at the door, which Lola answered. I heard the milkman's enquiry after Mrs Johnson, and Lola's brief explanation. A concerned 'I'm some sorry to hear that', followed in a moment by a breezy 'Some 'andsome weather, in a', you?' Lola called to ask how much I thought we needed, and I joined her, nibbling a piece of toast. 'Couple of pints, is it?' asked the milkman, his eyes twinkling at my breasts. 'No, I guess we better have – four, honey?' said Lola to me, seriously. 'Hector likes a milky drink at night.' I twinkled back at the milkman; and felt uplifted.

4

It *was* handsome weather. All day, only wisps of cloud interrupting the blue, but with a gentle cooling breeze around the coast. Snug in our borrowed Viva, we drove – I drove, to Hector's instructions – unhurriedly from spot to spot. We struck south across the Penwith moor, enjoying, as we crested the moor, the splendour of Mount's Bay off Penzance, its immense clear blueness 'charmed' by St Michael's Mount, a tiny offshore island rising into a monastery or some kind of fortress. Milton's 'great vision of the guarded mount' certainly described its magical, veiled, shimmering quality. His angel was there. We branched off right to avoid the holiday jams of Penzance, crept sluggishly uphill again through Newlyn behind a heavy brewers' lorry, passed a black taxi speeding down into Penzance that I thought for a moment was the one we might still be waiting for, and levelled off through narrow and quieter roads west.

We stopped for a shandy at the pub in Paul hamlet (Lola's quaint phrase, which I said sounded like a cousin of the famous prince); glanced at a memorial tablet to Doll Pentreath, the last native speaker of Cornish, that we found in the church wall opposite; and walked downhill the short distance to Mousehole. We sat for a while on the quay of the impossibly crowded old fishing village. A Glaswegian holiday-maker had caught a baby shark, and a crowd had gathered round. It was probably the finest moment of his life. I took a snap of him, and the baskers in his glory. Sun dazzled on the water, between lolling boats. We agreed it was all so beautiful we must come back when it was quieter.

In the short time we were there, Lola contrived to embarrass us. She got talking to two fishermen landing their catch. What fish was it? she asked. Mackerel, they told her. Lola told them it sure as hell was not mackerel – she bought mackerel at her local market – it was a different fish altogether. One of the fishermen rubbed his stubble. 'Well, missus, we been took in,' he said sadly. 'We been

28

catchin' they all summer and we thought they was mackerel.' He gave me an imperceptible wink. I turned away, ashamed. Hector was walking away from his mother. He was blushing. I felt very sorry for him.

Having coped bravely so far, Hector became distressed at the climb back up the hill. Deceptively quick and easy had been the walk down, but it was, in fact, a very steep hill. I wished for his sake we had brought the car down – or missed this place altogether, since we would never have been able to park on the quay, and the village roads were more like the narrow passageways of Venice. I lingered behind with him. Ahead, Lola sang short gasping spasms of *The Sound of Music*, and was soon lost to view round a bend. Puffing, Hector had to stop every few yards, turn and pretend to be admiring the view of Mount's Bay beyond the roofs of Mousehole. I too wasn't sorry to rest on a wooden seat by the roadside halfway up; in fact, to spare him more embarrassment, I said I felt exhausted; was unfit, cockney born and bred. He collapsed beside me. 'It sure is a warm day,' he gasped.

I flapped my sweater to let the air get to my skin. The breeze that had been pleasant on the quay was not getting to us here; the sun was trapped by the tall hedges, the semi-tropical and luxuriant trees. I regretted wearing a swimsuit under my clothes, and my tights stuck to me. But Hector, in light slacks and shirt, was so obviously suffering more than I. I asked him if his heartburn had returned, but he said it hadn't. He was fine. Dubious about Joanne's glib explanation, I glanced down at his groin for about the tenth time that morning. It was hard to tell. But there was a becoming smoothness at the taut triangle of slack-creases and nothing to dispel the possibility that he might be as bland there as a doll.

As if to prove his fitness, he stood up swiftly and braced himself. Spotting a dead branch in the ditch he picked it up, trimmed it and, as we began labouring uphill again, used it as something between a walking stick and a crutch, in the manner of Robert Newton playing Long John Silver. 'Yo-ho-ho and a bottle of rum,' he croaked, rolling his eyes. 'I miss my umbrella. I'm naked without it.' The little comedy turn robbed him of breath and he had to stop to take deep gulps. Some half-a-dozen pauses and admiring looks at Mount's Bay later, we reached the church and the pub car park, where Lola rested against the bonnet and repaired her make-up. As Hector and his stick manoeuvred into the front seat I whispered to her, 'He's not at all well.' 'I know,' whispered Lola. 'I'm awfully worried about him.'

29

Hector, recovering, started perking up on the renewed drive southwards towards the Logan Rock. He followed his map and called out the stones we should look for: the Pipers, the phallic stones we had located on our first day; and the stone circle, the Merry Maidens, that went with them; but we didn't spot them this time. As young maids and randy pipers are, they were unpredictable creatures: some days we spotted them, some days we didn't.

What is the sex life of stones? I wondered.

We reached Treen, the nearest parking place for the Rock. A pub, a small Methodist chapel, terribly old and given-up, a shop, a pottery, three or four houses – Treen hamlet, as Lola would have said and whom I imagined a very pretty girl cousin, about twelve years old. We found a space in the car park, unloaded the picnic stuff, and set off for the cliffs. I felt good in the beautiful day, and hungry. I blessed Lola.

We walked the straight National Trust path between strips of almost-ripe corn. The invisible sea drawing me, I soon outstripped mother and son. It was a long walk but fortunately flat most of the way. They dwindled behind, out of sight. Family knots of tourists trailed back. I wasn't particularly surprised to glimpse Mr and Mrs Johnson, looking sunburnt and serene, moving back towards Treen from another part of the cliff. A part of them would obviously have stayed with their car, going whithersoever *it* went, continuing their enjoyable holiday and thereby annulling their daughter's tragic accident. The sea line beyond the bluff sent a lightsome spacious sense of its presence. The sun drenched me.

I paused by a gap in a hedge to let them catch up. Hector was animatedly talking to his jaunty mother. The wind blew her old-fashioned skirt up in a sudden gust, and she caught it with a giggle; an aged Monroe, with an all-American grin. They were surely discussing me, my square shoulders, my non-existent waistline, my ungainly walk. I felt estranged from them suddenly, and walked quickly on.

I couldn't help being sensitive. I was glad I was. Why was I always being criticized? Tears stung my eyes but I tried to fight them down, look at the scenery instead. The headland of the Logan Rock, though it could not have been more than two hundred yards long and a hundred wide, invited the isolation that descended on me. The greeny-blue sea, the violent high cliffs with tiny white nail-parings of beach, called one, now to the left flank of the headland, now to the right. And something else called one onwards to the pile of granite at the tip, where the balancing rock itself was hidden from all but the most intrepid. The grass under foot, and one's height above the slow breakers, created silence. Bathers and swimmers at Porthcurno, the next inlet towards Land's End, were silent, as were the herds of cattle grazing on the coast fields to the north. There was so much, and yet so little, to take in that it was difficult to walk around in couples or groups, to judge by the silent walkers. A few tourists sat on rugs or stretched out sun-bathing, but most drifted, slowly, alone, from point to point. The headland was calling everyone into his or her solitude. The steady, slow and silent dribble of people on and off the headland added to the sadness of its beauty.

I refused to eat, but took an apple away to munch. I went some way off and out of sight of them; though I could hear an occasional raised tone, or laughter. I squatted on a rock. Out to sea, white foam edged an unmoving ship. I wandered across the headland and sat on another rock. I caught on the wind Hector's voice, 'Jo', and then a pause, followed by laughter. I moved further towards the point, where I could not overhear them.

I felt sad and sole and destructive. I hated these humans who moved into my line of sight and out of it. I hated Lola with her pruriently billowing skirt and her coy aged hands pushing it down. I longed for Morgan le Fay's gift of turning people into the likeness of stones. Here on this headland we would not be missed.

And indeed the fat Lancastrian boy and his parents who came and spoke words near me had just returned from being stones. They had finished their thousand-year stint or something. The boy and his mother were more or less behaving normally, but the father, dazed in his long yellow cardigan, was still getting used to it and wondering where he was.

A woman was sitting on a rock, out of view of walkers, almost on the edge of a sheer drop. She was absorbed in writing postcards. Her face was bent over, very quiet and absorbed. It occurred to me – in the whimsical sense in which Hector had thought himself to blame for his father's death – that the perfect murder could take place when strangers or sisters were alone on a cliff edge. The sheer perversity of the act, the total lack of motive – perhaps even the existence of every motive not to – would ensure nothing but sympathy. I had no intention of toppling this woman to the foaming rocks below; but how easily it could be done if one wanted to.

I sat looking at the sea, its vast almost imperceptible surges, northwards along the jagged coast.

We swam in the clouding afternoon at Porthcurno; ate ice creams by the run-down tennis court as Hector enviously and contemptuously watched two young couples playing pat-a-ball

('Your whites should have dried fine, honey,' said Lola. 'Maybe you and Jo could knock a few balls around tomorrow?'); went back to the cottage to bath and change; and ended the day at the expensive Tinminers' Tavern (Lola had no sentimental qualms), followed by pleasant drinks and real tin miners – and fishermen – at the Trewellard Arms.

Lying lulled by the swish of wind and by the faint regular beams of light coming through the curtains, I heard a gentle knock and a soft 'Honey'. Lola wished me to open their window. Hector was already asleep and her wrists weren't strong enough. It was curious to see Hector asleep, humped awkwardly in the small bed, his mouth open. I raised the window. Air was certainly needed. Lola in her pink nightie was perched on her bed, rubbing in embrocation. Its sickly odour filled the room. I was glad I'd scotched the notion of sharing a room with her. I didn't know how he could stand going to bed in this odour of sweet crumbling senility. I sat with her for a while, massaging her painful wrists, and we chuckled in whispers about the jolly evening, and the Cornishmen's highly suggestive courtesies. She gave me a wet noisome kiss on the cheek before I left.

In my sleep the woman on the Logan Rock was broken into a thousand bone fragments lying on an auctioneer's table. They were white semi-precious stones brought up from a galleon salvaged off the Scilly Isles and I knew it was vital that I buy them, since I had sunk the ship. I would put them together with glue and she would shine as dazzling white as the sand of Porthcurno. But a huge boatman in his sea boots kept outbidding me. I cried in self-pity and anger, I couldn't bid any more, my purse was empty. I was relieved when the boatman got the bones knocked down to him since if the hammer had fallen to me I should have had to confess to being penniless.

The huge and jolly boatman gathered up all the bone pieces and slotted them into a piano accordion, which he proceeded to play with zest and charm. Everyone started singing. The woman had turned into a song, and I remembered in my dream a Red Indian dreamsong a visiting American professor of my (shortlived) College days had quoted to me as he pored quizzically over my vagina: 'I, the song, I walk here.' I knew she was happy to be absorbed into the piano accordion. I had done right to sink the ship, after all.

These last relieved thoughts came to me in half-sleep. It was faintly light. I knew I would have to get up, my bladder was uncomfortable. I got out of bed and met Lola in the passage. 'It's another wonderful morning,' she said. 'Why don't we go for a

32

swim?' So we went down the path to a little cove, stripped, and let ourselves splash into the sea. It was surprisingly warm for so early in the morning. I pissed blissfully into the sea, then we did the breast-stroke. Lola stood up in the waves. Her clitoris poked up between her thighs. She laughed. 'I don't mind if you sleep with Hector,' she said. I said, 'Does he have balls?' 'No,' she said, 'but he does have two cute little stones, that balance together like the logan stone.' It was faintly light. I knew I would have to get up, my bladder was uncomfortable. I got out of bed and went barefoot down the passage to the bathroom, and when I came back I recorded the accordion dream and the swimming dream before they could vanish.

The accordion-player was, in reality, scarcely half a boatman. Most of the time he was a lighthouse-keeper at Pendeen. We'd drunk with him at the Trewellard Arms. Someone had struck up a hymn tune, others had joined in, and from nowhere the lighthouse-keeper had produced an accordion that he happened to have with him. Lola had collared him, and Hector and I had to rescue him from her gush. He had bantered with me and chatted me up. I'd told him I liked young men with beards and blue eyes; but (tucking my arm in Hector's) I added that I liked mature men better. The young lighthouseman had invited us to look round his property: in one adroit movement saying 'Thank you, my 'and-some', as he stretched to take the pint from Hector's overstretched hand, and embracing both Lola and me in the offer yet singling me out with a laconic twinkle in his eyes. Lola said it would be wonderful, but I said I'd be afraid of stones. It wasn't just prudence; the idea frightened me. I would as soon have agreed to go into the sun. It would be terrible to find, even in a lighthouse, no light. 'If the salt have lost his savour, wherewith shall it be salted?'

After recording the accordion I dozed again for a while, and when I woke the morning had already clouded. Drizzle piled against the window, and the bedroom was damp and chilly. I felt, in a way, quite glad: I saw the three of us in front of a fire, closed off against the winter. I heard a comforting clatter of dishes downstairs. We could rest today; read and write; eat and drink before the cheerful electric fire. I enjoy cooking, when there's someone to cook for, and today would be my chance; I could make Boeuf Stroganoff, which

I do particularly well. We could get to know each other better, start to grow into a family. I saw the scene repeating itself in northern California: Lola cooking the flapjacks to feed Hector before he drove off into the snow; me coming downstairs to the warm kitchen, to help her and to see Hector off. Then in the course of time, when Lola died, I'd have learnt to cook the flapjacks. I wondered if astronomers went off to work at night, rather than in the morning. I'd ask him. It was quite important in terms of our intimate life.

When I got downstairs there was an air of imminent departure. Both were in their raincoats. Lola, stacking away the dishes, said frostily that she'd assumed I'd want to sleep on, after being out so late. I controlled my panic and didn't ask any questions. Questions are the great betrayers. Frightened, I watched myself calmly make tea, and sit with it. I listened intently to their curt conversation. I gathered they were waiting for a taxi, and it was late arriving; they had already missed the train they planned to catch. If the cab didn't get there soon, they would miss the next one, and have to wait hours. Lola was calling the cab-driver a motherfucking sonofabitch, and Hector, trying to pacify her, said maybe a lot of tourists were starting for home a day early, to avoid the Saturday jams, and maybe their cab had caught the resulting chaos.

It was a relief to know I'd only lost a day, but I was so full of terrified imaginings of what my impersonator had done that I had to hold my cup in both hands, and still it shook. Bit by bit I picked up that they were visiting Lola's distant relatives at Redruth, farmers called Uren. I knew they'd planned to call on them some day.

Seeing a hint of sunlight, Hector said maybe he ought to take his tennis gear after all. The dazzling whites were on the clothes-horse in the kitchenette, and I got up to fetch them for him. But Lola sprang to her feet like lightning, glaring at me, and fetched them herself. Hector put his racket on top of them in the holdall. They sat again in tense silence. Lola said curtly, 'Don't forget to take your balls this time,' and Hector muttered that he had them. My hollow belly caved deeper as I realized my mistake; Joanne had been right.

The glum silence was broken by the taxi-man's knock. I flew to the door to open it while they gathered their bags and baggage. But the breast-loving milkman stood there. His mood was doused. 'Some change in the weather 'day, in a', you?' He trudged off in his lifeboat kit. The fog horn boomed. Screw it, said Lola, unbuttoning her mac. Striving to keep my voice cool, I offered to drive them to the station. 'We don't want to interfere with your plans,' said Hector drily; then glanced queryingly at his mother, who shrugged an okay. While she was visiting the bathroom Hector melted a little. 'Don't take it personally,' he said. 'She's having a hot flush.'

It was a murky journey across the moor. St Michael's Mount, a blur in the grey bay, held no angel this morning, not even a fallen one. Nor did I. Hector, once, tried to lighten the atmosphere: 'I can smell the farm air already! It'll do us both good – huh, sweetheart?' – swivelling and smiling at his mother. Her face, in the car mirror, matched the horse pill she was swallowing. I risked asking how they planned to get back, offering to pick them up again from the station. Hector said they might stop over, if the weather stayed bad; and anyway they could take a cab. 'Huh!' snorted Lola. 'Hope you won't be lonely!' Hector grinned, with a droll sideways glance. 'A shame you're not coming with us; but we understand. I guess it can be a strain, being with the same people all the time.' I watched the oddball couple disappear, under his umbrella, into the station.

The drizzle had turned to solid rain from a black sky, and I drove back with the headlights on. The wipers were sluggish. I wondered if the battery or whatever was playing up again. Maybe the Viva was just extraordinarily responsive to human emotion. I drove much too fast on the narrow winding roads, wanting to see if my sister had written anything. I'd been afraid, earlier, to run upstairs and look in the notebook; but I might as well know the worst. I knew it was she because there was a fresh packet of Stuyvesants in my bag. The most that could be said was that she wouldn't have done anything violent or criminal, as Joe was capable of. On the other hand she was sexually obsessed and totally without morals. There was no limit to the harm she might have done in that sphere.

There was a scrap of paper trapped in the letter box, and pencilled on it were the words, 'Where 'ee to, my 'andsome?' I wasn't surprised. Inside, on the mat, was a blue air letter postmarked Penzance. I undressed and ran a bath, and didn't open the letter till I was well afloat. A bath helped to calm me at such times.

'Dear Jo,' it said,

I'm in the bar of the Pirates Rugby Club, shagged out.
I've been shagging all afternoon, under a blue sky, on a
cliff with one of the old mine houses lapping the water
while Tom's been lapping my cunt. An idyllic setting,
and I tingle still. Jesus, Jo, it was one of the, no three of
the, most beautiful fucks of my life. He's so *unjaded*, so

35

pure – he's a local preacher! and I'd guess he's a virgin, though he tries to make out he's a man of the world. There's this fresh-faced innocence, and yet it's all there, bursting to get out, and boy, it came! Things other men take for granted, like being sucked and putting a finger up their arse, had this extraordinary effect on him. And you should have seen him when I pushed his head down! Stout Cortez, with a wild sunrise. He didn't plan it, it happened. He was lying back telling me about some faith-healer in St Ives, and I practised the laying on of hands. I guess I kinda raped him, honey. One in the eye for your American friends – who I suspect, Lola anyway, may have encouraged him to take an interest in your spiritual and mental health (and maybe to get a rest) but didn't think he would take it so far. . . . He's had to go to a meeting (they're electing a captain), says he feels he's floating like a rugby bladder.

But I can't hold on at present. The bad things keep coming, even when we were fucking, Jo. You could be Joe reading this, or Joan, in which case – hi! But I think whoever arranges these things wants *you*, Jo, to, as I said, catch up. So catch up, but please don't *fuck* this up. Don't put all your eggs in Hector's basket, as you want to – I know you. I admit I set you up in the situation, it's my fault, and I'm sorry. If you must, screw him (in both senses) on the quiet, but let your light shine on the lighthouseman. You won't be disappointed. I can see from your dream you're interested in him. And for Christsake don't piss on him – hold back a little. Cleave to the handsome young Cornish cock. It's fated, I've read it in the cards.

I brought this air letter to write to Seamus, but I expect he's busy enough erecting electrified fences not to worry about me for a week or two. Isn't it frightening, Jo, to think Father's got a grandson out there, doubtless torturing the natives and thoroughly enjoying it . . . and who will beget others! It's the one consolation I have about my own son, that it won't happen, poor kid. Mother told me when she was dying (in her lucid moments between ophelian snatches in Gaelic) that Poppa first screwed her on a Sunday after church, by one of God's thousand blue glassy eyes. She'd just taken her first communion! Jesus, he liked them young! She had her honeymoon voyage on

36

the Rosslare–Fishguard ferry amid the stench of vomited Guinness. No wonder she was incapable of her own distress. He was mad too, Jo! it's the only charitable explanation. When I get things straight (this isn't connected) I want to write some stories based on that Witches' Museum – a witch in love with a warlock, a black witch and a white witch, ditto, a Spanish anjana-witch opening up her treasure chest to reward a kind act, etc. What do you think? Let's be friends. Love,   *Joanne*

I had anticipated the blue-movie scene with Tom. Joanne had enough Celtic witchery herself to ravish any man when she wanted to, and she usually wanted to. What shocked and upset me was the reference to the Witches' Museum, because it meant she either had an entry into my life or – at least – into my memories. This had never happened before. I had never felt so depleted. She usually had more life than I anyway, in terms of minutes and years. But when I lived, it was my own life. Now she had this two-way mirror, while I could only stare at my own fat reflection.

But I looked at my floating breasts amid the bath foam and felt a bit more cheerful. *I* was alive, and felt a certain confidence of continuity. I saw completely through the friendly tone: she was wheedling, desperate. As for the rugby-playing lighthouseman, I at least knew what I had to face, which rarely happens with us Poor Clares of a broken world. I'd tell Hector I only went out with Tom to make him jealous. I would get Hector. Shit on obsessions with the past. I had a right to a little happiness. Seamus had managed it. Whatever doubtful milk he sucked from Mother's nipple, and however uncertain his prospects of a tranquil old age, he had broken free, shown it was possible to achieve domestic happiness.

There was a little 'poem' in the notebook:

> He plays his accordion
> as he plays his woman.
> No strad
> but a bleddy handsome tune,
> bleddy handsome, you,
> God's truth
> you're bleddy right.
> His eyes twinkle and
> ash drops from his cigarette.

I sat in my housecoat, cross-legged in front of the fire, and brushed my hair. I enjoyed the luxury of having nothing to do but

37

sit, read and dream, on a wet day. My musings were broken by a knock on the door. I opened it to two bulky strangers. The bulky man-stranger resolved himself into Tom, without his beard. Irma Greuss said, did I want a taxi? Tom slid past me into the hall while I dealt with Irma.

There was confusion about the hour she should have arrived. Ten o'clock, I said; two, she insisted. I borrowed a couple of pounds from Tom to pay her off, and she shambled away in the rain. Tom lunged to kiss me and I turned my face at the last moment, and escaped into my lotus position in the sitting room. I explained why I hadn't been in to greet him earlier, and his blue eyes glinted at the thought of an empty house. I chirruped nervously about bad weather, hot flushes, faulty windscreens, incompetent taxi-drivers, and hair conditioners. He perched on a chair arm, lit a cigarette, dropped ash, gazed at me. We were both acutely aware I had nothing on under my housecoat. I asked him if he'd like a coffee, and leapt up to get it. He followed me into the kitchen and tried clumsily to get hold of me again. I stood stiff as he kissed my neck, then gently pushed him away. 'I'm tired, Tom,' I said.

'I don't wonder – it was a late night.'

I resumed the lotus, and buried my face in the coffee. Awkward and self-conscious, he sat again on the chair arm. Anyway, it was worth it, he said. It was bleddy good. He was glad I'd talked him into it. A wonderful experience. And all the better, he should think, for being out in the open, under the moon and the stars.

I mumbled into my hair and coffee.

Tom said he wouldn't want to go on living if *he* was castrated. I was taken aback, shocked that Joanne had revealed anything so personal, even about someone she didn't like. Hector would never forgive me if he knew. 'It isn't certain,' I muttered. 'And it needn't be castration or anything like that. Maybe it's a congenital deformity, or he could have been wounded in action.'

The young lighthouseman coughed into his cigarette. 'Well, he was wounded in action all right!' Then he looked puzzled. 'But we saw them coming up the cliff to cut them off. Because they were sleeping together. Did I get it all wrong?' I briefly saw Hector being set upon by lawless fishermen or wreckers, then it flashed into my mind what he was talking about. *Heloïse and Abelard* was playing at the Minnack, the open-air theatre on the cliffs above Porthcurno. I'd seen the notices, and suggested to Hector we might go some night.

'I was only joking.'

He breathed out smoke and threw his head back, amused with himself for having taken me seriously.

It was a bleddy good play, at any rate! I nodded agreement. But a good job you thought of taking a rug! 'Yes, it got really cold,' I said. He swooped to sit by me on the carpet. He nodded towards the window, where the rain pelted even harder. 'It'll be rained off tonight.' The rain became mixed with rattling sleet. 'What about this, then?' he chuckled, stroking his chin. I said, yes, I was wondering why he'd shaved it off, but hadn't liked to ask. Well, Mother was always on at him that it looked untidy; and I'd said I didn't *really* like beards much. So – He grinned. I pretended to agree with his mother and to find his clean-shaven chin an improvement. 'Why don't you try it then?' he suggested. I let him kiss me gently and stroke my hair. It would have been unkind, and odd, not to do so, after Joanne's gifts to him. But when he slid his hand under my housecoat I moved quickly away, and got up to sit in a chair.

Crestfallen, he asked me if I'd gone off him. That wasn't in question, I replied, meeting his gaze earnestly. And I begged him not to think that what we had shared had meant little to me. But for that very reason, because I cared for him a lot, I had decided we must put a stop to it. Otherwise I was likely to get hurt. I was fat and forty – much too old for him. He leapt across and sat on my chair arm. I didn't *act* like forty, he said (avoiding the fat part), and I had the beautiful hair of a young maiden. He stroked it to show what he meant. Yes, I said, but sooner or later he *would* see that I was too old, and by then it might be too late for me, I might be badly hurt.

He lowered his face, and sadly went on stroking my hair. I took his hand in both of mine, and comforted it. I saw the truth of my own lie. At the Trewellard Arms I had taken him to be in his early thirties, because of his worldly air, his banter, his bulk, his beard. Here, shorn of three of them, he had lost several years. It would have happened as I had foretold.

I could feel his tension easing, as I stroked his hand. He said he hoped we would be friends; and I gladly agreed. Would I still come to hear him preach on Sunday, he asked, and come to dinner after? His parents were looking forward to meeting me. I said I'd be glad to if he still wished it; and would his parents mind if I brought Hector too? The more the merrier! he said, after a short hesitation.

Now that we were good friends I could offer him a drink. I also boosted his self-esteem, after my hurtful rejection, by encouraging him to talk about his past love affairs. There was the young teacher from Nottingham, he said, last year, who night after night had fought him off at the last moment. Being a gentleman, he had stopped as soon as she asked him to. Then, on the very last night of her holiday, when the same thing happened, she had explained in exasperation that she had a rape fantasy and needed to be taken against her will. 'I hope you did, Tom,' I said, and he threw his head back in a hearty laugh: 'You're bleddy right!'

I was not ignorant of his charm. Indeed, as the afternoon wore on, it would have been easy to have fallen in with Joanne's choice, as I had done often enough before, as *she* had done often enough with mine. But my sister was right – I'm incorrigibly faithful, find it impossible to go with more than one man at once. Even though Hector, so far as I knew, had not even touched me, I felt 'committed' to seeing it through with him. I had been 'his', from the moment in the car when his dark profile had talked so sincerely about his innermost feelings: that dark profile framed by the dusk over the mine-laden coast. I'm the sort who can be faithful even when there is no response, no fulfilment. I'd have been a natural as Heloïse.

I asked Tom to tell me about the old mines. He glanced around the room and said, these used to be miners' cottages. He remembered being in this very room – as it was then – when he was brought in his mother's arms to visit a very old lady, 'Auntie Bessie'. She was nearly blind, and had given him a sour green apple, he recalled. The old lady had lost her husband in a terrible accident at the Levant Mine, round the turn of the century. Both of Tom's great-uncles had died in it too, when scarcely more than children. The man-engine had collapsed while the men were being brought up from their shift. The man-engine – in Tom's words – was 'a great iron beam, hundreds of feet long, down the shaft, with footholds every six feet. Pumped up and down six feet at a time. If the men were goin' down, they'd cling on for the downstroke, step back off on to little wood steps in the shaft wall, then step back on again for the next downstroke. Bleddy right, you! In the dark! Only their candles stuck on their hats. Some *thing* it was. Then one day the bugger broke in two. All the men were piled up at the bottom of the shaft. That was some disaster, *that* was. Took them days to get them out. And Auntie Bessie's husband was brought back *here*' – he nodded round the modernized room, his eyes aglow with the far-off drama.

When he had gone, with a hug from me for being so understanding, I baked a lemon meringue pie, which I knew Hector liked, and read from a paperback Emily Dickinson I'd found in my handbag.

I hardly noticed evening drawing in early, and the bang at the door shocked me. I expected Hector and Lola, and said 'Hi!' as I pulled the door open; but they had changed utterly, I was being asked if I was Catherine Joan MacDonagh, and my bowels gave way as they were saying how nice it would be if I would accompany them, etc., and I had to run up the stairs. The policewoman came racing up after me, and put a foot in to stop me closing the bathroom door. She kept her steely eye on me throughout; and continued to do so, as I fumbled my clothes on in the bedroom. She couldn't have fixed me with a more malevolent stare if I'd been Myra Hindley. Blonde, willowy and pretty, she glittered with the fury of Medusa. When I asked what I was supposed to have done she hissed, 'You're a shit-house. You ought to be hung. I'd put the rope round your neck myself.'

I was so out of control I gave myself a red moustache instead of lips. I looked at the pasty, double-chinned face in the mirror and wondered who I was. I wanted to tell her, 'Whatever I've done, it wasn't me.' I knew I had to pull myself together. I sent my mind across the moor, to the sloping field at Lamorna where the stone circle was. I sat cross-legged in the middle of the Merry Maiden stones. I felt quietened by the stone women of blurred identity.

The policeman waiting at the foot of the stairs wore a holster. I asked him if I could bring a friend, and while he hesitated I darted into the living room to pick up the Emily Dickinson. He grabbed it from me and examined it gingerly, as though it was a letter bomb about to explode in his face. Emily's wide and startled eyes grew wider and more startled under his touch. He handed it back, and I put it in my handbag. I hadn't read any of her poems before, having missed out on most of the American Literature course, but already I liked her and regarded her as a friend.

In the Panda car, where no one said a word, I had the queasy zawn-experience people must get when they know they're being driven somewhere to be killed, and can't do a thing about it. I also worried whether Hector and his mother had a key, should they return that night. I recognized Penzance, then Emily and I were being bundled out and whirled past a reception desk into a large deep freeze, where we were left, alone except for silent Medusa, for I don't know how long. Silently I asked Emily what I could have done, and she said it had to be Joe. Yet he hadn't been in real trouble since our spell in Borstal, and even in his young days he had done nothing to summon up Medusa; only speeding, car-thefts, minor larceny, drug offences. I shook with cold and fear, and so did Emily.

There was a bulky man in a double-breasted suit, who was quite kindly at first, glancing at some papers and enquiring politely if I was Catherine MacDonagh, and nodding amiably enough when I said I used my second name, Jo. With a puzzled glance at my grey sweater and black skirt, he showed me a photograph of four men playing cards in a pub I vaguely recognized as somewhere in Kilburn. Two of the men were in flak jackets and forage caps, and two in denim overalls. After staring dumbly at the photo for some time, I realized the two in overalls were women, mostly because their hair was cropped short. The kindly man pointed to one of them and asked me if it was me. I nodded. I asked him what I was supposed to have done, and he asked me to name the other persons. I couldn't. His placid face turned dull red and he thrust at me a sheet of notepaper. It was a short, passionate, badly-spelt love letter from Joe to someone called Moira. Shrugging, I agreed.

Her meagre features and round rimless glasses became familiar. I knew Joe was in love with her, and she with him. I recalled, between mountainous Miss Stove and my distressed companion on the coach journey, a few minutes when I shared a sleeping bag with the girl – she was in her late twenties – on the grassy slopes of a mountain. Maybe it was Snowdonia. I think they met at a women's group. I recall sitting cross-legged in a coven, in a bleak basement room somewhere, holding hands with her and another liberated sister, and chanting delicate spells, 'Nail their pricks to the floor' or something. Moira was a thin-lipped fanatic. She'd been sent from Belfast to join a Provisional cell in Kilburn. Whenever I found myself in her company, I had made a quick excuse to leave.

I said to the double-breasted officer there was no law against writing love letters to a girl. Brick-red, hardly able to articulate, he said it wasn't a question of love letters; did it please me that a child had been killed?

When I came to myself I was sobbing violently and his face was milder. I tried to say I, too, hated the Rose Dugdales and Ulrike Meinhofs of this world; women might be weak creatures but they ought at least to be stronger than men in compassion and gentleness. But when I said this I could see he had the shattered corpse of a child before his eyes; the knuckles were white as they gripped a pencil. It broke in two. I dried my eyes, my breath catching at times like a baby who has cried itself out. Quietly he asked if one of my great-uncles hadn't been executed in the Easter Rising. I nodded, but said we weren't all revolutionaries; much more important to me was that, also through my father, I traced a descent from Swift. Foolishly I quoted 'Savage indignation lacerates me . . .' His face went purple. 'Think of that lacerated kid, you bitch,' and strode out of the room. I asked the willowy blonde policewoman if I could go to the toilet. On the way along the corridor she rabbit-punched me in the kidneys, and I felt sick, so sick I just crouched on the toilet, holding my stomach, and forgot I had wanted to pee. When I was helped back, the double-breasted man started pounding the table and demanding confessions, and I was crying again.

He went out. A constable brought me a cup of tea and a sandwich, which I couldn't eat.

Then a thin, elderly, uniformed officer came in. He lit up a pipe, and was so pleasant I began to think it was all a mistake. 'How are you enjoyin' it down here?' he asked. Pendeen was a lovely little village. Quieter round there than here in Penzance; and as for St Ives . . .! He admired my silver shamrock brooch, genuinely, showing no trace of animus. He was so friendly I expected him to start calling me his handsome or his lover at any moment.

He had a pink folder in front of him. He started taking bits and pieces out of it, and handing them to me for comment, gently and genially, as if we were sharing holiday snaps. I saw they had been to my flat and searched it. There were a couple of badly-typed pages ending in mid-sentence. I glanced through it quickly and saw it was some kind of strangled argument about Marxism as a therapy for vaginismus, with offshoots into screams against imperialism. I confessed I was ashamed of it, adding that I really much preferred Spenser to Marx. I had to explain who Spenser was, and the nice policeman, re-lighting his pipe, said he loved reading too; he especially liked Arthur C. Clarke and John Wyndham, and did I enjoy their books? We had a literary conversation for a few minutes.

He slipped me photos and cuttings from my cardboard box. There was Joanne, semi-nude, in a ten-year-old copy of *Penthouse*, which made me blush. He said it was quite artistic, and he could see nothing wrong with it. A newspaper photo of my father, white-haired and wise, in front of a microphone at the Annual Dinner of the London Irish, just a few months before his death. The caption referred to the distinguished biochemist who had been knighted for

his contribution to DNA research. The nice policeman asked if I
didn't feel I was letting down the memory of such a man. I nodded,
choked. An old snap of my mother, still pretty, but fading and
apprehensive, her arm round the waist of a tall young man proud
of his Battle of Britain wings. Snaps of various boyfriends. A kind
of 'These are your Lives' – I couldn't see the point of it. Then
he slipped me a photo of a baby boy without arms, and I shrieked,
and blacked out. I was signing a long statement, the kind policeman was advising me not to get mixed up with villains again, and
to ring my doctor in London tomorrow. I think I remember
also the willowy blonde helping me to undress, at the cottage,
tucking me into bed almost tenderly, and bringing me a hot-water
bottle.

At the snack bar where I ate a toasted cheese sandwich the lady
said it was always quiet like this in Mousehole on a Saturday
morning, because most of the holidaymakers were either snagged-
up at Exeter trying to get in, or at Bodmin trying to get out. I sat
on the harbour wall, watching the fishing boats, the gulls. The few
people who strolled about didn't know whether to put on, or take
off, their macs. But it was pleasanter than at Pendeen, where the
sky had been black. On this peninsula there was usually, on one
coast or another, at least an illusion of brightness; and I was glad I
had found it today, on the south.

The red kiosk next to the public toilets kept attracting my
attention. I was drawn to ring Dr Salmon – he'd be at home,
waiting. He had both got me into, and out of, trouble. I could hear
him telling the police I was a hysteric, a disintegrated personality,
but not cold-bloodedly vicious. On the other hand, but for him
they would never have found me; for I assumed they had traced me
through the silly telegram I had sent him from the hotel.

His warm, dry voice would be comforting. He had been my most
constant friend for fifteen years; we had grown old together and he
might well painlessly expire one day while I lay, also dying, on the
couch. He was a compassionate man, who understood the need to
switch identity; after Dachau, he himself had never been able to
bear his old name, Solomon. It would be good to hear his infinite
relief, expressed as scolding. My hand lifted the phone to dial. But
he wouldn't be able to hide his disappointment that I was me. I put
the phone down.

A burst of warm sun started a heavy shower, and I wandered into
a harbour studio. I was very tempted by a graceful black unicorn's
head in terracotta. The spiral horn was separate, settling erogen-

44

ously into a hole in the head. I fingered my credit card, but I knew I really couldn't afford such an expensive thing. I settled for an ice cream cornet instead. In another studio there was a small exhibition in honour of Doll Pentreath, on the bi-centenary of her death. One of the pictures of her brought back to me startlingly a dream, from the forgetful hours between being tucked up in bed and pouring myself a coffee. In my dream I had brought a cup of milk to a dying woman propped up on pillows and wearing a nightcap. She had waved the milk away, irritably, muttering in some foreign language. I had thought the nightcap might be Hector's nightly milky drink – but there was old Doll, in the picture, hunched like my old woman, and wearing a lace nightcap.

Keenly I read the programme note on her. The last person to speak Cornish, she had eked out her last years selling fish, telling fortunes, and occasionally gabbling in Cornish to pompous visitors – a kind of aquarium specimen. Once, when a gentleman refused to believe anyone could still speak the ancient tongue, she burst into a torrent of Cornish abuse. I felt very drawn to her. If anyone lived on a peninsula, Dolly Pentreath did. We were sisters across the ages.

In increasingly pleasant sunshine I drove to Porthcurno. Tiredness and depression crept over me again as I sat on the white, damp sand. I was determined not to let the day die on me; and since there were few people about to see me I stripped to bra and pants and waded into the sea. Its iciness shocked away my depression. I felt languidly relaxed, and ready for anything. I swam out beyond the furthest swimmers and surfers. The bloomer-tucked grannies and trouser-rolled granddads paddling on the sea's edge had become sexless blurs. The surges started taking me like fairground waltzers. I was at the point where I wouldn't be able to make it back, yet I had no inclination to stop. I remembered Sylvia, and how she had swum out and out. It seemed a beautiful thing to do – not when I was suicidal but when I felt so good and *funny*, and in such lovely surroundings. I giggled. Everything was so good, it was immaterial whether you lived or died. Round the headland of the Logan Rock came a boat, skimming rapidly across my vision. Tom was there, crouched by the outboard motor, and there was a grey-haired lady in black who was probably Lola. She cradled someone in her lap. It seemed obvious they were sailing from the bitter salt lake of Loe Pool – I felt a little sad I would now never visit it – to the Scilly Isles, Avilon. The small boat vanished round the coast towards Land's End.

I was out in the realm of sharks and liners. I gave myself up to being drawn under. I collapsed on the hot sand, and lay panting, the dappled blue and white sky wheeled above me. Then I put on my dress and sat hugging my knees, staring out to sea.

Only Joe was a stronger swimmer than I, and it did not surprise me when his dream came into my head, a dream I knew I was dreaming. He dreamt it, I knew, recurrently, but wouldn't admit to it because it was an abortion dream. I was in bed, and two voices were whispering at my feet. One of them said, 'Let's get rid of her.' My feet were gripped and they were pulling me out between the brass bed rails. I clung on to the bed head, screaming. But they were too strong, they pulled me through.

Joe and I, being twins, shared the longest border. That meant we hated each other and feared each other. I hated his aggression, pigheadedness, humourlessness and intolerance. He hated my compliance, weakness, talent for distraction. But the guarded border brought us close. He was very close, now – so close that, for the first time, I felt we shared the same flesh at the same time. We conversed. I asked him about the explosion, and he grew very agitated, his body shook. Truly he hadn't known, he said, that human lives would be lost. I must believe him. He had only been on the edge of it – a couple of phone calls to safe houses. He'd even botched the calls up, which had contributed to his friends' capture. He wasn't sorry about that.

I accused him (at long last) of being a murderer already, killer of the foetus in my womb; it wasn't murder, he said, because the soul does not exist, it was just like putting down a rat. I said the oak already existed in the acorn. He accused me of bearing a child I was too sick to look after, even had he turned out normally; I admitted my sin, and accused him of mutilating me by having me sterilized; he said it was the only way to avoid further disasters, as Joanne and I weren't to be trusted. I confessed it was so. He accused me of the crime of loving men. I confessed it was so. I accused him of betraying our sex's dignity, and he said, look where our dignity has got us.

The tide had gone out a long way. Between that distant surf and me there was only a little boy in a yellow swimsuit, by a sand castle. I gave him a big smile (my heart tearing in two with grief) and slowly he turned his attention back to his sand castle, sinking on to his knees and turning his gaze aside. My stomach felt sore, and I wondered if the punch in my kidney had damaged my insides in some way. The weather had grown chilly, and I got up. As I stood, I saw a damp patch on the sand. I felt my skirt behind, and it was wet; there was blood on my hand and on my thighs. I cursed at my curse's coming, and so without warning. I opened my handbag to check if there might be a loose Tampax, and found instead the spiral horn from the unicorn I'd admired in Mousehole. Its tip had turned bright red.

I hobbled away up the beach, with one of Lola's hot flushes running through my skin. I didn't know which to be most shocked by – the violation, the sadism, the kleptomania or the exhibitionism. As if suspicion of terrorism wasn't enough. I could be in the dock for shop-lifting and indecency. I had a picture of me haemorrhaging on to a rubber sheet while two policemen took statements.

It was at least a minor consolation that I wasn't menstruating. It's quite a problem guessing where one is. Joanne and I used to keep a diary, but Joe wrecked that idea by drawing savage red stars all over the place. He'd blow up the moon if he could.

Somewhere on the way my brother had managed to buy, or steal, a pair of patched jeans, a holed fisherman's sweater, canvas shoes, a windcheater stuck with camping emblems. My clothes were lying on the back seat. I didn't want to risk facing Hector in this outfit, so I drove on past the cottage to a public toilet in Pendeen, where I changed. I rolled the men's clothes up into a bundle to carry in, if and when the coast was clear. There was no point antagonizing Joe by throwing them away. Already, in the morning, I had found a devastation in my bedroom – drawers pulled out and perfume bottles overturned – from his annoyance at not finding any clothes. At first I'd thought the fuzz had had a look round, but the sickly-sweet scent of hash confirmed it was Joe.

In general, we all found it paid to be as tolerant as possible. Usually Joe put up with our make-up and high heels; Joe and Joanne with my cooking-herbs; Joanne and I with Joe's grass; Joe and I with Joanne's cigarettes. We always suffered for our occasional destructive impulses, but sometimes we just couldn't help it.

My horoscope for the day had warned I would receive worrying news from a friend or relative. I found now, not Hector and Lola, but the worrying news: a card – picture of the Minack – from Joanne. It was postmarked Penzance, and must have been sent after I'd dropped Hector and Lola at the station:

So you passed up my date with Tom. You shit-house.
You don't deserve this book, but read and devour – she's
fucking good. The Times is bad – see Joe's pals caught on
the ferry running back to the grey sunken cunt. Is he

47

involved? Jesus fucking Christ. But you see, it's not all our
fault. There is a pain – so utter – It swallows substance
– up. Love   *Joanne*

Somebody – presumably a sorter or a postman – had scribbled over
the message, 'Contact the Penzance Elim Church.'

I put a hot-pot on. I read a few pages of *Sir Gawain and the Green
Knight*. I beat up some eggs to make a sponge. I turned on the
television news and saw Joe's friends with raincoats over their
heads. I was walking, in jeans and windcheater, at dusk through
the mine ruins. I stumbled over rusty gear, put my feet in wet
holes, threw stones into walled shafts. Seconds passed before I
heard the splash. The coast was as full of holes as the day. Blind
windows of engine houses, billions of tiny holes between the drizzle, holes opening and closing in the dark grey sea. Holes between
the fog-horn booms and the light flashes. The holes in my life and
in my heart.

The cottage was blacked out. Maybe the Americans had deserted
me. A cat, whom Lola had been feeding scraps, squirmed in ahead
of me. I gave it the cinders of hot-pot; it walked away in scorn. I sat
crossed-legged in front of a Saturday Movie. I woke to the blank
test card, and stubbed the disgusting joint. I stood up (I was stiff,
and my back hurt) to get the air-freshener. The ginger cat was
miaowing at the door and I went to let it out. There was a yellow
telegram under its paw. My heart thumped with fear. I let the cat
out and slit open the telegram. It said, BACK TOMORROW
(SUNDAY) HOPEFULLY. HECTOR NO BETTER. KEEP
HAVING FUN. LOVE LOLA.

I puzzled and worried over it. 'Hector no better' sounded
decidedly sinister; its illogical intrusion, its air of euphemism,
created visions of him in an intensive care unit, breathing oxygen,
dying, dead! He had been borne to Avilon. And how long had the
cable lain there unnoticed?

I rushed out, leaving the door swinging, and ran to the call box in
the village. There were several Urens in the directory (which made
me want to pee) but only one with a farm address in Redruth. A
sleepy operator dialled it for me, and it rang about twenty times
before a deep ill-tempered voice answered. Hector was not at all
poorly, he said; only tired, and a bit under the weather. He
couldn't imagine why Lola had alarmed us. They had thought it
wiser to rest up for a day, and return tomorrow. Lola wanted to go
to their little chapel in the morning. No, they hadn't got a doctor
for Hector, and there was no need whatever. They were both tired

and trying to sleep – and by implication of the gruff Cornish voice, so was Mr Uren. And so, doubtless, was Mrs Uren, feeding her fourth baby. I apologized again, hung up, and walked back feeling guilty and foolish. I had as usual done the wrong thing.

Joe was back, sneering at my concern for a bourgeois yankee rapist, when his mother was worth ten of him. Crying, I asked him how he could have hurt me so. He admired and touched my breasts, and wondered if my cunt was sore – putting the horn in quite tenderly, and gently moving it about. My vagina was very sore and dry, and I made him stop.

7

The sun dropping like a blood-orange and the moon rising like limeblossom honey. Stretching a golden strip over black waters. Nuns climbing up from the sea, chanting, and bearing flaming torches. 'Mexico!' he cried. Peter Abelard and I driving through mountains, round hairpin bends, tyres screeching. 'Let's fuck,' he said, 'the way colliding galaxies fuck, drifting through each other infinitely slowly. Let's find an inn, Miranda!'

Most admired Miranda, I was a mermaid ashamed of my smoothness, searching everywhere for a vagina. If I didn't have one, I'd never be able to get a man to marry me. The Arno flooded and I reached the wooden Magdalen by Donatello, who said to me, 'I'm full of holes, take one.' But she was too old and haggard. I found a hole in Emily Dickinson's stocking and I said, 'This will do, it's not used.' She said No it wasn't, and she didn't know why the stocking had a hole in it, as it was a St Michael's and they were usually reliable. Her leg, clothed in black lisle, rose out of the Loe Pool. Hector Berlioz was lying in bed, dying. Emily tried to save his life by pumping fly spray, but it wouldn't work. She stood with her back to the bed, legs apart, and bent double, tossing her petticoats over her head like a can-can dancer. With her two tiny hands she stretched wide her white buttocks, till her cunt glowed orange. Berlioz, springing up in bed, began thwacking her with his umbrella, and singing *Le Spectre de la rose*.

I enquired of her why she stood it. Her eyes wide, solemn and frightened, she said, 'People must have puddings.'

I dressed as soon as it was light, and walked in the brilliant morning to the call box. I wanted to apologize to the Urens for having disturbed their rest. Mr Uren was quite affable, and handed me over to Lola. She sounded buoyant, and pleased to hear my voice. Hector *was* still drained, it was true. She put it down to sheer mental exhaustion. But there was absolutely nothing to worry about. They had been puzzling like mad over the reason for my concern: had the cable really said 'Hector no better'? The solution *had* to be this: she had phoned the message through while the others were starting tea. The awfully friendly but muddled telephonist at the local exchange had had great difficulty interpreting Lola's accent. And Lola remembered having called out from the hall, at one point, 'Hector, no butter,' because she thought the rich Cornish farmhouse butter would be bad for him. The telephonist must have picked up her aside and misunderstood it.

Anyway, they were enjoying the rest, and Myrtle's (Mrs Uren's) plentiful hospitality, and would see me this evening. She was just off to church. So was I, I said. Did I want to talk to Hector? He was having breakfast in bed. I said No, and that I'd look forward to seeing them.

Not having a watch, I sat poised by the window, waiting for Tom to turn up, to take me to St Just where he was preaching. It must have been an hour before he arrived, driving a large van.

More lapsed than Lucifer, I fell by habit to my knees and crossed myself in God's gloomy house, which looked and felt as if it had been condemned, and the owner moved to a tower block. From wherever he and his hang-ups were, he rewarded my piety with a splinter, and a hole in my tights. I almost cried from vexation, because I had taken a lot of care to look respectable and nice, with my good green suit and my black court shoes. I was vexed enough already, at having to spend a beautiful morning pretending to be a Christian, with about a dozen elderly people in a building that could have held three hundred. During most of Tom's long extempore prayer I was trying to pull my tights up higher so that the hole would be hidden by my skirt. I didn't know any of the hymns; I watched Tom, singing lustily in the pulpit to augment the frail elderly voices. I couldn't 'place' him at all; where was the groper and fornicator, with accordion and fag? He seemed to have grown and got older with the voice of his calling.

When it came to the sermon he was a revelation, and as it happens his text was Revelation too: 'Blessed are the dead which die in the Lord.' I enjoyed his homely parables; and one in particular which he saved till the end. It seemed there was a Huguenot priest in the eighteenth century who was appointed by the Bishop of Exeter to the living of Lanteglos-with-Camelford in North Cornwall. The poor fellow thought Cornwall was the end of the earth (perhaps it was), and set off from Exeter with servants, horses and mules, loaded with bales of silk and books and barrels of wine enough to last him twenty years. Unfortunately he knew no English, and when he crossed the Tamar at Launceston he tried to ask the way, sometimes in Latin and sometimes in French, but could get no sense from the inhabitants. They kept telling him he was on the right road, and it wasn't far – just keep going. In Lanteglos itself they told him the same tale, pointing on down. For Cornishmen, said Tom, hate to disappoint anybody. (I could imagine it: 'Just down the road a bit o' way, my 'andsome ...' 'Keep on as you're goin', my lover ...') Till poor Daniel Lombard found himself at Land's End: reining in his servants behind him, and gazing in extreme confusion beyond the last straggle of rocks to the vast Atlantic.

And from that point, Tom – burly, tall and dignified in a navy suit, grey tie and white shirt – mounted eloquently to his moral conclusion: 'It's no good us knowin' French or Latin, or even English, come to that. If you would sojourn in a foreign land, if you want to make it your home, you must learn the elements of the language before you do get there. Brethren, when you come to the Jordan and cross over unto the other side – how will you ask the way? – how' (his eyes rolling) 'will you ask the way? ... *Unless* ... unless you have learned the elements of the language. And here' (rapping the Bible) 'is the only way you can learn it. And it's not much use us studyin' it one day in seven. It'll be gone from your mind. A *little* a day ... a little a day. And if you find the language of the Holy Spirit difficult ... hard to master ... confusing ... remember, you're not learnin' it to go on a day-trip across the Channel. Nor *even* for a lifetime, like Daniel Lombard. But for Eternity. *Eternity!*' Tom bellowed the word exultantly; then dipped his voice into a soft, plangent tone. 'One thing more. You may believe you're gettin' there by drivin' on regardless – that new car, that wall-to-wall carpet, that colour television. But it idn' always so. You may be travellin' *away* from your destination. You may have been closest to it when you was a child, when you sat in the Sunday School and heard the sweet strains of Gentle Jesus, or when you sat on your mother's lap, and she taught you to say this prayer ...' And we hastily stood up and joined in the Lord's Prayer which Tom intimately intoned – snapping the great book shut at the Amen, and announcing the last hymn: 'Just as I am, without one plea, But that Thy blood was shed for me.'

Outside, my hand was pumped a dozen times, and I was asked unanswerable questions, like where I came from, and how much longer I had on holiday. But the surprise of Tom's sermon, the sudden bright midday sun and clean air after the bleak chapel, and these strangers' warmth and curiosity, made me feel glad to be alive; I felt vernal and juicy in my smart green suit. 'That was *good*, Tom!' I said, still surprised, when he came out of the vestry and joined me. He grinned, pleased. With him was a tall white-haired man who had taken our collection. He clapped his hand on Tom's shoulder and said, with a smile, 'He's no fool – silly bugger!' There was a scar on his lean, sunburnt, ascetic face. 'Mr Parkins,' said Tom, 'my boss at the lighthouse.' We shook hands. 'Well, got to get home,' said Mr Parkins. He took a few steps up the road, stopped, and set off in the opposite direction, giving us a vague smile. As Tom was unlocking his van, a rotund and crippled pensioner came round the side of the chapel, adjusting his flies. 'Didn't hear *you* 'day, Frank!' Tom called. The old man rolled across to us on his walking stick (one leg was shorter than the other), wheezing as he drew close, 'Bronchitis, you! Bleddy handsome sermon, ol' man.' Tom asked him if he'd like a lift home, and he said, no, he liked the walk, there was nothing and no one to hurry for. Yet he made good speed: in the couple of minutes it took Tom to get the motor turning he had gone out of sight. We passed him by the tall lush hedges on the outskirts of St Just. Without glancing aside, as though he knew the sound of the engine, he raised his stick in a brief greeting.

Tom and his parents lived in a simple bungalow, not far from the Meadery. Mrs Polglaze was small and plump, with fresh cheeks and curly grey hair. She said what nice things she'd heard about me; I said I'd heard the same of her – and her son had preached a wonderful sermon. She gave him a proud hug, and said she and Arthur were going to the evening service. They 'belonged' to Trewellard chapel, but they were going to St Just to hear their 'boy' tonight. He was the youngest preacher in the circuit, and the youngest lighthouseman. Tom smoked and looked out of the window, abashed.

His father came late home to dinner and ate his in an armchair – apologizing briefly and then eating in silence. He was a builder, and was working overtime to finish a new house for the mine captain at Geevor. Cement dust had settled into the deep creases of his leathery skin. His eyes looked kind and exhausted. We let him eat his dinner in peace. Mrs Polglaze brought out names like Anne Ziegler and Webster Booth, as if I'd know who they were; and to my horror, I did. I was closer to his parents' age than I was to Tom's, and in spite of my quiet insistence that he and I were only friends, I felt embarrassed. Still – as Mrs Polglaze said of her own advancing middle age – you were as young as you felt. Asked how I liked Cornwall, I said I envied them a beautiful landscape they were at home in, whereas I felt rootless. Tom though, from the way he gazed out of the window as he chewed his roast lamb, seemed to be expressing an opposite desire – to get away, see something of the world. He spoke only once during the meal, when he said laconically, 'Young boy drowned off Cape Cornwall this mornin'. Down on holiday with his mother.' We went silent with the tragedy of it, so close; Mrs Polglaze dabbed her eyes with a hanky. It was always happening, she said; people who were silly and didn't take care. It was a very treacherous coast. That dear child.

In our quietness we listened to the request programme coming softly from their old-fashioned wireless. An Etonian-sounding bore was being asked what he had missed most during his six months up the Amazon. What he had missed most, he said, was seeing the Queen at Ascot. Mr Polglaze – having drawn strength from his roast dinner – swivelled very slowly till he faced the wireless. 'Did you hear that?' he said. 'He missed the *Queen* at *Ascot*! . . . Elsie, get pen and paper. Draft that man a letter of sympathy. Tell'n we're some *sorry* to hear that.' His face did indeed express concern, astonishment, outrage, held for a long while as we chuckled, and shading at last into a brief tremor of a smile. I liked Mr Polglaze from that instant.

Rested and fed, and perhaps sensing that I liked him, he started to unwind conversation about his life and background as a miner's son. He was proud there had been mines here since Roman times; but alive, too, to the tragedies. His father had returned home from gold mining in South Africa, to comfort his mother after the death of her two younger sons in the Levant disaster. He had stayed, got married, produced a son and daughter, and died in middle age of miners' phthisis.

I said it must have been terrible to have *two* sons taken like that. 'Awful! Awful!' said Mrs Polglaze huskily, her eyes misted again. Arthur said, 'Mother do live very close to the waterworks!' and his wife chuckled, drying her eyes. She said her own mother had been engaged to one of Arthur's uncles – Jack – killed in the mine. I saw her in a strange light. She would not have been here if the Levant disaster hadn't happened.

Then there was the poverty and disease, continued Mr Polglaze. 'Did you know,' he said, 'the average age of death in these parts a hundred years ago was twenty-seven? . . . Twenty-seven.' He spoke of the miners' superstitions, such as hearing a 'knacker', a mine pixie, just before a fatal accident. Or the tale that if you forgot your watch when you went off to work you'd not return alive. I said I had a terrible memory and would always be leaving my watch behind.

'The man with the worst memory in Cornwall,' said Arthur slowly, and as if I was hungry for the information, 'is Stanley Parkins, head lighthouseman to Tom here.' I said I'd met him at the chapel: glancing at Tom to confirm it. Tom nodded, smiling, breathing out smoke. 'Yes. He was goin' off home to mother's, before he realized he was married with two grandchildren!'

His father opened his mouth in a short, silent laugh, then went on: 'Stanley went up to Plymouth one day in his car, to a congress of lighthousemen; came home by train, found his car missing from his garage, and informed the police it had been stolen. A constable found it the next day abandoned in a Plymouth car park.' His eyes rolled as though challenging me to disbelieve him and he threw his head back in a barked laugh, then another. 'He's a peach, he is, our Stanley!' Elsie and Tom chuckled, though they must have heard the story dozens of times. I smiled weakly, and stood up to help Elsie clear away. Forgetfulness was not a weakness that ought to be laughed at. 'He's some clever man, though,' said Elsie; 'a wonderful musician.'

Mrs Polglaze shooed away my offers of help, and ordered Tom to take me for a walk, it was such handsome weather. 'Take her down Botallack,' said Mr Polglaze, and his son said he'd already shown me it. Trying not to blush, I said I'd like to go again. Mr Polglaze's grandfather had worked there, going out half-a-mile under the sea bed; and Elsie's grandmother had been a bal-maiden there, working on the cliff top, breaking up the rocks with a mallet. I refused their invitation to come back to tea, saying I wanted to get a meal on for my American friends. It was an excuse. The more at home I felt with Tom's parents the more false it seemed; eating their lamb and arctic roll while thinking of Hector.

I pictured the bal-maidens swinging their mallets, as we inched our way down the cliff path. They could have had few psycho-sexual problems, I thought. We sunbathed on a blanket halfway down, in a grassy clearing. The cliff trapped the sun; we baked; we took our coats off, and Tom rolled up his sleeves. He pointed out Cape Cornwall, where the boy had drowned only this morning. The coast was savage, austere; the sea a glazed and dazzling blue, edged with pure white at the base of the cliffs. Few people wandered down to the old engine house, on the sea's rim, and back. It seemed, for a time, the Sunday to end all Sundays, complete absence of effort and the struggle to alter things. Only the all but soundless lap of water broke – not broke, but drove home more fully – the stillness. The ruins sealed the silence; men, women and children had toiled here, hammered wedges under the sea, and laid their mallets down. Their deaths were audible.

The sun burned my forehead, my cheeks, my throat, my arms. I wanted to take my tights off but feared giving Tom any ideas. But as I daydreamed on my stomach I let him brush his hand up under my blouse and stroke my back. 'I've got a fat back.' I laughed; but he said it was lovely, he liked a good handful. I sighed, and told him he had a very gentle touch. 'I would say,' he said quietly, 'you've never found a lot of tenderness.' I lay contented, my eyes buried in my arms. 'Would you like to tell me about it?' he said softly. He squeezed his hand down under my skirt band and I winced where I had been punched. He stroked in the right place. 'You've been hurt,' he said. I asked him if he really believed in faith-healing, and he said yes, quoting Thy faith hath made thee whole and Take up thy bed and walk. I unhooked a fastening so he could rub more easily, and let myself drift with the tide and with his touch. He touched me in the places where I hurt – very gently and tenderly, and I felt soothed and peaceful. I said to him he was not to think I had changed my mind from yesterday, and he said he wouldn't think that; what I had said about involvement had been very sensible.

I went back to tea, and his parents were glad I'd changed my mind. I sat between them for the evening service. Both, but especially Arthur, had strong, sweet voices, and I felt ashamed of my raven's croak. The congregation had swelled to thirty for the evening service, and they made a gusty noise. Not having any problems with my tights (Mrs Polglaze had lent me a pair) I was able to listen to Tom's prayer, and also watch him through my fingers. His eyes were closed, his body and arms on the move, his voice an eloquently persuasive singsong – a real Olivier. If I'd been God, I'd have given him all his requests without question. There were pleas on behalf of the old, the bed-ridden, 'all who cannot be with us tonight' – some three thousand million – the starving, and the acquainted-with-grief . . . 'We pray, dear Lord, for those who are bereaved. We pray for the dear woman who came down on holiday last week, with her little boy, and he was drowned this morning, off Cape Cornwall. Oh yes, dear Lord Jesus, we ask you to help that mother to bear her loss, for none of *us* can do it. "In Rama was there a voice heard, lamentation, and weeping, and great mourning, Rachel weeping for her children, and would not be comforted, because they are not." And *would* not be comforted. They tried to comfort her, but she *would* not let them, because they had no promise of eternal life to offer, and nothing else could help. Let Thy lovingkindness shine on the weeping mother today, dear Jesus, as we know you let it shine on Rachel, for You are our only comfort . . .' I couldn't stand for the next hymn, because I was in floods of tears. Mr Polglaze offered me his large handkerchief. I felt ashamed at making such an exhibition of myself.

But afterwards, having a cup of tea with them, Elsie said I was very tender-hearted, like her. She herself had been wet around the eyes, and so were lots of other people, because they put themselves in the place of that poor woman, without a husband and now her son gone.

Tom played his accordion, and Arthur his cornet, and sang Victorian ballads. When Tom walked me back to the cottage a crimson sunset was stretched along the coast. It had been a lovely day, I said, and his father and mother were lovely people. A station wagon drew up ahead of us, outside the terrace. I saw Lola getting out, and from the driver's side, a short, stout man in late middle age. Lola held out her arms to me and we embraced. 'My!' she said. 'You look well!' 'So do *you!*' I said. She vibrated bounce and health. 'Where's Hector?' 'He's in the back,' said Lola. The stout farmer – Mr Uren – was opening the rear doors, disappeared momentarily, then backed slowly out, manoeuvring a wheelchair carefully on to the road. Hector was in it, and, as he saw me, gave a weak smile.

I have a keen eye for girls caught in a Svengali situation, and I could see at once that the palely pretty shop girl at the Trewellard general stores was being serviced regularly by the proprietor. Tom had asked me to go in with him, to help him with his mother's shopping list – simple orders that might have been, for him, a German naval code. The girl was tense as she served us; and hare-lipped, cleft-palated Mr Harris bantered much too nervously with Tom. The atmosphere, thick with the coming lunch-hour screw after a weekend's abstinence, could have been cut with their ham slicer.

I told Tom so, when we were rolling along again in the big high van. He seemed to find it a great joke; said that Charlie Harris, far from being Trewellard's most reckless character, wouldn't even stock fireworks for Guy Fawkes Day because there was normally 'no demand' for them – and Tom imitated Charlie's cleft-palated grunt. And that apart, Veronica went home to dinner. It didn't matter, I said; it was happening; my instinct told me.

I even (though I didn't tell Tom this) thought it right and proper, in a way. During the short time I was a secretary, I had thought it only fitting that my abhorrent boss should want me to work late so he could screw me. It was a relationship (and a job) that Joe swiftly terminated. And I know he was right to have done so; I'm troubled by my own feelings. Mr Harris was being good to this girl by giving her employment, and deserved something in return. Every Good Boss Deserves Favour, as my old music teacher almost said. In my head I knew it was crap, but in my bones I opened my legs to authority. If I'd been a peasant girl in the Middle Ages and my lord of the manor waived his *droit de seigneur*, I'd have cried all my wedding night.

Tom's van bowled along the roads and lanes of Penwith. High off the ground, I could see over the tall hedges, to the brown furzy moor and hints of ancient earthworks. I quite enjoyed the sense of drama. It wasn't Tom's van, exactly: it belonged to the Pendeen Silver Band, who used it to carry their instruments. The body of it was closed off, like an ambulance or Securicor van. From the back, now, came the fine strong voice of Lola singing 'John Brown's Body'. She had risked a few bars at the pub, the evening we had met Tom, but nothing like so strong as this, so assured in the notes and breathing. No doubt the stacked music racks in the corner, and the 'reserve' trombone and cornet, had touched off the singing; also I had the feeling she was trying to cheer Hector up, because he had fought morosely against this trip; and indeed in a little while he joined in, tunelessly but happily; a frail elderly voice. Mrs Bolitho sang still louder, all but drowning him. One detected, for the first time, her Celtic strain, the love of singing.

What I *didn't* have an eye for, what left me feeling helpless, afraid and tearful, was a strong healthy man in the toils of a Gagool. After Mr Uren had carried Hector tenderly up to bed, I had had a tearful talk with Lola in the kitchenette, begging her to send for a doctor. She said he just refused to see one; and anyway, there was really nothing wrong except sheer physical exhaustion, after years of studying too hard. He did have a heart murmur, but they were sure it was nothing to do with that. As the Urens had a wheelchair left over from Myrtle's invalid mother, now deceased, it seemed a good idea for Hector to use it for a couple of days, so resting without being completely immobilized. He wasn't paralysed, she said, just so worn out he literally couldn't drag his legs around. All Hector said, when I took him up his cocoa, was 'I don't holiday very well.'

I'd begged Lola for this morning's trip. Lola rolled her eyes at Tom as if to say 'Oh brother!' but gave way under the pressure of my tears. She even agreed, reluctantly, with my argument that, whereas both of us had crawled through the hole, Hector hadn't deigned to, and this could be having some kind of psychological effect. Tom, who for the most part had listened silently to us, feeding me a chain of cigarettes, said he could take us, as he was on afternoon shift this week: we'd never get the wheelchair in the Viva.

Lola soared buoyantly in 'Climb Every Mountain'; her son's weak voice cracked and slithered into a crevasse.

'What do *you* think of it, Tom?' I asked anxiously.

'*She* got a good voice.'

'No, I mean, what do you think of Hector?'

'He don't look too smart.'

When we reached the parking place, I asked Tom and Lola to wait for us. *I* would push him. 'I want to talk to him,' I said, 'about seeing a doctor.' 'It won't do a bit of good,' said Lola. 'He's as stubborn as a mule when he wants to be.'

It wasn't easy pushing him up the lane, trying not to jolt him too much. He seemed to be quite enjoying the ride. He pointed to a puzzled white horse in a field of black cows. 'Lola's got a nice voice still, Hector,' I said cheerfully. His head dipped in a nod. 'Surely. She still sings solo in the Grass Valley choir. They sing old Cornish tunes, you know. It's surprising how much of this place is over there, back home. We met a guy called Pengelly in Redruth, and there's a shoe store called Pengelly's on Main Street back home. I got these there.' He poked his toe out of the rug.

When we reached the hedge site his face was grey from the pounding he had taken. He hoisted himself up the stone steps, on his behind, and then helped me lift the chair over. He asked if we could rest a while. It was a close, cloudy day, and I was glad to, myself. How beautiful were the colours, I said – the yellow gorse, the purple heather.

'You should see Grass Valley,' he said. 'It's at the gateway to the Sierra Nevadas, two thousand five hundred feet up, and richly forested. In the fall it'll be a riot of colour, the reds and golds of plane trees, sycamores, maples and poplars mingling with the dark greens of the silver-tip firs and the digger pines.' It was the most lyrical speech I had ever heard from him, and it swelled my imagination. 'It's called Grass Valley because of the lush grass that grows there. We get a lot of tourists; ever since the last gold mine shut down just before the war, it's been a favourite jumping-off place for them. You must come visit us if you're ever in the States.'

It was an easy glide over the short grass, through the heather and gorse. The hole was still there, and took us almost by surprise. Hector tumbled out of the chair and stretched flat. 'It's the birth channel, Hector!' I said. 'Get through it and you're out.' He squirmed; I seized his shoulders and helped yank him through. I felt the clouds lift, a joyous relief. He lay panting heavily on the grass, and I lay beside him. I watched his rising and falling stomach, where his shirt had come free to expose a triangle of pure-white vest.

'*Tell* me about your mother, Hector,' I said. I meant the possessive old woman, but his eyes softly returned to childhood. He picked a blade of grass and sucked it. 'She was pretty,' he said, 'very pretty. Wonderful to me. Always a song on her lips, and helping people. The life and soul of every occasion. Everybody loved her in Grass Valley.

'Then she developed Parkinson's disease. It happened so suddenly. It was one Sunday, between Sunday School and evening service; Mother was making some tea and chatting about clothes, and the next moment she was in a narcoleptic trance. Literally frozen. And she stayed like that for the next thirty years. Just quarter-waking to be fed. You can imagine what it did to us all. Father with three of us to take care of, and Mother a total invalid. He did his best, poor guy, but eventually she had to go into a special home, in Denver, Colorado.'

Expressing amazement and sympathy, I ruffled his thinning hair and asked if they'd had any warning of such a terrible attack.

'Mother had had a mild sleeping sickness as a girl. Not the tsetse kind – the virus. You probably won't know about it. It swept the world in 1917. It came out of nowhere, like Lenin in his sealed train. Maybe twenty, thirty years later it would burst out, as post-encephalitic Parkinsonism.'

There was pain in his unblinking eyes. I waited for him to continue. This explained Lola's posthumous lust for experience. He shut his eyes, and looked as if he was going to sleep. A young couple, crushed by rucksacks, had stolen up silently; they looked at the hole for a moment, then, embarrassed, moved away again.

'What happened to your mother, Hector?' I prompted him. 'When did she get better?'

He gave me a strange, half-startled look. 'It was fantastic,' he sighed. 'I won't bother you with the medical name, but a miracle drug known as L-Dopa came out in the late sixties. It brought instant recoveries. There's a wonderful book by Oliver Sacks, called *Awakenings*. You should read it. We got word one night that Mother was completely herself again. We drove over right away, of course, and there was Mother, overjoyed to see us, talking a mile a minute! Of course it was a tremendous shock to her, but she took it, took everything, with fantastic courage. Even humour. You won't credit this, but her last words in '37 had been "I think I'll wear –" and according to the nurses, when she woke up and turned her head she said "– my blue dress this evening." And, you know, she was still so pretty, she hadn't really aged at all, she was still so wonderfully pretty ...'

He was gazing up at me wistfully. I realized then *why* he was so bound to his mother, and that I would need a lot of love and strength to break the tie.

'Marry me, Hector,' I said.

He pulled himself up on his elbow, and smiled. The sun broke through the skein and made the little yellow gorse flowers glow. 'You know that's not possible, Jo,' he said. 'But if it was, I'll have you know, you'd be the first person I'd ask.' He ruffled my hair and winked, and I felt not unencouraged. 'We better get back,' he said. Hauling him under the arms I struggled him back into the chair.

With another short rest at the stile, we made the return journey in silence. Opening the front door of the van I had a startled impression, more than a vision, of mouths drawing apart – of stocking-tops – of hands moving to the wheel – of skirts adjusted. Tom leapt out and opened the back doors for Hector to be lifted in.

'Honey, you never told me it was Tom's birthday!' Lola carolled. I climbed into the back beside Hector, and told Tom, with my eyes, what I thought of him as his bland face hovered for a second, before the grey sky became the black doors. If flirting with old Jean Harlow was meant to pay me out for preferring Hector, it was disgusting and demeaning, a cruel joke.

I made one of my specialities, a rich cream-and-brandy sauce to go with the pork tenderloin for lunch; but Hector only toyed with his plate. He nostalged again about the beauties of Grass Valley. 'When I turn up my toes, that's where I want to be,' he said, gazing with shining, recalling eyes at his mother across the table. She responded with a soft look, for a moment, then dropped her gaze, saying in gentle rebuke, 'Our vacation's only just started, honey.' Turning to me, she suggested a swim in the cove, to freshen us up; I stalled on it. Maybe one of us ought to stay with Hector, I said. But Hector told us to go right ahead, he'd be quite happy resting and reading in the garden.

While Lola did the dishes and a selection from *Showboat*, I moved Hector into the little rose garden and tucked a blanket round him. It was hot in this sun-trap, and I took off my tights to complete my Botallack tan. Peacefully I lay at his feet, watching a green insect explore the stub of his brown Pengelly shoe. I asked him how he felt.

'Happy,' he said.

'I'm glad. Do you feel any better?'

'No, but it doesn't matter. I feel like an imploding neutron star that's turning into a Black Hole. Terribly dense and heavy. If a fly settled on me now it wouldn't be able to get away. I feel just great.'

'You've got too deep a mind for me, Hector,' I said, stroking his shoe. The little green insect hopped away. Hector asked me if I'd bring him a glass of water, Lola's sun glasses, and the journal on his bedside table. I went for them – meeting a grotesquely bikini'd Lola on the stairs – and when I took them out, Hector was asleep.

The next I knew, I was sitting on my bed, in my housecoat, and reading through a poem, with no sense of having written it:

> An old man is walking by high hedges
> on the road back from chapel
> to an empty house,
> his stick tapping on loose gravel.
> He has walked this road all his life,
> he is becoming the high hedges,
> he likes it this way.

Lola called to say she'd finished in the bathroom. I had a long luxurious bath, watching the top leaves of a tree sway in the breeze. I slipped into the frock with no sleeves.

When I walked through the screen of rose bushes, I stopped. Lola was there, in a garden chair next to Hector. I saw them in profile. They were too busy to see me. Lola had her dress tucked up high, and Hector, stretching, was stroking her thigh above the dark stocking; almost as if she was hurting there, and he was making the pain better. But Lola was chuckling, whispering. I backed into the bushes.

'It's okay, honey!' Lola warbled. She stood up and brushed her skirt down as I came out to them. 'We were thinking of lying down for a while. I may have overdone the swimming, my hands are stiffening up a little. I was just telling Hec how Tom enjoyed seeing my garters! I guess all men are turned on by them!' Her son blushed, and turned away his head.

Guiding his wheelchair into the house, she ruffled his hair and chuckled. 'He's got wandering hands – haven't you, sweetheart?' Her pre-Freudian coolness was amazing. 'We'll have a little rest and then think about some dinner.' 'Shall I cook Boeuf Stroganoff?' I said, hardly knowing what I was saying. 'That's a nice idea honey. Could you eat some of that, Hec?' He didn't answer, and she said, 'It's still early, honey, let's talk about it later.'

The sun was dipping when Lola came into my bedroom, in her housecoat. I had been lying with an unread book. 'Hector feels a lot better,' she said. 'He wants us to go out and eat. Somewhere nice; he thinks he could manage to walk, with a little help. Isn't that wonderful?' Her eyes sparkled. She plumped on the bed and rested her arthritic hand on my thigh. 'It's the old stone cunt,' I said, unsurprised though with sarcasm. 'You can say that again, honey –' she giggled – 'though it doesn't feel stony.' She slid her hand swiftly in and out of her housecoat. None of my irony was getting through to her.

She tightened a stocking with her gnarled, false-nailed hand. Nodding down, I said, 'You must find it difficult to buy them these days.'

She nodded. 'I let Hector get them for me in Sacramento. There's a store that caters for old ladies and frustrated guys!'

'So you've really hooked him on them, Lola?'

'Oh' – she chuckled – 'he's always been hooked on them. But I guess I *was* responsible. Hec puts it down to one Christmas when I did a hand-stand as a forfeit at one of our Sunday School socials. Gave him his first wet dream, he says, and made up for not having Santa any more!'

I asked her, with Cornish understatement ('he don't look too smart'), whether she thought it altogether healthy.

'Well, I don't know about that, sweetheart. Don't all men have a little something? I'll say this in its favour – it's helped keep us together, all these years.'

The words jammed in my throat, like cars at the Exeter bypass.

'Honey, there's one thing,' she said, dropping her voice to a whisper: 'I didn't tell him about the swim. I don't want to make him feel – left out. You know what I mean? When you and I had a joyful experience at St Ives, he was very happy for us, even though it wasn't exactly what either of us expected. But I guess when you told us about Tom, he felt a little hurt. He thinks it's something personal. Oh, I know he isn't Clark Gable, honey, but I know you're fond of him and he's gentle and sweet. I guess I'm not putting this very well, but you know you're welcome to if you *want* to. I hope you will, Joanne dear. I want him to experience widely. Something as enriching as we've experienced.' Smiling, she reached into her housecoat again, then returned her hand to my thigh, giving it a silky stroke and saying, 'I'm sure he'd love it with you. I guess he's a little disappointed you're not as accommodating as you said you were, in some respects. You know what I mean honey!' She squeezed the top of my thigh. 'Or we could have a threesome if you preferred it that way. But don't do anything you don't want to. You don't have to feel obligated.'

Hector tapped on the door, and popped his genial face around. 'Come along, Momma! Get your dress on. I could eat a horse!'

'Okay, honey, I'll be right with you!' His face withdrew. 'Men!' she chuckled. 'That's all they want, Jo, to make them happy – a screw and a steak!'

The head waiter, in the surprising Italian restaurant in a dour Penwith hamlet, commiserated with Lola on her 'husband's' illness, observing him tap his way shakily to the gents on his Robert Newton walking stick. I caught his seductive eye, as if to say 'You're a chancer'. Maybe he did believe it. Maybe, with his subtle Venetian nostrils (he *must* be Venetian), he could scent the sperm of Hector (the thought made my head spin) under her red-skirted lap.

Feeling a little giggly after two schooners of sherry, I said, 'Now there's a compliment, Lola!' Lola tried to hide her pleasure but showed a full mouth of teeth. 'These Italians could charm the birds off the trees! My God, what amazing eyes! Did you see the way he looked at us while putting in the corkscrew?' And we covered our hilarity by sipping our red wine as Hector subsided, shakily, into his chair. 'What's the joke?' he smiled. 'We were just imagining,' said Lola, 'what Mario Lanza over there must be like in bed.' Her eyes sparkled into mine and we giggled again. Out of sight, Hector's hand, I was sure, gave her thigh a squeeze, while with the other hand he summoned more wine. A distinct 'twang', a harp note from the mysterious moors, came from beneath the table-cloth. Lola smiled into her wine glass. Hector looked innocent.

Over our main course Lola told me about *her* Mediterranean blood. Her great-grandfather William-John Moyle and his bride had come over from Redruth in the Gold Rush; but she wasn't by any means of pure Cornish descent. Supposedly she was descended from Lola Montez, the Irish-Spanish girl who became a German king's mistress. Lola Montez retired at one stage (from dancing and whoring) to Grass Valley. 'You can still see her home,' interrupted Hector, 'surrounded by red bougainvillaea and blue morning glory.' Lola's great-grandfather had a way with the women, and Lola Montez fell for him and bore him a child when well into her forties. Her husband of that era, a San Francisco newspaper owner, was enraged, and disowned the boy. So William-John took the boy into his own home. His wife had nine children and didn't seem to mind one more. The boy, when he grew up, married a Queenie Uren, also from Redruth, who in turn produced Lola's father.

That was the story, said Lola; and she personally believed it. So evidently had her parents, in giving her Lola's name. 'She used to dance beautifully when she was younger,' said Hector, squeezing his mother's hand. Lola blushed, and lowered her eyes to her plate, clearly touched by his compliment. Hector, I couldn't help notic-ing, had been gazing at her almost in adoration all through her long list of begettings.

'She's a wonderful woman,' he said to me, as she staggered to the ladies. 'Don't you think? She keeps me going. Her father was an alcoholic, you know. A bum. It's wonderful she's turned out as she has.'

My head was spinning with too many things – the wine, the bedroom intimacies I had overheard, Lola's lewd suggestions, her Montez fantasy, above all the need to rescue my knight from this crone with her magic girdle. The head waiter brought us two red roses, and we pinned them on. 'You'd love Italy!' I said, extolling the Bridge of Sighs, and the gates of paradise at Florence. I'd only had four hours there, after saving up for a year, but it remains one of the richest experiences of my life. Flushed with her rose and my remembered idyll, Lola begged Hector to let them take in Italy after France. Over coffee and chartreuse I read her childlike palm, and entertained them with stories of foreign disasters, like the pasty-faced German student I met in Venice. I sent him a Christ-mas card saying 'Come sta?', and he rang me from Munich to ask when he could come. They chuckled loudly when I explained what the words really meant.

Hector was very tottery as we made for the car, and neither Lola nor I was in much of a state to help him. We were in high spirits at his recovery; Lola sang, I whistled, and Hector croaked, as we headed back over the moor. Lola persuaded us to take up Tom's invitation to the Trewellard Arms, where he and his cronies would be celebrating his birthday. The pub was in full swing, crammed with boozy singers. I said 'Hi!' to Stanley Parkins, who sipped an orange juice, and he courteously stood to let Hector sit. His shock of pure-white hair drifted away above the sea of heads like a sailing ship. Lola was soon in full but tremulous voice, surrounded by a male quartet who swayed towards her as if she was the central pole of a wigwam. Tom finished playing his accordion and shouldered through to congratulate Hector on his recovery. 'And what do *she* want?' he asked, nodding towards Lola. 'Apart from a glass of water!' (He was amused, and a little irritated, by their insistence on iced water with everything.) 'I shouldn't worry, she's pissed,' I said. But Lola, at that point, tripped across – literally, being stopped from falling on her face by two burly fishermen catching her flying friendly bust.

Chuckling, she plumped down on Hector's lap. I could see him turning grey under her weight and the relentless gush about the Italian restaurant's décor, and her plans to redecorate their home in the same style next spring. Tom was being pawed by a pert brunette, Charlie Harris's lunchtime mistress. 'Where's her luncheon vulture, Tom?' I enquired, when he'd slipped out of her clutches. His eyes sparkled when it clicked. 'Home plannin' their escape route!' Last orders were called, and Tom was shouting fresh invitations to all and sundry to bring a bottle and come down to the lighthouse. I saw Hector sag deeper at the thought of still more merry-making, and I offered to take him home. I felt tired too, I said, after the walk to the Men-an-Tol, the swim, the drinks. Lola clearly was not going to miss out on the party.

'I'll bring her back,' said Tom. 'I'll look after her.' Hector's face had turned from grey to red. I feared for his blood pressure in the hot smoky atmosphere. 'Okay.' He shrugged to me. His face resumed a normal shade as Lola got up off his lap.

She brought close to me her alcoholic breath. 'Look after him, honey,' she whispered. 'Will you let me give you a tip? Put on a garter belt.' I said I didn't have such a thing. She looked drunkenly taken aback, as if such improvidence was beyond her. 'Oh well, take one of mine, honey. You know he'd appreciate it.' She shut a saurian eye in a coy wink. I said I didn't think I'd need any props, and that if he didn't want me for myself, it was tough luck. The old bird looked suitably chastened.

I sensed his trembling beside me as I drove home, and I whistled 'Are the stars out tonight?' We lurched together into the cottage and collapsed on to the sofa. His head fell back, his eyes closed. He unlaced his shoes. I loved him as he *was*, I felt: the sad, tired eyes, the sallow cheeks that filled and sank as he recovered his breath; I loved his V-neck pullover with its dribble of gravy. I loved his thinning hair and anxious brow. I opened his palm (he'd fought shy of it in the restaurant) and told him he had a strong line of Fate. I asked him if he'd had a serious illness. 'Not yet,' he said faintly. He wondered what was on TV, and asked for a hot drink. 'I'll make us one later,' I said. I thought I'd better take his mother's advice. I turned on the TV and said I wouldn't be a minute.

I went to my room and had another search through my suitcase. Coincidentally, I'd noticed in Tintagel that Joanne had thrown in a skimpy garter belt. I knew she sometimes indulged one of her weird men-friends. Perhaps she'd spent an afternoon, on the trip down, with the car salesman from Bath – an odious character who'd abused me abominably. Noticing Hector light up at a TV ad, I had, in fact, vaguely thought of wearing it for our night out at the Meadery; but the belt had vanished. I searched again, more thoroughly, but it wasn't there. Nor the stockings. I assumed Joe had quietly disposed of them. I'd have to make do with Lola's.

When I switched on the light in their room, I saw an astronomy journal on his bed. There was a photo of a galaxy on the cover, and Hector had doodled on it, presumably while Lola and I were chatting. With a red felt pen he had sketched suspenders on to the galaxy belt, which now cut into a generous female torso. It was a not unimpressive demonstration of the power of Hector's fetish. I *was* impressed. It was really no different from the Druids worshipping the Logan Stone. I liked the thought of a magic symbol. Love *ought* to be magical.

I began to understand how, after his mother's recovery, after L-Dopa, he had become sexually obsessed with her; both out of a guilty compassion for her lost life, and because she was about the only woman in the world who still wore stockings and belt. But the belt could be taken over; she was offering it to me.

I uncovered Lola's nest of fangs, and picked out a green garter snake and a pair of black fishnet stockings. I struggled with unfamiliar fastenings. Everything fitted, to my relief, though I could

66

scarcely breathe. It was a peculiar kind of *déjà-vu*. The turnabout to tights had been, for me, a strange elision. One moment I was crying about the news from Aberfan, strapped up as usual without being consciously so, and the next I was at a party jiving to 'Sergeant Pepper', with a panicky feeling that my suspender belt had broken. I looked down and saw I was in this indecently short skirt, and some kind of Shakespearean tights. Then a second panic: I'd forgotten my bra. My surprise at this liberation was quickly overtaken by the knowledge, picked up from Joanne's friends, that my father had died during the intervening months. I felt, in every way, unsupported.

So here I was again, in the crucifixion of the two-way stretch, for Hector. I gave myself an injection to bolster my courage. Feeling terribly exposed, I went downstairs, half floating, half reined-in.

Hector was watching cricket highlights, his eyes glazed, I snuggled beside him, making my skirt ride up my thighs. 'You okay?' he said, and returned to the screen. 'What's going on?' he asked eventually. He seemed not to have noticed I'd changed. 'Why do you like suspenders, Hector?' I asked. Furrowing his brow he said he didn't, he hadn't worn them for at least ten years; then chuckled as he realized his mistake. 'Oh, I guess that was Mother, in the beginning. When you're little, you need a strap to hold on to!'

'Lola told me about the hand-stand at the Christmas social.'

'Oh yes, I remember.' He snickered. 'But that was later. Not only that, though. Just living with her in the house, when we were growing up. Living with a good-looking woman who was very free-and-easy. Father told her off once for showing us too much; but as she says, it was just the give-and-take of family life, there was no harm in it. She had terrific legs in those days and you couldn't blame her for showing them off. Betty Grable's weren't any better. They're still pretty good, don't you think?'

I told him there might not have been harm then, but there certainly was now. Very great harm. I could understand him feeling sorry for all she had lost, but that didn't mean *he* had to compensate. 'We all have our own life to lead, Hector, and I'm afraid she's destroying you. She's a succubus.' Hector shrugged and sighed, staring at the fading screen (I had switched it off), as if he could see something there I couldn't. 'There's no harm in fellatio,' he murmured. 'Though as a matter of fact we don't practise it very often.'

I stood up, with my back to him, and bent over, flinging my skirt over my waist as I did so. It wasn't very subtle, but I wanted to shock him. Between my legs I saw his eyes pop. 'Jesus, Jo!' he gasped. 'You don't shoot junk, do you?' I said no, I'd had injections for a bad virus. His upside-down head nodded. 'How do you like it?' I asked. 'Swell!' he said. 'Swell! The stockings are a little short on you, and the garters should go under your panties.' Apologizing for not remembering, I straightened up and made the necessary readjustment. I promised I'd go to Penzance tomorrow and buy some longer stockings. 'But not too long,' he said.

'Shall we go to bed?' I said. He looked at his watch. 'You go ahead. I'll wait up for her.'

'I mean *together*. Your mother won't mind. She *wants* us to. You're not a child, Hector, you can do as you want. *She's* enjoying herself. She's probably doing a strip,' I added ironically.

Hector cackled. 'You really think so? I guess she might be! Showing them all this,' he said, leaning forward, squeezing my thigh and sending a strap zinging. 'I guess you're right.' He said he thought he could manage the stairs by himself. Panting up behind me, strap-hanging occasionally, he made it to the top. I felt a little triumph that the holed stone or stoned hole was already doing him good; and I told him so. 'I guess you're right.' He collapsed on his bed, drawing deep breaths. I helped him undress. He wasn't as smooth as a doll between his legs, and now that I had led him to the 'overwhelming question' I was quite glad about that. He looked very thin – I was sure he had lost weight – but saggy at the stomach beyond his years. It was all a part of not looking after himself. I took his penis in hand, but it stayed limp. 'That feels real nice,' he sighed. I stripped to the magic girdle.

He lay on top of me, and we kissed. My bird, my cock, stayed limp for a long time, and he had to rest a lot; consequently there were more words than thrusts – as, for instance:

I'm sorry, I've lost you again.

That's okay, let me sit on you. It won't tire you so much.

I guess I shouldn't have had so many drinks.

Just rest.

I guess his prick must have jumped when he saw she had garters on.

Oh yes it's in me now! That feels good. Does it feel good to you?

Not quite so hard. Just stroke them softly.

Is that better?

That's nice. Are you on the pill?

No, but it's okay, you can come inside.

Why, have you menopaused?

Shit, no!

I'm sorry.

I've been sterilized. For health reasons. But I'd want us to have a child, Hector. We're not too old to adopt one. Perhaps a little Vietnamese child. Would you like that?

Maybe I'd better get on top again. So you like old Lola's garters, eh? They feel good on you.

Where am *I* in all this, Hector? What do *I* mean to you?

You're very much present to me as a person.

I'm glad you like me in them, Hector, and I love the feel of them, the way they tug on my stockings. Did you come?

A little, I guess.

We lay quietly, and he asked if I'd enjoyed it. Very much, I said, stroking his thigh; even though I hadn't come. That was only to be expected, so early in our relationship. I needed time to get used to someone, and there'd be no problems later on. He'd find me sexy, and loving, and boringly faithful. 'That's great,' he said enthusiastically, and squeezed my hand.

He must always tell me what pleased him, I said. Kissing his throat, I said I was sorry if I'd hurt him. There *were* some red love-bites, for I'd felt Joe's presence, angry at being with a man, especially underneath, and wearing chauvinist underclothes. It just so happened *I* liked being bitten, I said, so *he* needn't feel afraid to do it, if he ever wanted to. He'd remember that, he said, and after a pause, he swooped and rammed his lips round my breast, taking nearly all of it in, and bit hard. I screamed. Ripples spread through my body and I felt close to coming. 'Love me again, Hector,' I whispered.

'I wish I could, honey, but I'm bushed. Feel,' he said, taking my hand and putting it between his thighs. There was nothing there.

Then he unclenched his thighs and let his little cock pop out and let out a great laugh. (Hector let out a great laugh.) It was the first and only time I heard him really laugh, joyously. The idea of Hector as a joker threw me, and I lay confused.

'Do you mind if I read for a while?' he asked. When I came back from the bathroom he was sitting up in bed, Lola's housecoat round his shoulders. He looked very solemn and distinguished. I snuggled in beside him again and looked over his shoulder at the complicated cosmic diagrams. It was the galactic suspender belt issue. 'Tell me about it, Hector,' I said, kissing his cheek. Clearing his throat, he told me about the colliding universes of matter and anti-matter, the one hurrying to the end of things, the other

69

hurrying backwards to the beginning. 'Thank you,' I said. 'You've a lovely voice, Hector. I bet you're a good teacher.' 'No, I hate teaching,' he said. 'But science is wonderful.' Reverently he stroked the glossy pages of his journal.

He looked at his watch again and wondered where Lola was. I felt him shivering, and asked him if he'd like that hot drink and a hot-water bottle. 'That would be real good. And a glass of water,' he said. Just then we heard a car draw up, doors slam, and a female trill. Hector whipped out of bed and fumbled into his trousers. A fist was pounding on the door, and Lola's trill continued. I fetched my housecoat and followed Hector down. Tom, grinning sheepishly, was holding Lola up. 'She idn' feelin' too smart,' he said. Hector invited him in for a nightcap, but Tom said he had a friend in the car, and vanished. I took Lola's weight. Her eyes were rolling as if they didn't belong to her; her dead weight was worse than Hector's. He came puffing upstairs behind, giving us a steadying push now and again. I dumped her on her bed and hauled up her legs. She was breathing very shallowly, and I asked Hector if I should get her some black coffee. The old lady's eyelids unglued a shade, and her lips broke into a smile as she saw her son. 'Hi, honey!' she murmured, stretching out her hand for him to take. 'Tom screwed me. And Stanley Parkins.'

Hector's fury took me back to the double-breasted policeman. I thought the vein in his neck was going to burst; his clenched fist was ready to strike his mother. But instead, he was fumbling with shaking fingers at the hooks of her skirt. I helped him tug the skirt down. Lola, chuckling, her eyes gone again, said we were tickling her. I went to unhook her stockings but Hector stopped me. 'It's okay,' he said in a thick, slurred voice, 'I can manage the rest. Thanks.' Lola grabbed my hand. 'Thank you, my sweetheart!' she said. 'Why don't you stay?' I thought maybe I should, if only to protect her against Hector's rage. I looked queryingly at him, but he shook his head and said 'No' in his strangled voice; 'No, I'll sit with her till she's asleep.'

10

Croquet mallets were knocking at my head. Hector's fascist mother, Lili Marlene in a black plastic mac, stood over me, holding a cup of tea. 'I didn't want to disturb you, honey,' she said. 'So I let you sleep on. Tom and I are just leaving.'

70

I pulled myself up with a groan, and took the tea. I asked where they were going, and she reminded me that when she'd had her hair done in St Ives she'd booked herself a facial, as she didn't want to go to gay Paree looking a fright. By a lucky coincidence it turned out Tom was going to St Ives to see about some gear for his boat. She'd be back for a late lunch.

She didn't need a facial, I mumbled. How could she look so well after such a night? She said, maybe the swim had helped – they'd been for a midnight bathe at the cove. 'Gee, the water was cold ... but I guess I feel the benefit. And other things ...' Her old eyes sparkled. 'But I need all the help I can get. You can't be first and last.'

Her glance fell on the green belt, lying on a chair, still attached to the fishnets. 'Aren't you glad you took my advice, honey?' she said. 'You may find you look and feel better for it, too; I guess we can all do with a little gentle support, as the years go by.' She perched on the bed, and put her hand on my arm. 'I want you to know I'm deeply grateful. You're making Hector happy. And I hope *you* didn't find it too unpleasant? Boy oh boy, was *he* horny after you'd got to work on him!' I asked her to hand me my handbag, and I took out a pound note. I said would she see if she could find any larger-sized stockings in St Ives. 'Sure, sweetheart,' she said, refusing to take the note. 'He likes black, or dark flesh-coloured.' I said I knew.

The toilet flushed, and Tom's face grinned at me round the door. 'What *ho!*' he called genially. 'Coming honey!' she said, and squeezed my arm. 'Have a nice day.'

I felt depressed by Tom's carefree indifference to me; sickened, too, by his interest in such an old slag. Normal though he was, in most respects, I simply didn't understand him. He was such a changeling.

When they had gone, I knocked on Hector's door and heard him say, 'Hi!' He was sitting up in bed, housecoat round his shoulders, finishing a breakfast tray. We agreed how terrible we felt; but as I sat chatting with him and stroking his face my headache cleared and I started to feel happy. We had all morning together in which to build on the previous night's delicate *rapport*; the beginning of a new life. We heard a knock downstairs, and I went to answer it. A postman held out a letter, saying it was unstamped. It was addressed to H. Bolitho Esq., and I took it up to him and went back down with my purse. I clambered up again and Hector handed me the letter. It was from Mr Johnson, saying he'd be coming down for his car on Tuesday – today – arriving by train at 12.30. If we could pick him up, he'd be grateful, but we weren't to spoil our plans. If we weren't there he'd come on by taxi.

I felt sullen about the interruption to our morning together; then guilty at being so selfish. His grief came back to me – no wonder he'd forgotten to stick a stamp on. He intended driving straight back; it would hardly be a pleasant day for him. I suggested to Hector that he could pick him up, if he felt able to, while I cooked some lunch. Hector said he felt okay to drive, and he'd better set out early to see if he could hire a car for the next few days. Maybe he ought to get dressed? I said there was plenty of time, and should *I* go and put some clothes on? He looked at me uncertainly and I nodded, smiling. I put on the belt and fishnets and climbed into his narrow bed. His body seemed to lose itself in my embrace. I told him he needed feeding up and I'd make that my first duty. His little cock stayed small, even when I took it in my mouth (gently this time because he said it was sore). We lay quietly. Dreamily he played with a green suspender.

I was going to tear up all my tights, I said. I loved this captured, uncomfortable feeling. I said I'd like *him* to wear them too.

'You really *would*?' he asked. 'I really would.' With sudden energy, startling me, he whipped out of bed and went to Lola's drawer. In no time he had fastened a black suspender belt round him, and was pulling on nylons. His legs were so skinny, the black nylons came up surprisingly high. He stood there, swaying slightly, looking like a divine fool. 'Don't feel shy,' I said. 'I love it. It makes me feel horny just looking.' And it really did.

I rode on top of him. We were twin sisters plunging our hands into Christmas stockings. It was good. And I felt Joe's hands too, exploring; for although he burnt his bra and threw his girdle in the dustbin he has too many memories of the rock era of swirling skirts and petticoats not to find them magical in the object. For a few moments the skinny match girl and the plump pastry cook came together. Roughly he stroked my breasts and I begged him to bite them. Grunting, he bit a nipple sharply. 'It's beautiful,' I gasped. I asked him if he believed in sacred marriages. We were made for each other. Why didn't we get married today by special licence? Mr Johnson could be our witness.

'Lola –' he gasped, saying her name as an incantation, like Gē or Cybele, as his cock vanished. I got really angry. 'Screw Lola!' I said. 'She's not a mother she's just a selfish randy old whore.'

'You're right, she is, she is!' he said, choking, and his penis hardened again and I thrashed up and down on it.

．　　　．　　　．

He lay resting on the other bed while I pulled out the soaked sheet. 'When I come I come very heavily, I'm afraid,' I said. 'I hope you didn't mind. I've an overactive gland.'

'I guess whatever turns you on.'

I sat beside him and took his hand. 'We came together,' I said. 'Already. Isn't that wonderful?'

'I guess it is. It was quite an experience.'

I took the wet sheet downstairs to drape it in front of the electric fire, and when I came back up, Hector was thumbing through a magazine. I glimpsed a corset and a grease stain. 'What's that, Hector?' I asked. 'Soft porn,' he replied; 'you know the type. Nothing offensive. There's a letter in it from my father. I thought maybe you'd be interested.'

I said I was – deeply. I wanted to share everything. Above all I wanted to hear about his father. After his confession on the way to the Meadery I had felt reticent about bringing him up.

'He had a fetish too,' said Hector. 'Almost the same, I guess, only heavier. Corsets, corselets, that kind of thing. And he loved garters too. I only found out when I was sorting through his effects. It was kind of a shock. He's always appeared somewhat puritanical. Maybe fetishes are inherited.'

'Well,' I said pointedly, 'you both shared Lola.'

'Only briefly,' he said, then coloured. 'Oh, I see what you mean.' He threw back his head, and nodded, as if stricken by revelation.

'Read it to me, Hector.'

'You can see the mine captain, the fascination with how things work – underground. It's too long to read all of it. This bit reminds me of Sunday evenings round the piano. Pop loved music. It got lost in me somewhere. . . . "Often these corsets used to make the most delightfully erotic little sounds as the wearer moved her body, and with the close-grouped arrangement of front garters, a skilful exponent of the art of such audible titillation could accompany the soft seductive sound of her silk-sheathed thighs chafing together, with a most thrillingly intriguing clickety-click" (that's in inverted commas) "as the metal fittings of the garters at the front on one leg momentarily caught the corresponding fittings on the other leg."'

'That's poetry,' I said. 'Your dad could *write*.'

Hector shrugged but looked pleased, and continued reading. His voice, the tremulous bearer of his father's letter to the world, lulled and excited me as if I was on a train journey across America, titillated by soft springs that rode the clickety-clicks of Mr Bolitho's steely journey. I felt Joe stroking me as I registered odd phrases like small towns flashing by: Corseted Glory ... Back Lacings ... Amazon Maiden ... High Tension ... Tea Rose ... Apron Front ... No Nonsense ... Chastity Shield ... Soft Slither ...

Hector choked on a cawing laugh, stopping me between stations. 'I love this bit – "This is why some female devotees of this style have said to me, I love my garters. They are a woman's best friend."' I chided him for laughing at his father's dear obsession, and he effaced the laugh. 'There are a couple of drawings, also by him,' he said – offering me the magazine. I looked at the back and front view of a severe woman, distinctly Lolaesque, clad in a severe corselet.

'Lola,' I said, looking fixedly at him. Hector shrugged. 'Maybe a little. Pop knew her a long time before she'd give way to him, and I guess he had to make do with a lot of heavy petting. In postman's knock at church socials, that sort of thing – back in the twenties ... Maybe it's Mother. A little. But mostly I'd say it's Grandmother, when he was young. It's heavily Edwardian. We Bolithos are always light-years out of date. My grandfather had a fixation on farthingales. I'm joking,' he added hastily. 'I remember my grandmother as a stout, wise old lady, well-known for her original, pithy sayings – "a stitch in time saves nine", "look before you leap", "too many cooks spoil the broth". Many of these have become proverbial.'

He enquired if I couldn't see the delicate economical lines of an engineer in the drawings. I could; and pictured the iron-faced prim man striding the mined hills, hearing the little sleigh bells of women under their dresses, ghostly percussions.

'You miss him a lot still, Hector.'

'I guess so,' he sighed. I reached for his hand.

'This is beautiful,' I said. 'And deeply religious.'

His father was, said Hector, a God-fearing man, who had put his family's welfare before his own. After the collapse of the great Empire Mine in '41 he had built up his own engineering business and made sure his sons had a good education. One of Hector's brothers was the pilot of a Boeing 707, and the other a computer expert working in the space programme. All from a simple Cornish tinner, Hector's grandfather, who had emigrated to the States at the turn of the century. 'In three generations,' said Hector, 'we've moved from the rocks underground to the earth's surface, to the stars and constellations. Where can we go from here?'

To a good wife and a good home, I thought; but I'd have to let him find out for himself. I flicked through the magazine. It was full

74

of fuzzy amateurish pictures. I showed Hector a low-angled one looking up a woman's skirt, and asked him if it turned him on. He whistled through his teeth, and I said I could see the appeal of posing for such a photo. I told him the story of my first, or one of my first, sexual experiences, just after the war. I was coming home from school, on the top of a red double-decker. There was a narrow draughty gap between the seat and the seat-back, on those buses; and I suddenly realized a beady eye was pressed to the slit in front of me and was staring straight up my gymslip. The schoolboy who had been sitting there was obviously stretched out flat on the long seat. Instead of feeling angry I was excited, and (I blushed to recall it) reached a hand under my skirt and pulled aside the gusset of my navy knickers, as though they were chafing me.

'But he must have known that you knew,' said Hector. His penis had grown more engorged than I had ever seen or felt it. 'Oh yes, and he knew I knew he knew I knew.' 'Jesus!' said Hector. 'Could he see your garters?' he gasped. 'He could see everything,' I said. And in those days, he said thickly, they must have been wide and solid and with shiny bright clips; like most of Lola's still were. I said yes, I supposed so, yes. I had confessed my sin, and the holy father had told Mother. 'And he could see them plainly?' Hector gasped. My father had belted me for being a slut, and checked whether I'd been assaulted. 'Oh yes! Everything! My white thighs, my cunt.' His excitement was exciting me. My bounced thighs spread for the beady eye all the way home. 'Jesus!' His hand pumped. It was my first belt, white and with pink stars. 'And you just *let* him see!' gasped Hector. 'Well, of course! He obviously wanted to, so much.' 'He knew you wanted him to see them,' Hector gasped. 'Oh yes! He couldn't have had any doubts about that, Hector!' 'That's wonderful!' Hector ejaculated, sending thick jets of sperm on to his chest. He lay exhausted, his eyes closed.

He opened his eyes, glanced at his watch, and said it was time to fetch Mr Johnson. 'No, keep them on,' I said. (He was unhooking his suspenders.) 'Wear them under your trousers. Nobody'll know but me. I'd like it. It'll be a kind of link between us. Just the two of us.'

Hector shrugged. 'Okay.' Chuckling to himself, he pulled wine socks over his spliced nylon heels. My head started a dull ache. I guessed it had had too much excitement on top of the night's alcohol. I shut my eyes. When I opened them they saw an old miner fastening up his pit trousers (he still had buttons), and in the surprise it was a few moments before I adjusted to Hector. He

75

buttoned a loose fawn cardigan over his grey vest and asked me if I felt okay. 'You get some rest,' he said. 'You look pale.' He said he'd make some coffee, and I asked him to pop the chicken in the oven at the same time.

A small panic crossed his face. 'I don't know if I can do that. I'm afraid I might get it wrong. I'm not used to cooking.'

When I came back from putting in the chicken, my head was throbbing and I'd started to feel sick. I shut my eyes and concentrated on not moving. I tried to take my mind back fifty years to the miner and his family who had slept in this room.

But instead I was Vanessa Redgrave flying swiftly through interstellar space. Outside the space ship it was pitch-black, but it was warm and cosy inside. There was confetti all over the controls, and a pair of black and tan boots tied to the tail of the space ship. I heard from somewhere a clatter of crockery and a kettle being filled. I floated on top of my dream. There was a crash as Hector broke something, but there was only a little blood. Now there were stars accompanying our flight. Mr Bolitho was with us, in a pit helmet, leaning over our shoulders. Now the stars that were travelling with us were threaded through by stars drifting in the opposite direction. Hector said, with a fascinated chuckle, that we were entering the suburbs of colliding galaxies.

Mr B. said he hoped we didn't mind him coming along on our honeymoon, and I chatted to him brightly, setting him at ease. I showed him the hose my father had given us for a wedding present, to make up for belting me and making me sore. 'They're American nylons,' I boasted. 'Terribly dear!' Mr B. nodded, his jovial eyes glinting.

'Look at that, Pop!' said Hector, pointing.

He looked. The stars had thinned out in our drift. But there were other space ships, in which we could see ourselves, hanging in the black spaces. Hector said we were in a Black Hole.

'We're going backwards in time,' he said.

'No,' I said, 'it's too late, Hector, it's your mother's cunt.'

They quietly observed the blacknesses spinning by. Mr Bolitho nodded gravely. Hector said, 'Oh yes!' excitedly. I asked them how long it would last and Mr Bolitho said for ever.

And now, though it was still the Lolan vagina, it turned into the Grand Canal in Venice. We were waiting at the railway end, surrounded by cases chalkmarked *Just married*, and a crowd of well-wishers. I was embarrassed by the photographers, annoyed that no vaporetto had showed up. Hector assured me it was okay, as

76

there was a regular cervix. Just then, one hove in sight around the bend of the Canal. We were aboard and travelling in high spirits towards San Marco. Tom was at the wheel and so I knew there'd be no danger. Passing the magnificent decaying palaces we all sighed in rapture. Our Italian guide gave a long speech in which he said Venice was the supreme fetish of civilization, beautifully absurd and absurdly beautiful. Hector and I thanked him for it. We leaned on the rail as he pointed out the haunts of the famous. There, Byron had lived, and there – pointing – the child had drowned in the film *Don't Look Now*.

I glimpsed Joanne swaying her hips on the Bridge of Teats. Joe had joined us, much to my annoyance. He sneered at the tears in my eyes, telling me I really hated children and wanted them dead too, only I put the blame on him. And we could stuff the Grand Canal; it was built on the bones of starving peasants, and it stank. He leaned over the rail, pissing through his clitoris. The water turned yellow.

'You are speaking of my wife's vagina,' said Mr Bolitho, with a kind of New World stiffness and decorum. 'Chauvinist prick,' sneered Joe, and turned his beam of urine on him. Mr Bolitho pushed him overboard and we laughed and applauded as he swam away. I hugged and kissed Mr Bolitho. He was crying. 'You must miss Lola a lot,' I said.

'I guess so.'

I said we must find her a new husband. There was a red-headed man on the bank near the Rialto who looked like my father. Glimpsing me, he said proudly and affectionately to his customers, 'That's my fucking daughter!' I thought it would be a good idea if I could get Lola to marry him, he looked so sad and lonely.

Now there were gouts of blood, the size of gondolas, swimming past us. Mr Bolitho explained that, like the biblical Sara, she was getting hot flushes and had re-started her periods. The sun was setting through clouds, the sky grew Turneresque. And the water became choppy as the Grand Canal widened and we saw the Salute, the Doges' Palace, the domes of San Marco. The vaporetto bucked and our well-wishers were thrown about. Tom held on to the wheel, swearing. Spray coolly drenched our faces. 'Mother's coming,' Hector shouted over the hubbub. Good humour swept the decks. I giggled as Hector was thrown against me and we clutched each other. I saw a frock-coated man sitting on the window ledge of a third-storey window. I giggled again as I knew what was coming. Suddenly he toppled back, his frock coat flying, and fell into the Canal. Our vaporetto exploded into laughter. 'That's George Henry Lewes,' I explained to Hector. 'George Eliot's "husband" – husband's in inverted commas.' His fall had been so absurdly beautiful we laughed till we cried.

11

Waiting for the chicken to cook, I stood turning the pages of Mr Bolitho's girlie magazine. Crude husbands were proudly showing off crude photos of their crude wives, most of whom were old, fat, and ugly. But this, judging by the slavering letters, was just what was wanted: 'I've been drooling for days over Mrs E.C.'s truly corpulent belly and slack pendulous tits hanging down below her waist . . .' There was hope for me yet. There were, in addition to a wide variety of Bolitho turn-ons, women in rubber, leather, satin; in bloomers, camiknickers, nursing bras, gas masks, hair curlers, ropes, chains; pregnant women, women on toilets; whipping and being whipped; men in women's clothes, men in nappies and sucking dummies. And contact columns begged, or offered, more of the same, together with fantastic electronic comforts. I'd glanced at English magazines of a similar kind, but never one that spawned so many needs, or gave such a sense of opening up new frontiers, in the hope of finding a place to settle.

I half-expected to stumble across 'Ex-miner, musical, artistic and generous, wishes meet stern, firmly-corseted lady', etc. Had any of them, I wondered, ever found what they craved? I recalled some of the ghastly situations Joanne had got us into by answering such ads, or sending her own, for love and other deaths. She had drawn a very flattering self-portrait – and yet she might have done better to have exaggerated her faults. 'Middle-aged outsize tart, greying red-head, with wrinkles, stretch-marks and varicose veins', would probably have drawn them in droves. Each offered lady in Hector's father's book was older and uglier than the last.

And the last (that I had eyes for) was Lola. Behind her was the floral wallpaper she now wished to change for contemporary. In spite of unfamiliar clothing she was unmistakable. And there was a letter:

> The latest edition contains some very nice comments
> about me from Donald, Colorado, and I felt I had to send
> some more photos for him. Two of them are in my
> nurse's uniform for Donald and the other is displaying, as

he described it, 'My magnificent cunt'. The thought of arousing your readers with an unashamed display of my intimate parts and underwear under my nurse's uniform makes me real horny. If you publish the one of me displaying all, including my rather large tits, my husband and I will have another wonderful session thinking of all those cocks like Donald's. I do hope your readers think my photos worth comment. As I get older, I find my sex drive has got stronger and I enjoy giving satisfaction to men, not forgetting my husband.

> *L.B. (Mrs)*
> *N. California.*

An astronomical journal lay on the coffee table in front of the couch where she was displaying her 'magnificent cunt'. It was the Lola of now, not thirty years ago; all the references elsewhere to Polaroids and vibrators slid into place. When I flicked back to Mr Bolitho's letter I saw it concluded with 'a reaction against these abominable pantihose is long overdue', and it was signed 'F.McT. (Wisconsin)'.

Perhaps Hector didn't need a reason for telling such lies. Wasn't it all of a piece with the pathetic charade of Lola's letter – the pretence of being a nurse, the pose of being man and wife? It was all unreal. Hector was unreal. It fitted in with his massive erection when I was describing a girlhood memory, in contrast with the difficulty he had staying semi-hard when we were actually making love. No doubt he'd brought the magazine across the Atlantic so he could masturbate every morning over his mother's photo. I wanted him annulled – anything of him that was real enough to annul. If Joe went ahead and joined M U M (Murder for Ulrike Meinhof) I'd start by stuffing Hector's balls in his mouth and stitching it up.

I was wearing Joe's old clothes and I was trying to pick up a conversation with Mr Johnson. 'My wife's taken it very badly,' he said, grimacing.

'You must expect it.'

When I came back from the kitchen with the bottle of wine, he was watching cricket. 'I hope you don't mind?' he asked. 'It's not that –' He waved his arm helplessly. 'Life must go on.' I recalled Hector's reminiscence about the ball game before his father's funeral; the real Hector that had come through. I started feeling a little better about him, and even found myself smiling at the way I'd been taken in. But Americans were so subtle. I expected to hear the toilet flush and Hector coming downstairs; but nothing happened. I made some excuse to slip outside, and the car wasn't there. I gathered they must have missed each other, and Mr Johnson had come by taxi.

He absorbed himself in the struggle as I finished laying the table. Mention of hooks, leg, and being restricted, in Richie Benaud's Australian accent, reminded me of the green belt and the black belt linking Hector and me; except that I wasn't wearing mine. The Test cricketers came in for lunch, and I said we'd better start ours too, but first I'd slip up and change into something decent.

Over the chicken and salad, Mr Johnson talked about Cordelia, and how he couldn't do a thing with Beryl and her mother, they were prostrate with grief, and often hysterical. He was an atheist; yet ever since their return to Redditch, a crow had perched on the window sill each morning. It unnerved even him. And the phone call responsible for their child's death had been a wrong number! (His face gritted with pain.) I crooned sympathy, and refilled his glass. It was a relief to hear the knock on the door. 'Hector's back,' I said.

But it wasn't Hector beaming there, it was a policeman. 'Would you be a Mrs Bolitho?' he said. The fear that had clenched at my heart relaxed; if it was trouble it was not mine (how selfish we all are when the crunch comes). I explained she was out at the moment. He was an elderly policeman, a kind of Dixon of Dock Green figure, grey-templed and rubicund. 'There's been an accident.' He had a wistful, boyish half-smile. 'Oh my God!' I said. Wistfully and half-smiling he was looking at my breasts. 'Her husband's had an accident.'

For a moment, in my confused state, I was going to say, She knows about it, it's stale news, it wasn't an accident it was his heart. 'I don't think it's serious,' said the policeman. 'He's just knocked himself about a bit. He collided with a lorry just outside Penzance. He's in Godolphin Hospital.' 'That's not her husband, that's her son,' I said. He looked confused and troubled, as if this was a complication he wasn't used to dealing with, in a quiet place like Pendeen. 'I'm just passing on the message,' he said. 'This is what I was told.'

Mr Johnson came out with his wine glass. 'Hector's had an accident,' I said; 'he hit a lorry.' He went white. 'Is there much damage? – It's my car,' he explained. 'I couldn't say,' said the bobby, smiling wistfully and boyishly, gazing at my breasts. 'He hit the side of a juggernaut, so I don't suppose it's done it a lot of

80

good.' 'Oh my God,' said Mr Johnson. The policeman gave him a number to ring, and he dashed out of the house.

I said I would tell Mrs Bolitho, who shouldn't be long. The elderly copper walked away, waving a cheerio, paused, came back, rocked on his heels. Was I going to the Carnival and Fête on Friday, he asked. I said it was unlikely. 'Pity,' he said, blushing; 'it's worth a visit.' He rocked again on his heels, and went off.

Mr Johnson returned looking wretched. The front was a mess, it would take weeks to repair. The insurance company was sending someone to see it tomorrow. He'd have to try to bribe him into declaring it a write-off. I said how sorry and guilty we felt – would all feel. He switched on the television and watched the cricket, miserably.

Lola and Tom arrived while I was washing the dishes. Mildly surprised that Hector had turned into Mr Johnson, Lola called 'Hi!' and trotted upstairs. Tom shook Mr Johnson's hand and spoke some quiet words of sympathy. Clearly we heard Lola cascading and thundering in the bathroom. When she trotted down I went straight into: 'Hector's a little concussed, but he's perfectly all right.' I know it sounded crazy, but it's so much better than saying 'Hector's had an accident' or 'Hector's in hospital'. There's an art in breaking bad news. (Lola, so Hector says, broke the news of his father's death by ringing him with chatty gossip about snow in the Sierras and the cat having had four kittens, before dropping her tone into 'Well, dear, I've some bad news. Your dear father has passed away.')

Reassuringly I filled in the details. 'Oh my gad!' said Lola. She rushed out to call the hospital. Tom made tea. Lola returned less agitated. He was conscious, and no bones were broken. They were keeping him in overnight for observation, but then he ought to be able to leave. She could visit him at seven, and should bring his pyjamas and toilet gear. We sat drinking tea in a mood of mentally exhausted relief – all except Mr Johnson, who had nothing at all to be relieved about. He explained to Lola about the car, and how he'd have to stay overnight now, to see about insurance and repairs. Lola, overcome with remorse at this second blow to him, insisted he sleep at the cottage. 'We can share a room for one night, can't we, honey?' she said, glancing at me. I nodded; it was the least we could do. All the hotels and guest houses would be full anyway. We were very kind, he said dolefully. He watched the cricket with glazed eyes. Tom, finishing a chicken leg, broke a silence with 'There's another bugger gone' as a wicket tumbled, stood, and said the lighthouse called. Lola hugged him, thanking him for the lift. 'Never mind, my lover,' he said; 'he'll be all right.'

On the early evening bus into Penzance, I admired Lola's new-look face. She said the only trouble was, it made her clothes look dowdy. She teased me about Simon Johnson, saying I clearly found him attractive. I vigorously denied it, and asked her how she'd got that idea. 'Oh, just the way you look at him, honey! The way you sit . . . all the old body-language! Not that I blame you. I just love that Oxford accent.' She advised me ('as a mother, honey') not to fall into the smoking habit. It was dangerous to the health. Hector hated even the smell of cigarettes.

We found the hospital, and the ward, and I sent Lola in ahead as I wanted to have a word with the friendly sister. She ushered me into her office and I told her I'd come for some underclothes they must have found on Mr Bolitho. 'That's all right, my sweetheart,' she said briskly, handing me a brown paper parcel. 'We get all sorts in here, we don't take no notice of it. We 'abm put they on the list.' I explained he'd been on his way to a carnival where he was to be dressed in drag, and he'd put these on to save time when he got there, and for us to help him with the fastenings. She nodded briskly again. 'Ess, well, it's holiday time, id'n it, you?' Dismissing a matter so satisfactorily solved, she said, 'Are you his daughter, my lover?' I said, no, I was his girlfriend.

She twinkled at me through glasses and tilted her head in the direction of the ward. 'Do his missus know about it, then?' I started to correct her, but checked. It occurred to me that, just at present, Lola looked so little like Hector's mother that the truth would be embarrassing for him. 'Yes,' I said, 'and we're the best of friends.' 'Well, that's all right 'n, i'n it? That's grand. You got 'ave bit fun, abm' 'ee?' I smiled and nodded, and went through into the disinfected ward. Lola was wrestling Hector into his stripes. I felt a few sick eyes on me, straying from their wives. I bent and kissed Hector and asked him how he felt. 'Better,' he smiled.

He looked awful. There's something about pyjamas, anyway, that ages a man into senility. His jaw had been badly bruised and they had taken out his dentures for comfort. I hadn't known that he wore them. The shrunken cheeks and puckered lips called atten-tion to the sparseness of his hair, and the amount of grey it held. What normally looked distinguished now simply looked elderly. And all this was thrown into obscene relief by Lola's tinted blonde mane, newly-bought freshness of complexion, and rude bronze health. She fed him black grapes, popping them between his gums and cupping her hand to wait for the spat-out pip. I whispered into

82

his ear, 'Don't worry about the undies, I've explained them away,' but he didn't seem bothered, or maybe he didn't hear me. We found we had to speak up for him to catch our words; he was still obviously more than a little dazed. I tried to cheer him up by saying Tuesdays were always unlucky. Tomorrow would be better.

With pauses for recovery of breath, he explained what had happened. For the first time in thirty years he'd gone through a red light and hit a truck. He could only explain it by the fact that he'd been thinking of Gill Green, a girl he'd won the Grass Valley mixed doubles with, ten years back. He'd been thinking of her, maybe, because she looked like a younger version of me (Lola looked at me, and nodded). The name Green must have suggested to him subconsciously that the lights were green.

He didn't say much more. The explanation had worn him out. I told him not to worry about the car, and he replied, 'I've got to pick Mr Johnson up.' Lola chattered frantically about her ozone spray, mask, and plucked eyebrows, but he wasn't really hearing it. He gazed up at her with a seraphic smile, and said, 'You're beautiful, honey. You look like Sophia Loren.' Even Lola had the grace to blush, and her turkey throat wobbled.

For all our love of Hector – or perhaps because of it – it was a relief to us both, I think, to get to the bar of the Western Hotel. Lola had a few tears. Taking her hand, I told her not to worry, he'd feel like a new man in the morning. I wished I felt as sure as I sounded. At least it worked on Lola. She smiled, chuckled reminiscences, complained affectionately of his absent-mindedness, his helplessness without her. I found myself warming to her. She seemed genuinely to want me to have him, to break his dependence. We exchanged confidences over his little ways, including in bed; I recalled that childlike palm of hers, and somehow her innocence made me forget we were referring to the primal taboo. She was handing on the succession. I became suddenly tickled by Lola's having bought me support stockings by mistake in St Ives – the memory of her face, when I took them out of the paper bag. I grew helpless with laughter, and mine infected Lola. Women aren't supposed to roll about with laughter, and the crowded bar stared at us disapprovingly, and we didn't care.

We clung to each other, still giggling, as we walked up the road. We spotted Pendeen faces climbing aboard a coach, and controlled ourselves. 'We must remember that Hector is unwell,' said Lola. We collapsed into hysterical laughter again.

Tom had said to us there'd be a coach leaving the St John's Hall for Pendeen at about nine o'clock, after a band contest. If we wanted to we could have a lift back. He'd tell his parents to look out for us. They saw us coming up the road, and waited by the steps of the coach to say hello and see us safely aboard. 'Did you win, Mr Polglaze?' I asked. He said they came third, the best ever. 'And Father here was second in the cornet solo,' said Mrs Polglaze proudly. 'That was *good*!' I said. I introduced Lola and they said how glad – and how sorry – and how *was* he?

The coach was as good-humouredly full as the Marx Brothers' cabin in *A Night at the Opera*. After a similar crazy scrimmage I ended crushed against the gross and crippled old man whom I had first noticed adjusting his flies outside the Methodist chapel. After saying 'How are you, my lover', he turned his face to the window. I was half on, half off, the seat, and Lola, standing, was pressed against me, and crushed in on all sides, totally unable to move. I looked up into her shadowy face and said, 'I wonder what's happened to the Waltons?' She looked down at me in a droll manner. 'John-Boy's had his first fuck,' she said. I went into another ripple of silent laughter and felt her stomach shaking against my face. A tall bandsman, crushed against her back, ribbed her, and I could sense her relief as it allowed her to break into a laugh. The instruments moved off and the coach followed, through the outskirts of the town and into settling night. We pitched and bumped at high speed round hairpin bends. I had to save Lola from falling. Her nearness left a pleasant scent of Scotch and Chantilly. 'Any rate we can't fall down, can us, you?' said the tall bandsman over Lola's head. The coach was lightheaded with triumph. Tribal male shouts to cronies punctuated the cicada-trills of women. The level of noise dropped as the coach settled into a steady speed along the main road.

Someone started a jolly hymn, and the infection spread rapidly from the back to the front of the coach. All I can recall is the refrain they kept returning to, endlessly and with relish – 'Amazing love, how can it be / That Thou, my God, should'st die for me?' It had a racy tune and a heady harmony. The women flew like birds and sustained the second syllable of AMAY–, and the men, who all seemed to be basses, posed themselves and then gravelled in with four staccato growls: a-maz-ing love! And the women flew again on HOW CAN–, and held it, and the men more softly, swiftly, how-can-it-be; and higher yet, louder, the women, THAT THOU–, and the men with exultant glee, strong mallet-blows, that-Thou-my-God. It was stirring. They sang as if they believed it. And on the second chorus my gross and taciturn neighbour amazed me by joining in with the voice of Chaliapin, though he still gazed vaguely out into the semi-dark, oblivious to everyone.

And in the third verse, Lola sang. Richer, clearer than I had ever heard her, dominating the sopranos, a lark soaring to the zenith on THAT THOU–. There I was stuck between Chaliapin and Nellie Melba and feeling horribly inadequate. I had no voice. I could do nothing but transmute the energy flowing from Lola. Her legs embracing mine, I let my hand finger the hem of her skirt. I moved my hand between her legs. The coach turned from the main road and the lurch caused my hand to touch her stockinged thigh. I moved it away. The road curved and my hand touched her again. I kept it there. As she sang just as lustily, I let my hand stroke gently up and down her leg. I reached the cool flesh. I froze as the hymn ended, to mutual appreciation – 'handsome, you!' – but Lola said only 'That's a great hymn!' to the man pressing into her back, and coyly thanked him when he said she had a handsome voice.

Then Lola burst suddenly into 'Your tiny hand is frozen'. The coach fell silent, drinking in the superb voice in the unexpected popular classic, as well they might. Her tone, that reminded me of limeblossom honey, resonated into her thighs. I was vaguely aware of the shadowy presence of one or more of the others; Joe certainly, and possibly Joanne or even Joan. But I also felt lost to myself in a wider and more beautiful way; I wanted to stroke like this everyone in the coach, give of my depleted spirit to everyone; and through Lola I was somehow doing it. I was even in touch with lonely stone cottages we were invisibly passing, the lives of people who lived there, and of the dead whom they loved. I was in touch with the moor stones. They were flowing into my fingers through Lola.

I felt, less a specific desire for this juvenescent pensioner, Lola, than a beautiful greed, for the possible, the impossible. She was swaying to the coach and the song and my fingers. (A delicious tremolo.) My fingers walked about in her, wet through. Loud applause as Lola came. 'Handsome, you!' 'Encore!' 'What 'ee mean, encore? – same woman sing again!' (Laughter.) I explored her belly under her thick belt. (Lola singing 'Amazing Grace' on request, the rest humming or singing quietly in harmony.) I delved again, wanted to throw her skirt over my head like a photographer's black cloth. I returned to her thighs, they trembled, their vibrations passed into my fingers, I thumbplucked a dreamy guitar accompaniment. The song dying into silence, the night-shapes of mining gear, I withdrew my hand, the coach slowing.

We were invited for a cup of tea by Tom's parents, but explained we had a guest staying. 'I just love these friendly people!' carolled

85

Lola, as we walked the short distance home. She slipped her arm through mine. I said I felt embarrassed at what I'd done, and hoped she forgave me and wouldn't start imagining I was a lesbian. 'You don't have to apologize for it, dear,' she said. 'I've enjoyed all our experiences, so much.' She added: 'It was the closeness. The guy behind came off against me.'

We walked briskly in the keen night air. She seemed thoughtful. 'Honey,' she said, as the cottages came in sight, 'Hec had this funny dream when he was knocked out by the crash. He's not a dreaming man, as a rule, but *you'd* be interested. He told me about it when you were getting the clothes. He was a tiny baby, and sliding down my cunt. His little prick erected because of the rubbing – it was tremendously erotic, he said. When he got outside, the nurse spanked him and he was so mad he pissed on her – only it was spunk. Her lap was covered in white. Wasn't that a strange dream, honey? Could it have a meaning?'

Mr Johnson was curled up into a question mark on the sofa, watching the day's highlights. I didn't want to waste time speaking to him, said I had a headache, and went up. Lola, reporting on Hector's condition, stayed to chat and make a drink. I lay in Hector's bed; Lola's scent was still on my fingers. I remembered the package stuffed in my handbag, and took it out. There was a grey stain on the panel of the black belt, which hadn't been there this morning, from Hector's wet dream in the ambulance, or while the nurses were undressing him.

12

It was a beautiful day. It could have been morning, afternoon, or evening. At the best of times I have little sense of time. It was a beautiful day, and we were scudding along about a mile off shore, and I was fiddling with Tom's outboard motor. Tom was saying, 'You're a bleddy surprise packet, *you* are!' I moved away from the complicated motor before I could do too much damage, saying weakly that as a single girl living on my own I needed to know a bit about everything. 'A *bit*! You bleddy know more than *I* do!' Lola, bare-legged and in her stillvext Bermudas, came to join us. 'Oh it's *beautiful*!' she said. 'You want to see about those eyes, honey, as soon as you get back home. Our sight is very precious.' Joe, I knew, had a nervous tic, a constant embarrassment.

I took her place at Mr Johnson's side. He was engrossed in the *Guardian* sports page, and having trouble keeping it from blowing away in the breeze. Knowing he was a lecturer in English I wanted to ask him what the green girdle symbolized in *Sir Gawain*. I was reminded of it by the greenstone cliffs gleaming in the distance, and as Joe would never have brought it up (*Spare Rib* is about his intellectual limit) it was a safe conversational opening. But before I could open my mouth Simon was saying curtly – his eyes still devouring the cricket report – 'I don't think that was very fair.' 'I don't know what you mean,' I said.

'Beryl has a lover too. It wasn't just me. It wasn't one-sided. I'm *not* a callous man.'

'No,' I said. 'I'm sorry. Maybe I jumped to conclusions.'

At my penitent tone he relaxed, folding the newspaper into his lap. He stared unseeing towards the cliffs. I trailed my hand in the cold water, and waited for him to unburden himself.

'We're just not very compatible. We've been close to splitting for quite a long time. The holiday was my idea to see if we could –' he waved a hand – 'find a *modus vivendi*.'

I touched his hand sympathetically. 'Maybe this will bring you closer,' I suggested.

He sighed. 'I doubt it. She blames both of us too much. She thinks if we hadn't *sinned* by having affairs we wouldn't have arranged the holiday and Cordelia would still be alive. She says she never wants to see her lover again. But her going away with him now and again has been the only thing that's made life at all tolerable to me.'

He leaned his head back, closing his eyes. Different from my father in almost every respect, this clip-lipped Englishman, he reminded me of him in that weary pose. The knowledge that – hooked stupidly on a fishing holiday in Connemara – he had mortgaged his life to a woman who was, at best, shallow, unpredictable, exhausting; who had held him back in his career – *he* ought to have had the Nobel Prize, not Crick and Watson: how often I had seen my father throw his head back wearily and bitterly, like that, and close his eyes. But Lola broke Simon's dream or emptiness, calling to us to look down in the water, you could see stone hedges, and tree trunks. 'The Lost Land of Lyonesse,' called Tom, nodding to me, knowing my interest in such things. We looked, and could see nothing.

'She's a wonderful woman,' said Mr Johnson. 'Even the birds came to her hand to be fed this morning.' And, considering her age, what incredible legs she had. He gazed at them admiringly.

'She's very fond of you, Jo,' he added. 'She feels you're like a sister to her.'

As if drawn by his admiration, Lola came back to sit with us. 'Isn't it wonderful he had a restful night, Jo?' she said enthusiastically.

'Yes,' said Simon, 'it's a *very* comfortable bed. I'm grateful, Jo.'

'No, honey!' Lola smiled. 'I meant Hector! I just hope they let him out, when the doctor eventually gets around to seeing him. He'll be mad at missing this trip. My! This ought to inspire you, honey! I read a poem once about white sea horses running in to land.' She touched Mr Johnson's gleaming white shirt. 'It's come out real nice, Simon.' 'Yes,' he said, 'I'm awfully grateful.'

She trotted back to Tom again. Simon commented how awfully worried she was; she simply couldn't sit still. I put on my windcheater over the thin, ragged sweater, and Simon put on his sports jacket: it had turned fresh. The water was choppier. To our surprise the blue sky was covered with small white fleecy clouds; but there was no threat of rain.

I finally got round to asking him about the green girdle in the poem, and he said he hadn't read it. 'You ought to, it's beautiful,' I said. He smiled: 'That's a pre-systematic judgment.' I said I didn't know what that meant. I only knew it was a beautiful poem. Simon said he really didn't know much about literature, nor care for it all that much. When I expressed surprise, since he lectured in English, he explained that he taught linguistics. He had studied literature, and taught it in school and at a College of Education, but it hadn't been his cup of tea. He had a scientific bent, really. 'I felt a bit of a fraud,' he said sadly.

I could sympathize. I'd started courses and never finished them. I still had the Royal National College for the Blind I could try, but little else. 'Fortunately,' Simon went on, 'linguistics came into fashion. I took an M.A. in it, and landed this job at the University.' I asked him what it involved. 'My own specialism,' he said, 'is stylostatistics. Literature does come into it, but as a code rather than anything else. I mean, it's irrelevant whether the literature is good or bad. In some ways it's better for analysis if it's bad. I'm doing research in phonological aspects of style. Both segmental and suprasegmental.'

I delicately – but one should *talk* about the dead – brought up Cordelia. 'That was Beryl's idea,' he said. 'She used to be an actress.'

An icy wave splashed me, saturating my jeans, and Lola put on her black plastic mac. Tom gestured that he was turning back in.

As we turned we met the full force of heavy seas, the hammer of a fierce wind, and we were clinging on to the sides as we were thrown violently around, the boat bucking and rearing. Tom, standing by the motor, had no difficulty keeping his balance. He broke into a laugh, seeing our sudden confusion. 'Shan't be long,' he cried. 'Hold tight!' Then the engine stuttered, and he bent over it. It returned to normal; stuttered again. 'Jo!' he called, beckoning me. I went and pretended to have an expert look. 'What's wrong with the bugger?' he asked. I shook my head. 'I don't know, Tom.' The motor cut out, dead. We were plunging, silently, in loud seas.

Simon crawled forward, clinging tight for dear life, and had a helpless look. Tom tried to re-start the engine but nothing happened. 'It's a bugger, ol' man!' he said to Simon.

Simon helped to get out the oars, and dropped one overboard. The seas were mountainous now; every other second we were drenched. We had taken in a lot of water. Tom started baling furiously. Lola was almost blown overboard when the wind took her mac. We all crouched as near the bottom of the boat as we could. It was a ridiculously small boat, of a sudden. 'Hold on!' cried Tom. 'She won't overturn.' But I could see he was worried. One moment we were climbing a mountain, and the next on a slalom-slope. Clinging hold to a seat, I kept my eyes tightly clenched. The words of the *Pater noster* sprang into my mind. Lola was audibly praying, though the words weren't distinguishable. Pressed close against me, Simon's body shook.

Then Lola took a grip on herself. 'Hold on, honey!' she was saying to me. 'Trust in the One above!' She was clutching Simon's arm and telling him that, at the worst, he would see his beautiful little girl again. She started a hymn, a Salvation Army chant – 'We have an anchor that keeps us whole' – beating time to its vigorous cheerful rhythm. I felt just a little less terrified. It was her finest hour.

I saw Tom, balancing erect on the prow, being whirled up high then plunged into the deeps. I saw he was afraid. He was so little in control I was gripped with certainty of death. But, on the crest of the next mountainous billow, he gave a shout, a triumphant cry, that stopped Lola in mid-phrase. We stared up at him as he came plunging down again. His face held a seraphic expression. 'The Lord is coming!' he cried. 'The Lord is coming towards us!'

A beautiful, childlike grin spread across his features. Simon was being sick, but Lola and I couldn't take our eyes off Tom's face. If it was madness it was a blessed madness. I was filled with irrational

89

hope. The boat was swept up again, and again Tom stared over the waves. 'He's coming!' he cried again. 'The Lord is coming towards us! He's seen we're in trouble.' Lola started to snuffle. 'He's comin' to help us, my sweetheart!' said Tom. 'He do know we're in trouble. The Lord is comin'.' Lola's snuffles turned into deep sobs. I started to cry too. Simon was curled up, motionless, his face the colour of his shirt.

I heard a growing, throbbing roar underneath us. It flashed through my mind it was the Day of Judgment. Once, Mother had taken me to church to wait for the end of the world, but we had had to go home again. It had come now. Tom crested the waves again and cried out triumphantly, 'The Lord is nearly here! We're goin' to be all right, my lovers!' And the next moment I had a vision of a big man in sea boots and a heavy white cricket sweater; a man with a beard and a bald head. He was only about twenty yards away from us, and under him was a powerful launch. He was shouting to ask if we wanted a tow. 'Yes, sir! Very kind of you, sir!' Tom bellowed. 'Can you throw a rope across?' Turning to us, Tom mouthed, 'It's Lord St Levan.' The hint of a gleeful smile haunted the corners of his lips, and in that expression I recognized his father.

The snowy bunched-up cloudlets had drifted apart. I sat in pleasant warmth in the pebbly cove. I tried to write a poem about the morning's experience, but it was still too close; besides, I felt too relaxed and dreamy, and, in a strangely pleasant way, apart from myself. A young man in wine swimming trunks, picking shellfish on the rocks, incuriously watched the large middle-aged woman taking off her stockings to paddle.

I read vaguely, distracted by the sun, the swift wavelets, and the lithe young man picking shellfish. The strong breeze off the sea had a chill edge to it, and I decided it was time to go. I wondered how I'd greet Hector.

A gleaming new blue Avenger was sitting by the gate. I assumed an affluent son visiting one of the derelict old ladies who haunted the windows of the other cottages in the terrace, twitching lace curtains. I heard Lola's 'Cooey! we're in the garden!' and walked through the rose bushes. Sun-glassed Simon, and Lola, basked in garden chairs. Lola smiled. 'Hasn't it turned beautiful again? Have you been swimming?' No, I said, but I'd paddled. 'Where's Hector?'

She grimaced, and sighed. 'He's still in Penzance, honey. I've had the most terrible afternoon. Simon dear, we need an extra chair.' I told him not to bother, and sat on the grass.

'When I got to the hospital,' said Lola, 'the doctor had done his rounds and made up his mind Hector shouldn't leave just yet. It seems the police had been to see him, to take a statement about the accident, and it gave him a slight temperature. The policeman was very rude, so Hector says. But the doctor wasn't sure *why* he had the fever, and thought he should be kept under observation for a day or two, to be on the safe side.'

'You should have insisted on bringing him out,' I said indignantly. 'Hospitals are no place for a sick person.'

'Well, maybe. But it's not so easy when you're a stranger in a strange land. I strongly inferred there'd be fireworks if I didn't get to see the doctor tomorrow, supposing they still want to keep him in.'

'One has to trust their judgment,' said Simon pompously.

I had my own reasons for not trusting the science of medicine, but I held my peace.

'You haven't heard the all of it, honey. They'd moved him into a different ward. The one we saw him in was a sort of overnight ward, for vasectomy patients and so forth, and they needed the bed. It was a nice, bright ward, I thought, didn't you? And the head nurse was nice. You could tell from the way the patients whistled at us that they were happy. But Jesus, sweetheart, they'd moved him into a geriatric ward! Boy, was it geriatric! I've known some crummy geriatric wards but this one was a peach. I could hardly stand the smell of piss when I walked in. Not a man there was under about seventy-five. And plastic bags of – well, you know. You can imagine how I felt, seeing poor Hector in the middle of that lot. No wonder he felt depressed and feverish. He looked really miserable, Jo, it nearly broke my heart.' She searched her handbag and found a lace handkerchief to dab her eyes. 'About the only nice thing that had happened to him was your card and poem, honey. That was a lovely thought – you didn't tell me you were sending it. Hector was really thrilled about it; he was showing it round the ward when I got there. Jo wrote a poem for Hector, Simon, on the back of a funny card. It had the little coloured nurse who brought it to him in stitches, apparently. Wasn't that a kind thought?'

Somewhere above my quickened heart I heard Mr Johnson say dully, 'What is it about?'

'It's about me getting humped by Tom and Stanley Parkins at the lighthouse. He's the head lighthousekeeper. It's a really nice verse, I'd say, though I'm no judge of poetry. Hector likes it. It's very frank and direct. It wasn't *in* the lighthouse, it was at the cove.

But we'd been in the lighthouse, Simon. We'll treasure it, honey; it's the first time anyone's written any poetry about either of us. It was the only bright spot the poor boy had. I simply couldn't leave him there. I asked them about a private room, but the head nurse was a bitch. What right did we have, she said, to special privileges? I assume she meant, as Americans. I said, Fuck your socialized equality! She attacked me for using bad language, so I said, Screw you! and marched off to see the registrar. Fortunately he was more sympathetic – a lovely man, reminded me of Raymond Massey – has a brother in Detroit. My Moyle blood was up, by this time – my grandfather was a wrestler. I'm afraid I went for him.'

Simon interrupted her with a curt sardonic laugh, then gave an apologetic wave of his hand as she looked at him in puzzlement. She continued: 'I took the key out of his office door and said I wasn't budging till I got satisfaction. Well, he was terribly nice about it. I'd say he's a great asset, strong but gentlemanly. He arranged for Hector to be transferred to a private nursing home not far away. The hospital uses it for convalescent patients who have no one at home to take care of them, and a doctor looks in every day. I went with Hector in the ambulance and stayed with him while they got him settled. It's a lovely place, Jo, and Hector's got a private room overlooking the – what were they called, honey? – the Morrab Gardens. The room's nice and airy and with a lovely view. I feel a little better about it, and Hector felt happier. We can visit whenever we like, which is a blessing. But shit! I wish you could have seen that geriatric ward! Don't they have any feelings in this part of the world?'

Mr Johnson said, 'Perhaps our luck has changed.'

Let's hope so, said Lola. She added that Simon had also had a stroke of luck. Simon nodded. The insurance man had insisted the Viva should be repaired – which would take weeks – but when Simon had told him about the bereavement, and the need to get home to his wife, the man had agreed he could hire a car. That was it outside. It was almost new. They planned to give it a good run tonight, if I felt like joining them for a meal out somewhere. They felt we deserved a good meal after such a terrible day.

13

Desperate for advice, I had forgotten Tom would be at work; but his mother insisted I come in: 'The old ironin' can wait. Glad see 'ee, dear.' 'Yes, glad see 'ee, my handsome!' said Mr Polglaze. 'Shut that thing off, mother.' A reedy tenor was scaling the heights to 'take me up to God'. 'Best place for 'n', said Mrs Polglaze ironically as the voice went dead. She offered me tea and a piece of pasty, but I settled for the tea.

She perched on the arm of my chair and 'mothered' me 'And that was funny too, wa'n it, you, him havin' to use a wheelchair? Do 'ee think it's . . . mental?' I said it was; and now the accident on top of it; I started to cry. Mr Polglaze, to cheer me up, told a story about a man in the village who had become paralysed overnight soon after the outbreak of the war. 'A great stuggy young fellow he was, then. His wife had a job pushin' him around in his wheelchair – didn't she, Elsie? Then, soon after I'd come home, in 1945, she came rushin' into Charlie Harris's shop one day, saying there'd been a miracle. Mr Harris asked her whatever had happened. "Whey, Will have thrown away his wheelchair, he can walk!"' Mr Polglaze threw back his head and barked a laugh, and I snuffled and giggled.

'That's better, my handsome,' said Elsie. 'Did 'ee have a nice boat trip with boy-Tom?' Gathering that Tom hadn't wanted to upset her by admitting he'd nearly had to walk the waters, I said it had been very pleasant. 'That's grand,' she said. I apologized again for bothering them, but I hadn't known where to turn. It helped just to talk about it. 'You're very welcome, my handsome,' said Mr Polglaze, his mouth full of pasty, which he washed down with a gulp of tea. 'Any time. You don't need to be asked.'

'On holiday too,' said Elsie. 'Like Fate. How's *Mrs* Bolitho takin' it?' She pronounced the name, not Bol'itho, as Hector and Lola pronounced it, but Boleye'tho. She was taking it very well, I said. And it was nice that Mr Johnson was still with us and was going to take her out to dinner.

'Dear of her. Do her good. Take her mind off it bit. Hey, and some handsome voice she got, abm' she?'

I snuffled some more, feeling sorry for Hector and for myself. Mr Polglaze cleared his throat and said why didn't I go and see him, talk to him sensibly, try to make him pull himself together. I asked if they knew the times of buses. 'You don't want to wait for they old buses,' said Tom's mother; 'Arthur'll run 'ee to Penzance, wean't 'ee, Arthur?' I protested at taking him out after a hard day's work, but Arthur said it was no trouble, no trouble at all.

His hands on the wheel comforted me; they were large and work-hardened yet gentle. I enjoyed the quiet drive in his van. Every so often he pointed to a house and said, 'I built that.' I liked the pride and simplicity with which he said it, and wished I could say the same – of anything, however humble. He had also worked on the nursing home where Hector was; and hoped he would never have to go into such a place. 'Old age is a tragedy, my sonny!' he said, shaking his head. I asked him if he was going to have a drink while he waited for me, but he said, no, he would have a smoke and a little stroll around. I wasn't to hurry.

The home was shut. So much for the ever-open door. My ring was answered at last by a dumb night nurse. I breathed the familiar sickly-sweet smell of varnished old age. The inmates had been put away for the night, though it could only have been about eight o'clock. We rose two flights of a lift and along a long corridor. I glimpsed a lounge, homely as a furniture showroom. The girl knocked on a brown door and left me. I went in. Hector was propped up on pillows, reading. 'Hi!' he said. 'Hi, Hector!'

In his striped pyjamas he still looked pretty ghastly, but not quite such a tomb-haunter. I realized later he had his dentures back in. On his bedside cabinet was a half-full carafe which might have been apricot wine but was in fact urine. I laid beside it the bag of oranges Mrs Polglaze had sent along for him. A fruit bowl already overflowed with peaches, bananas, grapes. 'It's too much,' he groaned. 'It's too heavy, do you want to kill me?'

I perched on the bed and asked him how he felt. 'Fine!' he replied. 'Ready to play a five-setter against Connors. I don't know why the hell they're keeping me in.'

My spirit lifted at his sign of spirits. I kissed him and flashed my stocking-tops (a pair of Lola's). He smiled. 'You'll be out tomorrow,' I said. 'I sure hope so. Say, thanks for the card, it really cheered me up. And the poem – wonderful!' It gave me the chance to look at the card, which was resting against the carafe, by pretending a reappraisal of it. The Donald McGill picture showed a thin, leering, red-nosed man enjoying the view behind a fat lady with a hitched skirt (and stocking-tops) enjoying the view, through a telescope, of a lighthouse out to sea. And she's saying, 'How would you like to be holed up in that, blowing a gale of wind?' Joanne's choice would have amused me in other circumstances, and even now I could hardly avoid smiling. Hector chuckled too, looking at it with me. I turned it over and read the poem:

> Fucking in a lighthouse
> is not so terrible.
> It's not like throwing stones
> in a glasshouse.
> It's a discreet place
> for a ménage à trois,
> where God
> 'with Jesus Christ
> and the Holy Ghost liveth
> and reigneth for ever'.

There seemed nothing I could say about it. But Hector prevented any embarrassment. 'It's tender,' he said, 'and straight to the point. There's a lot of truth in it, too. I've been thinking about it a lot. I'm not a literary man, but I'd guess it's publishable. I'd like to show it to the editor of our literary mag at Sacramento. I feel very touched, Jo. We both do.' His eyes shone into mine, and his dentures gleamed.

'I'm glad you like it, Hector,' I said. 'It's symbolic, you see.' He nodded. I chatted brightly to him, about Mr Johnson's replacement car (he was pleased), and Lola's bravery on the boat (he was proud). 'I don't deserve her, Jo.' I asked him if there was anything I could do, and he said maybe I could peel him an orange. He strained forward, searching, and said there was a plate and a fruit knife somewhere. They were under the bed. 'I'm going to have to get along without my hot drink, I guess,' he said pathetically, with a weak smile to make it seem a quip. His look was so hapless that I told him he really *had* to work on this mother thing, this clinging dependence – it was dragging him to destruction. I said I didn't want to labour it, but if we got married I could save him. At present he wasn't really a man. But it was not too late. I said I *had* thought maybe she could live with us, if that was what they both wanted. But now I truly believed he had to throw her off altogether. We could surely find her a little place of her own, not too far away. The door would be always open for her to visit, any time, so long as she didn't try to take advantage.

'*Shit!*' said Hector, sending his fruit plate hurtling across the room. I jumped back. Juice trickled down a white wall. A vein throbbed in his temple. I could see him trying to frame words but none would come, and the unspeakable words made his neck swell. Then they surged out in a ghastly spew. Bit by bit he calmed into

more familiar Hector-speech, illuminated by wry or genial smiles –
though also clouded once, briefly, by tears. But I was too stunned
by the opening to make any responses or interruptions. I just sat
very still, as the lava poured over and round me. It was a long
speech; nothing at all like *Morte Arthur*, yet somehow, in
philosophic and even amused restrospect, it seems right to call it

HECTOR'S TALE

Shit! You've got the nerve, after all we've done for you, to try to
break up our home. I've had just about as much as I can take. Your
perpetual sarcasm about my 'mother' this and my 'mother' that . . .
I doubt if anyone else but Lola and I would have put up with you.
We've had more than our share of being disappointed in people,
but I guess you take the gold cup. When we met you at the Coach
Station in London, over that unbelievable coffee and ham roll, we
thought you were a nice, friendly, amusing lady. We warmed to
you at once. At the hotel in Glastonbury you lecture us about
morals, like some kind of religious nut – which strikes us as pretty
weird in the circumstances – but at least you're still *talking* to us.
Then on the ride up to Cornwall you suddenly switch seats, make
as if you've never met us, treat us like dirt? But we felt sorry for
you, we saw you were desperately lonely, we saw you had bad
nerves and were depressed. There isn't much fun in being a
middle-aged spinster, we know that. I'll admit to you, *I* wanted to
back out, but Lola was all for taking you under our wing. Because
she's got a heart of gold. And she's never said a word against you,
even though I know she's been dreadfully hurt by your sarcasm.

So, I go along with it. And what happens? You practically rape
her in St Ives, while pretending to help her to bed, when you know
she's a sick old lady who was already exhausted with entertaining
you all day, on top of a long flight and the bus trip. It wasn't what
we'd been led to expect. Okay, as it happens she enjoyed it up to a
point, but it could have killed her. You have the gall to impugn and
insult my virility, I don't know on what grounds. Jesus Christ, you
shit on my tennis whites. You use up all the hot water with your
endless baths. We help you through a bad time and then find out
you've been screwing around when we could have done with a little
help, when Lola wasn't at all well. And *we* were paying for you! We
were always taught in Sunday School that he who pays the piper
calls the tune; but that doesn't seem to be in your rule book. You've
smoked dope, you've fouled the air with cigarettes. It wouldn't
surprise me if you shoot junk. You insist on carting me off on some

crazy trip across the moors, to crawl through a fucking hole. You nag-nag me into going to bed with you, when you could see I was worn out. Okay, it was nice, but you keep making a big thing of it when we agreed, right from the start, it was strictly casual. You make me wear women's clothes, so I end up not only half-dead but crucified with embarrassment in front of the nurses. Worse than that! I think that's why your police are hounding me. They obviously think I'm some kind of a *nut*, unfit to be driving.

Okay. I wouldn't want you to think it's been all bad. We think you're a good guy. You've got certain mental problems and we sympathize. Lola's worked a lot with the mentally sick and she knows you don't always mean to do what you do. And we've had some good times. But get this straight once and for all – I'm not interested in you, I'm not interested in breaking up my home. I love Lola. I get depressive spells myself, and she keeps me going. Oh I know she's got her faults. She gushes, and she's not very bright. But let me say this – compared with some of your adolescent tantrums, Lola is Golda Meir.

When she goes, I won't last much longer. I've known her nearly all my life. I told you about her tough start in life – *she'd* never bring it up. Brutal alcoholic father, too many mouths to feed, mother who died of cervical cancer when Lola was still in school. So she married early, to escape from her home environment, and it didn't work out. You can imagine what a scandal her divorce caused in a narrow-minded place like Grass Valley fifty years back. It's not easy to be a lively, attractive young divorcee; you tend to get left out of dinner parties and you attract a lot of unfair gossip. I guess Mother and Father were about the only people who took a truly Christian view. They kind of took her under their wing. As a matter of fact she was there taking tea with us when Mother went into her Parkinson's trance. Lola offered to help Pa and he was grateful. I remember her in those days as a wonderful warm-hearted provider, in spite of the Depression. She did everything she could to make up to us for losing our mom like that.

You can imagine, though, how it started up more gossip. There's always plenty of sympathy around but not much real charity. Father was only human and he had his needs. Probably he would have married Lola if Mother had been dead. I guess Lola loved him, and felt her position acutely. When I was a student at Berkeley she confided in me a lot. We'd always been close, because I was the baby, but we became even closer when I reached my late teens. We had a very friendly informal friendship. She confided in me her hopes and fears. How would I feel if Father divorced Mother and married her? At the time I wasn't happy about it. Anyway, it wasn't to be. Pop had always been hale and hearty, but out of the blue he had his heart attack. Forty-seven, that's all he was, the same age as I am now.

My brothers had moved away, one to college in the East and the other drafted and sent to Korea. I was working for my Ph.D. Lola offered to stay on in the house and keep it welcoming. It was a great comfort at such a lonely and unhappy time. Whenever I came home Lola was warm and giving. I didn't have any girlfriends and she'd let me kiss and hug her a little. Being away most of the time put an exciting kind of distance between us. I took to getting the bus home almost every weekend. In the dead of winter (I remember I grew a beard to help keep out the cold) I'd take off for home, after my last class. To receive food, affection, the warmth of her body – sometimes she'd let me come against her thigh. Then on Sunday night, after one of her hot Cornish pasties – you must try one some day – I'd go back to Berkeley, clutching a hot-water bottle to my stomach and thinking of the wonderful time we'd had.

Well, eventually I wore her down and we got married. I couldn't see any sense to her arguments against it. Okay, I was innocent and callow, yet at twenty-four an 'elderly' man in many ways. I found girls at college silly and immature. Whereas Lola, still in her forties, was buxom, beautiful, and full of life. Really she was younger than me. And *men* in their late forties married girls half their age all the time and no one thought anything about it. She thought I'd live to regret it. Not being able to have children, for example.

But we *did* have one! Lola was in her menopause but she got pregnant right away. A beautiful little girl with blonde hair. Tracy. Here's a picture of her. Wasn't she beautiful? She died at thirteen. Lola won't talk about it. Don't ever mention it to her. She thinks death is morbid.

Well, tears won't bring back my little girl.

Lola and I went through a bad time. She took up nursing to occupy her mind, and I threw myself into my work. I was conscious of sagging breasts, wrinkles, crowsfeet, yellowy wasting skin; in her, I mean. Women age quicker anyway, I guess, and here I was, married to a senior citizen. I developed a crush on one of my students, and even thought about divorce. I talked it over with Lola – we've always been able to discuss our problems frankly and calmly – and she thought I ought to go to bed with the girl first. Sort of try it out. That'll show you what a wonderful understanding person she is.

This girl made a really major effort for her big night – no jeans and sweatshirt, but a nice dress, perfume, earrings, the works. She was a bright, beautiful girl. But as she started rolling down her pantihose I discovered I had a fetish. Hector, old man, I groaned, you're in trouble. I couldn't make it. I had to tell her I felt too guilty, drive her home, and give her a good grade.

I realized I was high and dry. All women but Lola had been castrated by their own wish. In terms of our marriage, pantihose were a stroke of luck for Lola. I sometimes think she invented them. She's clever enough. She's as artful as a barrel of monkeys. She pretended she was too old to start wearing anything different – but I guess she knew she'd got me hooked. Her legs weren't improving any, but her garter belts stayed young. I felt kind of degraded by the trap I was in, and still felt maybe divorce would give me a new start. She said she wouldn't stand in my way – she's got a lot of guts, as you saw this morning. I even went to a lawyer. But it wasn't to be, and for the most wonderful of reasons. My old mother had her miracle recovery, thanks to L-Dopa. It was bad enough breaking the news of her long coma, Father's death, a dead granddaughter she'd never seen – without adding a divorce to it. Mother believed in the sanctity of the home, and she was so thrilled to see Lola again. I guess she was a little bit upset at first, hearing Lola and I were married, but Lo had a good long private talk with her, and when I joined them at her bedside Mother gave me a big hug, smiling through her tears. We brought her home for weekends, and the doctors were saying she'd soon be well enough to come home for good.

But it wasn't to be. She had a few months of beautiful happiness, then the drug started throwing up bad effects. It happened in nearly all the cases. At first just nervous tics, like adjusting her glasses about twenty times a minute. Then a whole clutch of frenzied symptoms, like walking faster and faster with ever shorter steps, endless repetition of the same phrase, head jerks, orexia, satyriasis – that's overwhelming sexual desire. Most of the patients masturbated openly in the ward, but Mother, poor dear, wouldn't have known how to. Lola wanted to fix her up with someone on one of her weekends at home. But Mom still felt in her heart she was married, and it wouldn't have worked.

She had to be taken off the drug, and sank back into stupor. All she could do was write us little messages with her left hand. It broke our hearts visiting her. We went as often as we could since my brothers lived so far away, and were wrapped up in their own lives. That hurt her, I guess, only seeing them once in a blue moon. The last time I saw her was three years ago come Christmas. She wrote down, 'I'd like to move west.' I said to her, 'Momma, this is the best place for you.' I felt I was tearing in two. She could move her eyes and that was all. She passed away a week later. They couldn't find a cause of death. I guess she was just tired, and wanted to be with Pop.

Lola brought me through that grief, as she's done so often. I hope you can begin to see why I could never leave her. We've had our ups and downs, what married couple hasn't? I've had my share of feeling ashamed to be seen with her. She tends to be mutton dressed up as lamb sometimes. If I were you I wouldn't regret too much never having married; believe me it's no bed of roses. There have even been times – though it's an awful thing to admit, and I wouldn't tell *her* for the world – when I've gone along with the impression people had, who didn't know us, that she was my mother. Till this week we haven't had a proper sex life for years. Not since Tracy died, I guess. We took up swinging, in a small way, soon after my fiasco with the girl at the motel. And we've met some nice people through it. Particularly on vacation it's fun to share things and make new friends. We still get Christmas cards from as far away as Bermuda and Vermont. But sexually it's never really worked out. By the second cocktail, usually at least one person in the foursome has decided to call it off. Lola's heart has never really been in it, I guess, she just hasn't wanted me to feel tied down. Her advanced age and poor health have been a drawback too. Quite a lot of men like mature women, but there is a limit. You can't judge a person too well from a photo and a letter. Shit, no! We've found that out. We've met some real kooks. It's always risky, don't you think?

Most of the women have been too pantihosed or trousered for me, or else they wear garters as though they're fancy-dress. Incidentally, if you don't mind my saying so, you err a little in that direction. Not that I'm not grateful, but you sort of *wave* them about, and it takes all the fun out of it. There's a great difference between titillation and crudity. You watch Lola. It's just natural with her. She doesn't flaunt them. Just the occasional flash, maybe, when she crosses her legs. It's got to be natural. I don't think this Johnson guy responds to blatancy either. You should learn to keep your legs closed. I'm only saying this for your own good. I hope it doesn't sound mean, because I really appreciated the gesture; even though it took you a heck of a long time to get around to wearing them. I hope you don't have any regrets. It was good. I'm sorry I don't get turned on by water sports. Don't get me wrong, I wasn't disgusted by it. Nothing's disgusting in sex. If people want to urinate on each other, that's okay by me. It just doesn't do much for me personally.

I guess what I'll surely take back home with me is the story about the school kid looking up your skirt. You've got such a wonderful way with words, Jo. But then, you're a poet. It was terrific, I want to thank you for that.

This vacation's done wonders for Lola. I've felt prouder of her, and closer to her, than I have for years. The leisure, the sea air, the change of scenery, have made her a new woman. I just hope she isn't overdoing it. Nothing would make me happier than to buy her expensive lingerie, and see some other guy take her out and give her a good time. To watch her swan around our bedroom in a sensuous haze, waiting for her nail varnish to dry; maybe hoisting up her skirt to dab some perfume on her thighs; knowing she was going to be wined and dined and then fucked crazy in the back of some rich guy's Cadillac. . . . Well, we all have our dreams. Let's face it, she's no beauty queen and it seemed impossible. But Tom screwed her – right? And the other guy at the lighthouse. Okay, maybe they were drunk, but they screwed her. They *wanted* to screw her. It's been like a second honeymoon. We've had a couple of really crazy fucks.

And nobody can fuck like Lola. Leastways I can't imagine it. You're only the second woman I've ever actually slept with, so you can see how much I think of you. I'm sorry I sounded off. We're both tremendously fond of you, I hope you realize that. I wouldn't be talking to you like this if I didn't care a lot.

I'd hate to think the sex part with either of us has been bad for your health. Lola and I talked this over very seriously when we saw what a sick girl you are, but we figured after St Ives you enjoyed sex and so it couldn't do you any harm. And your one-night stand with Tom reassured us further. Don't misunderstand me, Joanne. I'm not suggesting we thought you were promiscuous, because it's not for us to judge. But let's say we could see you weren't averse to – screwing around. We don't blame you one bit. It can't be much fun. You've got to take what chances come your way. Not that we can understand why you're still on the beach. A woman like you deserves to be married. You're no oil painting, but you've got personality. You could do something about your weight. Have your sight checked – that twitch you get when you're tired and irritable doesn't help any, because you've got nice eyes. Your dress-sense leaves a lot to be desired. That's a nice dress you're wearing, but you should avoid pants. All women should, but you more than most. That blue pants-suit you wore at the Meadery was

– well, I've never seen anything like it. People were staring at you – I just had to get out. I'm sorry. You could get your teeth looked after, take some posture-control lessons – it's not too late. You're not *together*: sometimes you mince about like you were Ginger Rogers; other times you slouch around like *Roy* Rogers without his horse. You could learn how to cook decently. I'm only saying this for your own good. It could help your mental health, getting yourself into shape.

14

We were parked on a seafront. Across narrow water loomed St Michael's Mount, a black pyramid in the moonlight. To the left of it, across the bay, the Lizard Light pulsed.

Mr Polglaze asked: 'Are you feelin' better now, my love?' I nodded, and he patted my knee. 'You done your best,' he said. 'No good upsetting yourself like that.' He stubbed his cigarette and started the engine. It must have been late; the narrow road through Marazion was deserted, and even Penzance was quiet, and almost lightless. Mr Polglaze asked me if I enjoyed herbal cigarettes – he had never tried them. Hastily I wound the window down and threw away the joint.

As we reached the open moor Hector's insults came flooding back, and I began to sob. Mr Polglaze pulled out his large handkerchief for me, but it was soon wet through. Hector was right; he had even expressed himself too mildly, had been holding back out of kindness. I reached into my bag for tissues, and touched the cold unicorn's horn. I was convinced, then, that Joe had committed some terrible violence. There seemed to be dried blood around the tip. I asked Mr Polglaze to turn on the inside light, but it wasn't working. Crying silently into my tissues, I wept elsewhere too, for a part of me found the memory of Hector's insults terribly arousing.

The Avenger was drawn up and the key in the door for me. The house was in darkness, and I crept upstairs with my shoes in my hand. In a daze I pushed open my bedroom door before realizing Simon would be there, asleep; I closed it gently again and crept into Lola's room. Her bed was empty, so I switched on a bedside lamp, and started to undress. Absorbed in myself, I felt no curiosity as to where Lola was; and certainly, since the bathroom door was closed, she was not *there*. I opened the door and was struck by tropical heat. The wall heater had been left on. I heard faint lapping sounds, and then, adjusting to the dull red light, saw Lola, naked, hair hanging down over her breasts, in the pose of a circus snake woman, crouching between toilet and bath. The thin, coiling snake was held by the throat. Simon was poised naked on the side of the bath, his legs submerged in froth. They were both frozen, holding their breaths. I froze too, my fingers on the heater cord. 'Hi, Jo!' said Lola with a nervous laugh. 'We thought it was locked. Sorry, honey. Simon's been a bit constipated. Did you have a good time? We went to the Lobster Pot in Mousehole. We had a wonderful meal.'

A unicorn's horn had been driven into Hector's eye. Mrs Polglaze said softly, 'Dear of 'm.' I heard Tom say, 'It's all right, my lover, it's all right. He id'n dead. It's the Levant – the east, or possibly the yeast.' Lola was pulling the curtains back on to a blindingly sunny day. She was in clothes I hadn't seen before, a tight-fitting high-cut pair of white shorts and a red top that showed off her figure. 'It's a fantastic day, honey. I brought you some tea. We're going beaching. You wanna come?'

'Have you rung the home?' I asked, dreading the response.

'He's had a peaceful night. The big nut cut himself shaving last night. I don't know what the heck he was doing that for, or where he thought he was going. Maybe they're right to keep him in for a day or so, honey. Don't you think? He's not behaving like Hector. He's not badly cut up, but it could have been nasty. Luckily he had the sense to ring the bell. We thought we'd go for a swim at Porthcurno, as it's such a lovely spot and Simon hasn't seen it. Then we'll drive on to see Hector.'

I said I felt like a lie-in. Lola leaned over me anxiously and stroked my hair. 'Are you going to be all right, honey? You really freaked out last night. It could have been dangerous. You could have got Simon electrocuted, you know that? We're concerned about you, sweetheart.'

I tried to recall what I'd done that was so bad. Apart from Hector; and it was a huge relief to know he wasn't badly hurt. Memory only started to return when she said she was sorry I'd had such a fright – she knew how upsetting it could be to find someone in a room when you thought it was empty.

'Simon's screwed it back in,' she said. Searingly I recollected his expectant buttocks and the tube. 'It's working okay but I'd leave it alone if I were you. You can never be too careful with electric. We'll call the hotel manager and ask him to get it checked. Anyway it's such a beautiful day you won't need to turn it on. I just wish you'd

103

come with us. . . . Well, okay, honey, if you'll be all right. You really *must* join us at the Lobster Pot tonight, though. I shall insist. Hopefully Hector'll be out and we can celebrate. And guess who spent his honeymoon there, honey? – Dylan Thomas, the poet! I said to Simon, "Jo will be thrilled to eat here." Promise me you'll come, sweetheart.'

When they'd gone, I lay looking at the colour snaps Lola had picked up in the village and left by my tea cup. Most of those she had taken hadn't come out at all, but the one of Hector and me at the Men-an-Tol was a success. I gazed at the tall grinning man, pulling me closer to him with an air of tender ownership. Seeing his clean boyish good-natured face, I felt guilt and remorse in the pit of my stomach at having attacked it with a fruit knife, and prayed it would not bear any scars. It was noble and touching that he'd defended me by pretending he'd been shaving. He was a good man, who wanted me to believe he wasn't. And that was because Lola had screwed him up, and he didn't think he could make me happy.

Remorse gnawed still deeper as I thought how hurt he'd been by my rejection of him for younger men – first Andy, then Tom. He'd hinted as much. I'd hurt him too by my – so many – references to his 'mother', which had come through to him as biting sarcasm. How generous he'd been, to stay good-tempered for so long, and how understandable that finally, ill and overburdened, he had felt goaded beyond endurance. Then there was the dead child – that was an overwhelming new dimension. He'd grown a mask of frivolity to hide his wound. I had seen him weep. The very few times he had called Lola 'Momma', I recalled, had been in those tender or jocular moments when couples with children normally use such terms. Mr and Mrs Polglaze did it all the time; but it was deeply moving, and sad, that Hector's mind occasionally annulled the years, believing his daughter to be still alive.

Could he forgive me? I tried the tea leaves and they seemed hopeful. I gazed at him in the photo again and knew that – perhaps for the first time – I truly loved him. If I was to be honest with myself, I had to confess there had previously been an element of 'making the best' of Hector, in my anxiety to achieve marriage and companionship. Now, I passionately loved him; none other but Hector could I love. I would gladly do anything he wanted, even to sharing him permanently. I would fulfil his most secret fantasies, loving them as my own. I would swallow his sperm. I would let him lace me into an hourglass shape, until I fainted. I would dress in schoolgirl clothes and he could lift them up to cane my bottom. I would even give him an enema, if that turned him on – though he

104

was too fine and clean to share the uptight Englishman's kink. There was nothing I would not do for him. If only he would give me the chance.

I compared myself and Hector, at the holed stone, with Lola and Hector in a snap I'd taken for them at the Logan Rock. I felt a little reassured. Maybe her legs were shapelier, but my breasts were fuller; my shoulders were too broad, but my smile was surely nicer, and her hair (especially peroxided as it was now) could not equal mine. Tom had said what beautiful auburn hair I had. Though her eyes had improved, mine had a shining spiritual quality he must prefer.

I wanted to see him right away, beg his forgiveness, pour out my love to him. I'd catch a bus into Penzance and get there before she had a chance to poison his mind further against me. I jumped out of bed, had a quick wash, and started to dress. It was a strain, this morning, to fasten my suspender belt. My breasts felt tender too. I felt mildly headachy and oppressed, and knew my period would come soon. I slapped on more make-up than usual because I was in a hurry and because I knew Hector, with his fondness for womanly women, would like it. I thought about putting on the black suspender belt too, so that I could lift my skirt and blind him with a vision of the sun; light flashing off all the clips ('pulsars' he called them). Surely he'd have to forgive me then. But I remembered: 'It's got to be natural.'

Then it occurred to me, in a flash, that Hector didn't really *want* someone who would pander to his childish whims. Rather, he was yearning for someone who was womanly enough in her natural, naked self to embody the magic, and lead him to adulthood. With that happy discovery, I stripped off the uncomfortable garment.

As I washed off my make-up, I had another revelation. Hector's outburst had been a declaration of love. The passion he had repressed, for Lola's sake, during our times together, had jetted out in the guise of hatred and hostility; he had not wholly covered up his despair, over a dead-end marriage, with extravagant expressions of need and love. He had been saying to me, wistfully, 'I love you. I don't know what to do. Help me.' And surely he had recognized Joe's thrusts at his face as a passionate response? We had, in a way, exchanged vows, we were married. Verbally and with a fruit knife, a white-hot consummation had occurred. He was probably lying there waiting for me to come and drag him out of that deathly home.

Buying Tampaxes at the shop, I caught myself humming 'Are the stars out tonight?' I found I had a little time to wait for the bus,

105

and as the last *Mail* had gone I sat on the seat by the bus stop, writing a love poem in my notebook. My headache had vanished; I felt so light-hearted in the blue day that words flowed easily. It was about our dialogue under the Meadery stars. Chaliapin from the coach ride waddled by and said how handsome the day was, but I was too engrossed to hear till he had gone.

Then I was in my room, in my bed, my biro still in hand and my notebook on my knees. 'Dear Jo,' she had written,

> that's a terrible poem. I used to think we were *all* talented but now I'm not sure. Isn't he an ass-hole! (Hector, I mean. Simon's full of shit too but he won't be for long.) I had to save you from yourself, dear. He'd have thrown more crap at you, and you'd have licked it up. The more they shit on you the more you like it. That's why I shat on Hector's tennis whites – to build up some capital. I warned you. You should have stuck to Tom, you're a cretin.

> *Found-poem from Hector's comic book* ...
> She sleeps in a rubber night-
> dress between rubber sheets
> and we make love
> both dressed almost completely
> in rubber. We love to walk
> in the long garden
> dressed alike in rubber
> suits, rubber boots and rubber
> gloves with face-covering
> rubber hoods and macs and capes
> so that we share a rubber world.

> Granite is God's fetish (at least around these parts). He loves it 'cause we rub away too quickly. Othello had a hanky fetish, he killed her 'cause she had a headache and wouldn't wank him off with it. Shit, they're back, but I've locked the door and told the old dear I'm having a quiet wank. We don't get better, Jo honey, till we tell 'em both, dear father dear mother you prick you cunt.

I dressed and went down. Lola was baking an angel cake and Simon buried his face in the *Guardian*. Lola gave me a hug and said she was sorry she'd disturbed me in a private moment, and she didn't think we needed five packs of All-Bran but it was sure a good joke. There was nothing I could say except to ask if they'd had a good swim, and how was Hector. Lola's face was like a Victoria plum. 'My!' she said. 'It's like Death Valley out. You were probably wise to stay indoors, honey. Would you believe it, we never even *made* the beach. Did we, Simon? By the time we'd done some shopping it was time to visit Hector. He's okay, Jo. He looks worse than he is, with all those bandages. But they're so *vague* about him. No one had seen him when we got there; no doctor I mean; the police had called again. So, anyway, I stormed up to the hospital while Simon had a look round the museum, and I had a long talk with Mr Blight, the registrar. He's terribly nice, and he was really sweet to me, especially considering he's not a well man himself. He had a stroke, Jo. He doesn't seem to know why poor Hec hasn't been released! It's really turned me against Medicare.'

I said it was inhuman, and Simon, from behind his paper, said it was characteristic of the times we live in. Yes, sighed Lola, and the police were hounding poor Hector to death, no wonder he felt depressed. The end of the Cornish part of the vacation so near – such a wonderful experience – to be missing the best weather ... Even if they let him out tomorrow he'd be plunged into packing and goodbyes.

'Honey, it was so kind of you to visit him. I know he really appreciated it. *We* didn't go last night because Hec said not to bother, he needed a good long sleep. All the same' (coyly) 'he was glad to see *you*!' They planned another visit this evening, before dinner in Mousehole. And this time, I simply must come. She turned to Simon for support. Emerging from the *Guardian*, and clearing his throat, he said yes, I simply must. It was nonsense to think I'd be in the way. Lola flashed me a glance that said, 'For Chrissake help me out with this guy.' 'Thanks, Simon,' I said. I wondered if I should apologize to him for my violence of the previous night; but it seemed best to drop the whole thing.

Lola fumbled in her shopping bag, saying she'd bought me a little keepsake, from Hector and her. 'As a thank you for being such swell company.' She looped the silver chain over my head. 'You are a Cancer, aren't you?' 'Thanks, Lola,' I said. 'It's beautiful. I've always wanted a birthstone.' She had also – producing a box – bought a gift for Hector. 'He adores Scrabble. I thought it would be nice to have a game with him tonight. And if the worst comes to the worst, it will be something for him to do, till he's out.' She fumbled in a large package and came out with a garment, a short flared linen skirt, wine-coloured, and held it against her. 'Do you think it's too short, Jo? I took to it and Simon likes it.' I saw him looking at her legs appreciatively. 'If I've got nothing else I still have good legs.' I said it looked nice. 'And I bought a leather coat which I've needed for ages. And a few other things to go with it, shoes and a purse, and so on.' She sighed. 'It never stops once you start. I had to buy pantihose,' she said. 'I've resisted for years, but I suppose one has to move with the times.' She flourished a packet of black tights. 'Well, I'd better run a bath. And you promised to call your wife, honey.' Simon nodded.

Hector was not in his room and we checked back in the lounge. A familiar head overtopped its chair back, watching *Look Westward*. 'Hi, Hector!' I said, startling him. 'Thanks for the pendant!' I said, fingering it, and he looked surprised again. I smiled brightly at a couple of old-stagers who briefly moved their heads from their chests to see who had disturbed their sleep. I felt oppressed by a huge weight, and the worst of it was that Hector didn't seem incongruous.

I wanted to whisper, 'I love you, you big fool.' But the others were helping him from the armchair and assisting him to the bedroom before I had any chance to speak.

Lola helped him off with his dressing gown and back into bed. 'Gee, it's nice to rest,' he sighed. 'Do you know what, sweetie?' said Lola. 'We've been pronouncing our name wrong all these years! According to the registrar – who's a real dish – it's Bol-eỹe-tho! Would you believe it? Don't you think it sounds nicer, honey? From now on we're Mr and Mrs Bol-eỹe-tho. Okay?' By way of answer, Hector took hold of her hand and asked how *she* felt. Lola said, better now for seeing him; she'd had a bad stomach ache all afternoon, and guessed it was worry. He gazed at her glowing face, dipped his eyes to her miniskirt, flicked sideways to Simon; Lola, flushed, dived into her shopping bag; pulled out grapes, bananas, apples, angel cake, two monster bars of chocolate, and placed them beside the brimming fruit bowl and carafe. I saw his eyes turn inwards despairingly.

We perched uneasily on the bed, asking him if they were feeding him all right, if he'd watched much TV, and other such questions; and didn't listen to his answers, so unreal is the life of the unwell to those who are healthy. Conversation dried. Simon apologized for his error in not, after all, being insured for any other person to drive the Viva but himself. Hector shrugged, wearily and forgivingly. After another awkward lull Lola produced the Scrabble. We slid the meal trolley in front of him, propped him up, and laid out the game.

I started it off with *ill*. I knew it was tactless but it was the best I could do. 'Don't worry, Hector,' I said, 'we're all sicker than you' – searching his eyes through the white plasters to see if he'd truly forgiven me; but his eyes were expressionless. Lola made *hill*, and Hector, looking pleased with himself, enlarged it to *anthill*. Simon cut across it with *copula*. 'What the hell's that?' asked Lola. He explained it was a linking verb, which left us little the wiser. Not having a dictionary, we agreed we wouldn't challenge but just trust each other. I turned it into *copulate* and collected thirteen. Simon glanced quickly at Lola.

She heaved a sigh and added *n* to the *a* of my word, and asked me, with a shy childlike glance, to forgive her for being so dumb. Hector met *anthill* with *belt* and our eyes met. Simon greeted *copulate* with *proform*. Lola said didn't he mean 'perform', and Hector suggested 'pro forma'; but Simon explained that 'pro-form' was a term in linguistics for replacement words, such as pronouns – 'when we know what the item is and don't have to state it in full.' Simon collected eighteen.

I capped Lola's *an* with *anjana*, and Hector said it was spelt with a 'gi'. No, I said quickly, it was an *old* and *ugly* witch in black, who would become a lovely girl in green and give you precious gifts, if you showed her a little kindness. Crossing my legs and swishing my black skirt, I showed him a green suspender. (It had struck me that he was too sick to be re-educated yet.) My sarcasm wasn't lost on him; I saw him wince. Lola, after a long hesitation, made *clit*. Simon and I protested it was an abbreviation but Lola said it was becoming commonly used – glancing at me swiftly under her plucked eyebrows. Hector ran *star* across *anthill*. Simon turned *clit* into *enclitic*. 'For fuck's sake,' said Lola. 'Like the "s" in "he's" – enclitic negation and operator,' Simon explained. I ran *nigredo* down to the edge of the board, explaining that it was an alchemical term for black, symbolizing the dark night of the soul.

Lola created *dog* from it; and Hector, scouring the board, look-ing weary, eventually crossed *dog* with *go*, right in the corner. Simon transformed *belt* into *seatbelt*, glancing at Hector. Hector said he didn't want to play any more, and would like a sleep. Simon said the scores were much closer than the words suggested: he was just ahead of me, and Lola and Hector were still well within range. Lola said Hector had better not tire himself. We packed the game away, Lola and I gave the sick man a hug, and he gave us, for his part, a sad little wave as we left.

In the cooler, clear-blue evening, we drove in thoughtful silence. It was Simon who broke it, by remarking, in his clipped cultured tones, 'Well, he seems perfectly normal.' The words sank into my mind like a stone, and conjured up the memory of Hector's face peering over the bedclothes; bandaged like a mummy in a Hammer film; and after a short but painful inner struggle, in which only the soft purr of the engine was audible, I exploded into hysterical laughter – with which Lola immediately joined. After a puzzled meditative pause Simon gave forth deep staccato laughs of mirthless hilarity, and in a mutual dementia we entered the fishing village. We quietened into ordinary good-humoured well-being as we walked along the quay to the hotel. The salt air refreshed us. Colourful sails, bobbing merrily, busy fishermen and strolling holidaymakers, made a lively scene. We murmured our pleasure. But when Lola joined me at the wash basins outside the ladies' cubicles, I saw she had been having a little weep. 'You go on, honey,' she said huskily, 'I'll join you.'

Ill at ease with each other, Simon and I read the menu half a dozen times. I was reduced to asking him if the cricket was over, and he said, yes, England had won. We only relaxed when Lola appeared – brightly smiling with fresh eye-shadow.

I only realized how hungry I was when I smelt my thick well-done steak. Lola ordered champagne, saying it was her treat; though personally she must watch her step as she had drunk rather too much of the registrar's sherry. His fork poised with a piece of steak, Simon put it back on his plate and stared into nothing. Like a fool I had called attention to a dear little baby who was being dandled in her mother's lap at another table. I laid my hand remorsefully on Simon's. He pushed his chair back and shambled out of the dining room.

I asked Lola if she thought one of us ought to go after him; and she said to let him be. 'He's in a terribly emotional state – there's a real volcano there.' Then she whispered, 'Honey, I don't suppose you've such a thing on you as a sanitary pad?' She looked at me with the wistful childlike manner I'd noticed in Hector's room. 'Why?' I asked, startled. 'I've got – a slight show of blood,' she said, dropping her gaze, and giving a short sigh. I recalled – Hector had told me – her mother had died of cervical cancer, and I was all concern and compassion. 'I'm sure it's nothing, Lola,' I said tenderly. I did have a Tampax in my handbag, in case I started, but Lola said she could never use such things, she'd be terrified it would get lost up in her. She was only spotting at the moment, and she'd probably be okay till morning. Then she'd buy a proper box of pads and a sanitary belt. I murmured how easy and convenient it was, and told her how. 'Well, okay, I'll try,' she said; and just as Simon returned I slipped her the Tampax under the table. Lola squeezed his hand and hurried out.

Simon resumed his eating. 'I'm sorry, Jo,' he said, almost with a groan. 'I know it was stupid of me. I'm very fond of Lola. She's wasted on him. She's got so much to give, that she's having to hold back. She knows instinctively what I need. New life. New life.' When Lola returned (nodding at me, and smiling) he took her hand and bent his moustached lips to kiss it.

She looked so radiant in her wine skirt and black and white striped blouse, that it seemed to me ludicrous I could ever seriously have mistaken her for Hector's mother. Stumblingly I said I'd heard from Hector that I'd upset her; and I was sorry. 'Don't believe everything he tells you, honey. He's basically not a very serious man. He loves a leg-pull. He gets that from his grandfather. He was a lovely man, his grandpa. Smart – he could have gone far if he'd had any schooling. And full of fun. He used to tickle and tease me when I was in pigtails.' Her eyes were lit by a recalling smile. 'I guess he passed on his wandering hands, too!' Simon swivelled his face to the window, muttering an inaudible word. I saw into unimaginable vistas of time, saw Dylan and Caitlin laughing, with flushed faces, over their pints.

A shrivelled Salvation Army woman, about ninety-five years old, hobbled to our table with a toothless smile, a money box, and a bagful of *War Cry*s. 'They do a wonderful job,' Lola warbled as the little old lady hobbled away to the next table. 'Her faith is keeping her active.' Glancing down the menu, she said she was going to have a Peach Melba again, with Cornish cream. My! she'd be putting on weight! – and she pulled in her stomach, thrust out her bosom and patted her waistband. Fervently, almost orgasming as he peered at her sleek black thighs, Simon claimed she looked younger than ever and trimmer. 'No,' she sighed. 'I feel awfully fat and heavy this evening.' She agreed short skirts did have a youthful effect; and admitted she didn't feel as 'floppy' as she'd expected, without a belt – her tummy muscles must be tightening up, probably from so much swimming.

She smiled as at a private joke, and Simon asked her what was amusing her. She rolled her eyes at him mischievously. 'I was just thinking, honey, you may have to – split the honours tonight!' She slid her thickly mascara'd eyes to mine, and held my gaze archly as she sipped from her glass. Her mouth quivered, suppressing a giggle. 'Pardon me!' she said, belching.

It was a windy night. I had eaten too richly and drunk too much champagne, and lingered on the shore between sleeping and waking, vaguely aware of hurt and rejection. My farts and Lola's called to each other – I'd learnt to recognize her mellow saxophone tone. Simon's were rarer, a curt tuba. Had the fog-horn been blowing it would have been a spectacular quartet, but the sky was clear and starry – I wandered to the window once to look out.

I was in a hospital visiting a patient. She was naked except for a white shawl and a nightcap. Only her eyes were alive. They darted about restlessly. We talked by eye movements. She was saying she had become a Carmelite. She must give up everything, even her ring. She motioned me to take her plain gold ring from her finger. She quoted from Emily Dickinson – the Bride – without the Sign.

There was a power failure. All I could see was a pinpoint of light in each pupil of the Carmelite's eyes. It was enough to talk by. It was very black, she said. I fumbled my way to a phone booth to ring up the power company. With a lighter I was able to comb the directory. The owner's name, I found, was Nigredo. A silky prerecording said the emergency supply had failed, and they were switching to gas. The lights went on. My mother was sitting on the floor, covered in excrement. She licked it, cackling. There were wax dolls round the room, and pictures of Jesus, with blood pouring from his heart. 'You slut, Tracy,' she said, 'you've got grass on your skirt. Take it off. You wait till your father gets home. He won't take you to the pictures.'

It was a hospice for derelict women. I was an old whore playing Scrabble with myself, only I couldn't join any of the words together. Lola (Montez) came to me and started to wash my feet. 'What's your name, honey?' she asked. 'Magdalen,' I said. 'Oh, that's the name of this hospice too,' she said. 'Isn't that a coincidence! I've been a whore too, but I love this most of all, tending the sick. I'm going to die soon, in great pain, but I don't mind. This could be my last hospice.' There were other old women groaning and cackling, besides my mother. 'It's not old Mary's fault,' said Lola. 'He's so full of crap.' I saw Mr Johnson going around the ward, thrusting a rubber hand up between the old ladies' thighs. 'It's all the stuff he's shoving up them,' said Lola Montez. 'Girls are being born without wombs and without breasts. He's made it

112

fashionable – now all the women want it done. He's done so many hysterectomies and mastectomies he's rolling in it. But he's got it coming to him, honey!' she cackled. 'The next time he wants an enema we're going to connect it to the main reservoir and flush his heart out!'

Lola started to dance, and a huge Negress wearing a black corselet sat at a piano and accompanied her. When Lola finished her dance she said to the Negress, 'Will you give my husband a lay?' and the Negress pressed up against Hector's father. 'You can feel the bones.' He grinned. She squeezed him and he flattened against her udders. The silk panels of the corselet disappeared; what was left was the black thread and wire of the ghost-house. The Negress laughed in a deep voice and said, 'You can rest here, my handsome!' He said, 'Swell!' and she swelled so much she threatened to burst the ghost-house.

It was a milder day, still a blue sky overhead, but darker on the moor. Simon had had to be content with the *Sun*; he was scanning it avidly as he ate his All-Bran. In snug shorts, Lola bounced in through the door, apologizing for having been so long – Mrs Polglaze had caught her, and had wanted to know about Hector. 'He's coming out!' she said excitedly. We hugged each other like happy schoolgirls after passing their exams. 'The police came to see him *again*!' she added. 'While he was eating breakfast! Would you believe it? *Would* you believe it?' But she said it good-humouredly, and we began discussing what we should do to make his last day in Cornwall as pleasant as possible. 'We *must* get to Land's End! We still haven't been there!' She chuckled. 'We can't go back home and say we visited Cornwall but never saw Land's End!' And maybe we could take a last swim, somewhere. And then we would have to pack, as there was the Carnival everyone kept insisting we mustn't miss; and that would be quite enough, because Hector mustn't get overtired. There was a long train journey ahead tomorrow – and how wonderful they'd have my company on it – and then the flight. ... So Lola chattered on. She bent to stroke the ginger cat from next door. 'Gee, I'll miss you,' she said to it.

'Just think, Lola,' I said, 'you'll be in Paris in forty-eight hours! Aren't you excited?' Lola sighed. 'I guess so. But I'll be so sad to leave this lovely little cottage. And you, sweetheart. I just wish you were coming with us. We've had a wonderful time.' She said they'd be back in about an hour, ready to drive straight on to Land's End. We could have a pub lunch on the way. She asked Simon if he could get the Urens' wheelchair in the back of the car.

They didn't want it, any more, and some poor soul might be able to use it at the home.

As he was wheeling it out, Lola said to me confidentially, 'I'm sorry about last night, honey. It didn't work out as I'd hoped. He's a bit too – exclusive. He hasn't even liked borrowing my tooth-brush!'

Delaying the moment of packing, I browsed through the *Sun*. The photo of terrorists with coats over their heads made me shiver and thank my stars. Here was poor Hector, a sick man, being hounded by the police for a traffic offence, while they had let me go scot-free and lost all interest. And then, out of nowhere, came an irrational idea that had me lighting a cigarette with trembling fingers. Hector and Lola were not as they appeared. They were highly skilled and superbly trained members of the Anti-Terrorist Squad, who had been keeping a watchful eye on me ever since I left Victoria Coach Station. I even recalled a moment in the snack bar there when they approached my table hesitantly, as though I might pull out a gun. Conveniently they had left for a weekend's rest in Redruth at the point where the local police moved in. Simon Johnson was probably an agent too – how smartly he had turned up when Hector had his accident: assuming that, too, was not a part of some clever over-all strategy. No, I felt sure Hector's accident had been accidental. Between them, by this time, they knew more about me than I knew myself.

Lola and Simon came back, but without Hector. 'He doesn't want to come out, honey,' Lola said, dabbing her glistening eyes.

I was lost for words, and she continued: 'He doesn't want to come out. Says he doesn't feel up to it. He wants to stay there for a while.' She wiped her eyes and blew her nose.

'Didn't you talk him out of it?' I said indignantly. 'Make him see sense?'

'He's a stubborn man, honey. His father was the same. It's best to leave him be, and wait for him to make up his own mind to leave in his own good time.'

Mr Johnson nodded; adding earnestly, 'Some men can't be saved from themselves, Jo.'

'I try to do my best for him but it's not easy,' said Lola huskily. 'I've often felt like cutting the bastard's throat!' She looked at me, with a watery smile. Tears blurred her mascara.

But what of their plans? I asked. Lola said Paris could wait, it would still be there in a week or a month. Or maybe they'd never get to it, it didn't matter. She wanted to stay not too far from Hector. She and Simon had talked it over with him, and she planned to go to Birmingham tomorrow with Simon. 'I'm going to stay in their home. I've had a lot of experience of grief and I think I can help Mrs Johnson.' Simon nodded. 'Okay it's not Paris, but I gather it's got a nice shopping centre.' Simon said he hoped I'd drive with them as far as Bristol; he could let me off at Temple Meads Station.

There was a knock at the door, and Lola went. It was Tom, delivering an invitation from his mother for the four of us to come to tea. He was, surprisingly, in a blue tracksuit, which brought out the blue of his eyes; his stubble was growing again.

'It's a bugger, in 'a, you?' he said, when we'd told him about Hector. He stood irresolute. He was off work for a couple of days, and was on his way to Penzance to do an hour's training. He played wing forward in the Pirates second team. Was there anything he could do? Would we like him to go and talk to Hector? No, honey, said Lola sighing, but it was a kind thought; and she stretched up to give him a kiss on the cheek. He blushed.

I came to a quick decision. I'd take a lift into Penzance with Tom, if that was okay? I wanted to do a bit of last-minute shopping, I said, and check on train times. It was kind of Simon to make the offer, but we had lots of luggage, Lola and I, and it would be easier if I caught a train straight through. Simon shrugged disappointedly, greatly relieved, while Lola gave me a regretful, querying look with her eyebrows. I promised to meet them later at Tom's parents, after their trip to Land's End.

Bumping along in the musical van I tried to explain to Tom that I'd been stupid, and I hoped he didn't think the worse of me. 'That's all right, my lover,' he said cheerfully. He took his hand from the wheel to give my knee a squeeze, and I felt comforted. If there was only more time, I said, he'd find I'd behave very differently. We'd wasted – I'd wasted – so many precious days. He asked me to light him a cigarette. I lit it between my lips, and put it gently into his fingers. In the small touch, there was some kind of greeting after separation.

I asked him to drop me at the Public Library; and we agreed he'd pick me up there later. I went upstairs to the Reference Section. Lola's plans to go to Birmingham had more than ever persuaded me I was involved in a plain-clothes web. According to the *Sun*, a lot of police activity was going on in Birmingham, where terrorist sympathizers were said to be hiding out. It seemed to me there was only one way of getting to the truth: to check out some minor part of their 'cover' they couldn't possibly have rehearsed. In conversation I'd gathered quite a lot about Lola's supposed ancestress, Lola

Montez; and it was such a crazy, pointless detail it would tell me whether they were genuine or not.

With a little help from the librarian I found Lola's entry in the *Dictionary of National Biography*, under her baptismal name (Gilbert, Marie Dolores Eliza Rosanna). As I read through the article, I was ashamed to find all Lola's tit-bits confirmed (give or take a few understandable inaccuracies and exaggerations). Lola Montez had done just about everything. She'd danced, she'd whored, she'd been the mistress of a German king, and once dressed in boy's clothes to visit him in secret when his country was in revolution. She'd nursed sick whores (dying eventually of a disease picked up from them). She'd horsewhipped an editor for insulting her and she'd written a book about beauty care. She'd even ruled a country, wisely and well.

Everything but Grass Valley; and that was a minor detail one wouldn't expect to find, in a short life.

I felt terrible at having mistrusted the Bolithos. Truly I was crazy. I wanted to say goodbye to Hector, and I headed for the home. On my way I bought cufflinks for Hector and, for Lola, an LP of massed Cornish choirs conducted by Stanley Parkins, the sleeve note describing him as the 'quiet, unassuming genius of West Cornish music'. I felt pleased with that purchase. Then I heaved myself uphill towards the home. I felt fat. The zip of my skirt wouldn't reach all the way. A slim boy struggled to get out of the fat lady. I sat on a low wall to rest, and looked out over the grey harbour to St Michael's, taking in the gasworks closer to hand. I opened my purse and counted my money to make sure I had enough to get back home. I didn't have very much. I huddled in my coat. I was just a girl in an old coat.

When I arrived I asked to see the matron. I wanted to check if there was anything really wrong with him. Nothing at all, she said, except depression. She'd had to keep a close watch on him, night and day, for fear he did something to harm himself. And even then, he'd out-foxed her, trying to cut his throat with a fruit knife. One of the doctors had given him a good talking to, and she didn't think he'd try it again. How sorry she felt, she said, for his wife, so loyal and cheerful always. 'She got a cross to bear, that poor soul.'

Marriage was no picnic, she said, glancing at my hand. Especially where the husband was so much older. Like poor Mrs Bolitho, she herself had married an elderly man, and had lived to regret it.

16

He was reading in a bedside chair. 'Hi!' he said genially; finished a paragraph and put his book on the bed. I came over and kissed him. There was a strong smell of Hector to add to the varnish and polish. Bits of his body adorned the bed, floor and chest of drawers: nail-clippings, a comb and brush thick with greasy grey hair, the carafe of apricot wine, a glass of water with his teeth in it. Seeing me glance at the latter he apologized: 'My jaw still hurts a little from the crash. It's easier with them out.' I removed the filthy hairbrush from the bed and sat down. Noticing my grimace he said, 'Take of my body!'

'So you're not coming out, Hector?'

'Nope.'

I could think of nothing to say except 'I didn't think you wore glasses.'

'The accident hurt my contacts,' he said. He took off the steel-rimmed specs and examined them. 'These are Lola's reading glasses but she doesn't do any reading.'

'Do you like it here?' I asked. I looked around the naked cream walls, the highly-varnished flush door, the rectangle of drizzling sky suggesting winter. 'It's restful,' he said. 'It's a pretty room, don't you think?'

I went across to the window to open it a notch. On the sill was a snap of Lola in a Woolworth's frame, and another snap of a young man and woman in Thirties-style clothes posing proudly against a model T Ford. The young woman held a baby. 'Is this your mum and dad?' I said.

'Pardon me?'

I repeated it more clearly.

They were, he said. I said they were nice photos.

'Pardon me? . . . Oh yes! Well, it makes the room more homely.' He grinned.

I sat on the bed again and we stared at each other. He asked me if I was looking forward to going home. I said no, it got lonely living alone. He said, there was my teaching to look forward to, and I said I wasn't exactly a teacher, more a helper.

He nodded, blandly, picking his nose.

'Well, it's sure been nice knowing you!' he said, after a while.

We sat looking at each other. His eyes slid from my eyes to my crossed legs. 'I see you're still wearing them!' he said, with a small glint that quickly faded.

What about Lola? I asked. What about Lola and her good legs.

Hector shrugged. 'I guess I don't want her any more. Everything still revolves around her, but I don't want her any more. Sexually it's dead, but it won't stop breathing. Okay, we've had a couple of good fucks, this vacation. But only because of Tom, getting his hand up round her garters. And even that got spoiled. It turns out he isn't bothered about them particularly and when they fucked it was naked in the sea.' Hector brought this out in tones of deep cynicism and despair. 'And now she's wearing panti-hose. For this guy Simon. Right? Well I tell you, Joanne, I don't FUCKING CARE.'

He bellowed the phrase out, like a howl, at the top of his voice; then lay back panting in the chair. I expected half the staff to come running, followed by old men shuffling along in walking frames, but the home stayed silent.

'You get more privacy here when you go private,' he said. Then, coming back to his original theme: 'I guess if Lola gave me this garter thing I don't blame her. I needed something. You've got your poetry and Lola's got her choir. But it's not satisfying any more. It's moved from nature to burlesque.'

'So what now, Hector?' I said.

'I told you I don't holiday well. I want to learn. I don't want to be Newton picking up pebbles on the beach, I want to go into the ocean. Even if it means death. Staying alive doesn't bother me too much. Now Lola, she has an unstoppable lust for life. She'd want to go on living even if it meant being a microbe on somebody's gums.

'But I'm tired of nature's blind urges and fetishes. Did you know the penis of the male nautilus comes away and swims by its own instinct to nestle in the female? Well, screw it!

'I guess I want to be with my little girl, my golden-haired Tracy.' He put his bandaged face in his hands and sobbed.

He raised his head and rested, exhausted, against the chair back. 'It's hard talking without teeth,' he said.

I murmured that I was grateful to him for talking; I felt I knew him, for the first time. 'That's very good.' He smiled. 'It's peaceful here. Why the heck should I want to go climbing the Eiffel Tower with Lola, at my age? This place has got a surprisingly good little library. Small but select.' He nodded at the book and picked it up; I saw it was a Bible. Opening it at the bookmark, he started to read

118

but closed it again, saying he was tired and would I help him back into bed. His body felt extraordinarily far away under the pink-and-white stripes, and I ordered him to eat all his meals.

I had kissed him goodbye and was heading for the door when I remembered the cufflinks. He turned out to be childishly delighted with them, saying it was the nicest thing that had happened to him in days. The cufflinks seemed to give him fresh life. He drew himself up in bed and started to eat the grapes I'd brought. Munching, he said what a great guy Jesus was; and I sat back down on the bed.

'You know, Jo,' he said, 'when my mother went into her necroleptic trance, there was just nothing – nothing. She told us about it later. An endless series of nothings. Not as though she'd stopped moving but as though she'd run out of space to move in. Maybe I'm a kind of mental Parkinson,' he chuckled.

'How long did it last, Hector – for your mother?'

'Who knows? Years, probably. Then things cleared a little and she saw a face, bending over her. She thought it was my father, but then she realized it was Jesus. She said to me, "Hec, I suddenly knew it was Jesus. And I said to myself, Why, Jesus! you're goin' to take care of me, my sweetheart!" It was funny, but she spoke with a touch of Cornish. I guess when she said the words in her mind she was recalling her mother's accent. Normally she spoke in a soft American drawl.'

I nodded encouragingly.

'After that, he used to come regularly. And in between, she could see very clearly the places of her childhood, the grasses and trees of Grass Valley, the spring pools and flowers. She must have lived in those pictures for – twenty years and more, while the rest of us were going through wars and the Beatles. Just those pictures, and Jesus.'

'Did he stop coming when she had her remission?'

'For a time, yes. But he came again when it turned sour, when she experienced those terrible sexual longings I told you about. Once in a while Jesus used to come and, with infinite kindness in his eyes, take her old nipples in his mouth.'

I shivered, and said it must be a dreadful illness. It was, he said; and – I'd find this interesting – a colleague of his in the English Department at Sacramento told him there'd been a minor outbreak in the 1580s, and Shakespeare had written about it. Wasn't there a character called Yolande who went into a necroleptic trance for sixteen years?

He'd finished his grapes, and was tired again, and I sensed an air of finality about this goodbye.

119

As I was going out through the door he called 'Don't forget to look us up.'

There wasn't time to buy my train ticket. I guessed I was late already. I got Tom to drop me at the cottage, because I needed to pack, and sent apologies to his mother and Lola, saying I'd meet them all later at the playing fields. I started to worry about how to carry the Rousseau wall print of Hector and Lola all the way back without creasing it.

There was a card on the mat, from a local electrician, saying he'd called to check the bathroom-heater, but there was no one in. Lola came back to the cottage to collect me. She wanted to make sure I was okay, she said, and was really coming to the Carnival. I was touched by her thoughtfulness. I asked her where Simon was, and she said he had driven off somewhere, in a sulk. 'Oh, because I kissed Tom – you know – before you went off! *And* because – you know – I wouldn't let him touch me last night. I don't mind when it's only a little, but last night it was pouring out.' She rubbed herself dry after her bath then squatted. 'They're much more convenient than I imagined, honey, thanks for telling me about them. I guess I'm almost over it, but I'd better make sure. As if he couldn't be content for once with what he had! He's an awfully difficult man, honey. In the long run I'd even prefer Hector! Oh, he's handsome, and has a gorgeous voice, and knows how to use his finger . . . but he's so *jealous*, it's unbelievable! Well, *you* saw how he behaved over dinner last evening when I mentioned having a sherry with the registrar! I had to get Hector to hide your card – he threw an awful scene about *that* episode.'

Lola showed me how badly her skin had peeled, just from taking her blouse off for half an hour in the boat. It was very sore, she said, and would I mind rubbing in some lotion. I had never seen her body naked in the light, and I noticed stretchmarks that confirmed the Tracy part of Hector's story. I wanted to take her in my arms and tell her I understood her hurt. She lay face down on her bed and I rubbed lotion into her firm slim flesh. 'That's soothing, honey,' she said, her eyes closed. 'I wish I wasn't so fat!' She sighed. I told her she wasn't fat, just nicely covered. 'I guess I *have* lost a little weight,' she said, 'in spite of the alcohol. I'm not used to drinking so much. I guess I've had more exercise though. I've noticed my belts were getting a bit loose on me, and my blue skirt. I guess Hector'll have to buy me some new garter belts when we get home. If I ever get him home.' She sighed.

'Sorry, Lola,' I said, as she winced. 'It's okay, honey.' Suddenly she twisted round to face me, smiling. 'Can you imagine what he tried to do this afternoon when you'd gone? He grabbed all my belts and stockings and said he was going to throw them in a shaft! Jesus, I had to run after him to the gate! Oh, because he thinks I prefer Hector to him. Also he hates them. The first time I undressed he closed his eyes, and you probably noticed when *you* undressed last night he rushed to the bathroom. Apparently his mother kept him on reins till he was five, and they remind him of it.' She was stepping into her black tights and drawing them up to her waist. 'He prefers the long, sleek line and plenty of ass when you bend over.'

'You don't think this is too gaudy, honey?' she said anxiously, putting on a bright cherry lipstick. 'It's what they recommended at the beauty parlour, but I'm not so sure.' 'My father would have loved it,' I said. 'He liked plenty of make-up, honey?' 'Yeah,' I said, 'with pencil skirts, tight sweaters, seamed stockings, and stiletto heels' (she nodded, pencilling in her brows) '– but he didn't look good in them.' Laughing, we grabbed our coats and handbags. 'He knows where to find me,' she said. 'I guess basically he doesn't like women. It's drizzling, honey. He's not going to think he can tie me down. Oh, no! That's why I lay it on a bit thick, about Mr Blight and so forth! You may have noticed. To show him he doesn't own old Lola! He'll have to take laxatives. I'll send him a bottle of California syrup of figs for Christmas!' Giggling, we set off briskly down the road, arm in arm, like girls off to a dance.

Sun flickered through the fine drizzle as we reached the recreation ground. Three-storey council blocks overlooked the field dismally at the back, their grimness hardly tempered by the Union Jacks draped from window to window. The field itself wore a dismal look: damp carnival floats and stalls where the rain drizzled into Woolworth tea cups, lost children wandering around haplessly as the rain ruined their lovely Victorian dresses and hats or made the letters run on their labels; a few Pacamac'd spectators, most of them looking like tourists killing the last dreary afternoon and waiting for tomorrow to come so they could get home. The damp Jubilee programme I bought from a damp boy promised a Procession at seven, through Pendeen and neighbouring areas, followed by the Prize-Giving at approx. eight and a Grand Open Air concert (if wet in the Methodist Sunday School). The open air concert included a cornet solo by Arthur Polglaze and a medley by Tom (piano accordion). Musical accompaniment to the carnival and fete was already being given by the Silver Band. Maybe the conductor saw Lola coming, because they broke into 'Amazing Love'. 'It's that amazing hymn,' said Lola, and made for the band, in the corner of the field. The sky brightened. Searching for Tom, I found his mother. 'Goin' be lucky with the weather, are us, you? Like fate, i'n it? Yesterday was some handsome day.' I apologized again for missing the tea, and she expressed amazement at Hector's folly. 'Some *thing* for poor Lola to put up with. Poor *speed* he is, you.' I bought her a cool cup of tea.

Lola was getting some excitement going around the band. Over the rising noise of the floats being made ready, we could hear her singing 'The Sound of Music'. Confusion and excitement were also growing round the flower-decked Carnival Queen Float. A big white box was being tossed from hand to hand and the two pretty flower girls were crying. Word spread across that Veronica Treloar, the queen, had been taken poorly, and her mother had brought the dress back. Mrs Polglaze said she wasn't a bit surprised. 'I said to Tom, she'd be more trouble than she's worth. There's always *somethin'*, with our Veronica. She do catch every germ that's goin' the rounds, and she *won't* look after herself. When she near enough caught her death of pneumonia last winter, Olga still couldn't get her to wear a vest. Mr Harris d'say she d'come to work half naked.' Elsie went off to speak to Olga, to find out what was the matter with her daughter this time. I went to throw darts and rings, in the shadow of the pre-cast housing units. The sun went in and the air dampened.

The band had stopped, the field was thick with people. In the hubbub there were shouts and laughs and bursts of clapping near the Queen Float. I pushed back towards the centre and saw Lola being hoisted aboard the float, between the smiling flower girls. Tom appeared at my side. 'She's a bleddy good sport!' he said. 'We figured she'd have a go, and would be about the right size. Don't look bad on her, do it?' Lola spotted me, waved, shrugged, and spread her arms. She arranged her hair so that it flowed down over her bosom. The sun came through and flashed off the yellow dress, the gold crown. 'Some handsome hair she got, abm' she?' said a faded woman to Tom. 'Where she come from, you?' America, said Tom. The band broke into a Souza march and led the way out through the gates.

It was wet and chilly and I had started to bleed. Tom had joined the band, and Mrs Polglaze was selling sponges. I thought of escaping back to the cottage. 'Cold are 'ee?' said a deep voice over my shoulder. I looked round and it was Chaliapin. I asked him why he wasn't with the band and he said his bronchitis wasn't good for trombone-playing – wheezing to prove it. I told him to be careful of the damp. 'Ess,' he said, 'I believe I'll get in the warm for a bit o' while. I do live up there,' he said, indicating the top storey of one of the council units. He winked. 'I got a drop of the hard stuff; like a drop, would 'ee? It'll warm you up. You can see when they're on their way back.' It was just what I could do with, I said.

He led the way through a passage and, wheezing strenuously, hoisted himself on his walking stick, one leg at a time, up two flights. 'It's the bleddy fags, you,' he wheezed. Eventually we were in a tiny sitting room that was chillier and damper than it was outside. He bent over with a groan, to switch on the fire. While he rolled himself towards the kitchenette to get some glasses, my eyes moved from the cheap Victorian figures on the mantelpiece to a display case on the sideboard. It held rocks and minerals, including streaks of silver, sapphire and emerald. Mr Wearne was back at my shoulder, catching his breath before opening the whisky bottle. '*These* are nice, Mr Wearne!' I said. 'Ess,' he said. He had picked them up from various places where he had worked. He pointed out where each specimen had come from: a gold mine in Colombia, a copper mine in Michigan, a silver mine in Mexico, even a *quicksilver* mine in California. 'New Almadén. That's where I got this bleddy limp, you' – feeling his leg. 'Fell off a ladder.' Thirty years he had been abroad, he said, surprisingly; and had only come home to retire four years ago.

'Why did you come back, Mr Wearne?' He stooped, and reddened into a coughing fit. 'Well, it's *home*, in a', you?' He drained his glass and offered me a drop more. 'And do you know what *that* one is called, my handsome?' he said, pointing to a black lump. I shook my head. 'Botallackite,' he chuckled. 'Ess,' he said, nodding to the window. 'Come from down Botallack, and named after it!' He seemed to find it an astonishing thing; his sunken, bleary eyes shone.

'Can you see Botallack from here?' I asked. He said, no, it was a bit too far down the coast. But you could see Levant, where he had started work as a boy. I went to the window and looked out over the playing field to the village, the head-gear of Geevor, and the broken shapes of the Levant ruins on the cliffs. The sea was lost in the sky. For all the disasters, I hated to go. 'You've got a nice view, Mr Wearne,' I said, turned and saw – my bird, my cock.

We were on benches in the Sunday School, listening to two young brothers, tenor and bass, singing 'Watchman what of the night . . . when the de-ew shall fall?' . . . And Elsie Polglaze was whispering that Veronica Treloar had cystitis and I was replying

that Mr Wearne would probably get it too. I thought I'd handled it
– or not handled it – very well, after the first shock. She whispered
that he wouldn't hurt a fly, he only wanted you to play with it a bit,
he was a very lonely man.

Pulling the window up I'd told him a seagull would peck it off if
he didn't put it away. Blushing to the roots of his pubic hair, he did
so, and I had had another whisky and one of his woodbines.

The M.C. announced an extra item: a soprano solo by Lola
Bolitho. The announcement was almost a song in itself: he was so
struck by it that he said it again. There was loud applause. Lola
came on stage; she was back in her new wine skirt that showed off
her legs, and there were whistles from the back, followed by a
ripple of chuckles, quickly stilled. With her long tinted-blonde hair
and trim curves, with the glamour of distance and subdued light,
she could have passed for thirty. I felt proud of her, as of a young
sister who's winning all the prizes. The M.C. said what a live wire
she was, and – as they all knew from her name – really a Cornish
girl: and lots of them had heard her marvellous voice, and he was
sure we were in for a treat, and they were sorry she was leaving
them before they'd got a proper chance to get to know her. Lola
acknowledged the tumultuous clapping with a wave of her arm and
a big grin, and when it had died down she said she was deeply
moved and she brought them warm greetings from their cousins in
Grass Valley, California. After more claps and whistles, she signal-
led the conductor; the band made a low, uncertain entry, feeling
their way, and then Lola hit her first high, throbbing, golden,
perfect note of 'Summertime . . . when the living is easy . . . !' It
was so beautiful and tender and poignant that I – not alone I think
in the audience – felt tears in my throat. My head spun with
timeless beauty, and the hungers and derelictions of life, and
having to leave – and for where? And at the heartbreaking descent
of Lola's last 'Do-on't you cry', I blacked out.

17

I had survived the dew-falling night watch. There's not much (east
of the Falls Road and west of Prague) that's more terrible than
waking up in, say, a bedroom in Welwyn Garden City, and not
knowing where you are, or why. (I guess it's happening all the time
to the babies of Welwyn.) Still comparatively a baby, twenty years
ago, I woke up in Welwyn, to immortelles in cellophane from a

departed boyfriend, a sore shaved padded cunt, and the timid knock of my dead infanta in the tree branch at the window. I'd had the weightless, sick feeling of travelling on a luxury coach.

But this at least wasn't Welwyn, it didn't have the feel of Welwyn, and I wasn't afraid. It was a plain room, with a rugby team on one wall and a ship on another. Rain was pelting the window, and I huddled deeper.

Mrs Polglaze came in with a bright smile and a breakfast tray. Was I feeling better? Yes, I said, pulling myself up to take the tray; it was only my period starting. I often had blackouts when my period was really bad. 'Well, dear,' said Elsie, 'you're to stay *here* for a day or two. The doctor said you're to rest. Boy Tom won't mind sleeping on the put-you-up for a night or two. Arthur have fetched your luggage.' I said it was wonderfully kind, and she denied it: we were put on this earth to help each other.

She would bring me up a nice pasty later, she said; and after dinner she would light a fire, as it was such a damp and miserable day. Then I could come down. 'A bit of rest and you'll be like a new one, dear,' she said. A new what, I wondered? After I'd been to the bathroom and eaten the scrambled egg, I snuggled back down in bed, listening with pleasure to the rain, glad I didn't have to lug cases about, struggling back to an empty flat.

I was almost asleep again when Lola and Simon called to say goodbye. Simon just asked how I was, from the doorway, and waved, before scuttling downstairs. Lola sat on the bed and said how wonderful it had been, and how she would miss me, and I must look after myself. She herself didn't look good. She'd overdone the local wines at the Meadery, she admitted, and had a peach of a hangover. The old woman of the start of the holiday showed through the sunburn and hair rinse. Elsie brought us up a cup of coffee, and Lola said she hoped she hadn't kept Arthur out too late. 'He was kind enough to drive me home,' she explained, chuckling, when Elsie had gone. 'I don't think I'd have managed it otherwise!' He was a lovely man, she added; 'one of the best.' Simon had thrown another honey of a scene, demanding to know why she lingered in the van.

'With two lovely men around, honey,' she said roguishly, 'I guess you'll pull through! Don't think I didn't notice how eager Tom was to get you shifted to his place!' I protested weakly that we were just friends; yet feeling my colour come up, with pleasure at what she had said. 'Anyway, honey, you're a real good sport. Thanks a million for everything!'

I was touched, and embarrassed. I said I'd done nothing but try to break up her marriage. She leaned over and kissed my cheek. 'Honey, it would take more than you to do that! It's been a real experience. We expect poets to be a bit – bohemian!' The great thing about me was that I had a wonderful sense of humour. I could take a joke and I could tell a story against myself. Hector said what a lovely sense of humour I had. She spoke as though Hector was the authority on senses of humour.

I hugged her, and thanked her. 'No, it's for me to thank *you*, Jo dear,' she protested. I said I couldn't imagine what for. Lola smiled, and briefly touched my breast through Elsie's floral nightie. 'For that, sweetheart, apart from anything else! You know, I've never done it before.' She bent close to my ear and whispered, 'You'll never believe this, honey, but it's true – I never knew I had a clitoris before! Wham! It's made all the difference to me. I've had a whale of a time!'

Simon's horn sounded from outside. 'I'd better go. I've got to say goodbye to Hector and leave him his suitcase. We'll keep in touch.' She gave me a hug and stood up. I asked her if she had any idea when Hector would feel ready to leave; and she sat down again. 'I don't know, honey,' she sighed. 'I don't feel I know him any more.' She stared down at the coverlet with a look of gathering tears, and I pressed her hand. 'Honey,' she said huskily, 'I feel very close to you. I hope you do too. You remind me very much of my mother. She had a wonderful sense of humour – and needed it. I don't feel I can leave you under false pretences. The situation between Hector and I isn't as clear-cut and straightforward as it seems.' There was a swishing rustle as of a catch of fish being landed, but it was Lola's black mac being removed. It started with Hector's father, she said. At first, it was only innocent horseplay at church socials. They fought against it, because it was hopeless – Edgar (Mr Bolitho) had his lovely wife and sons. She (Lola) was a good friend of Edgar and Annie. But she was lonely and so was he, in a different kind of way. One day she found herself pregnant. 'I didn't know what to do, honey; I had no one to turn to.' She dabbed away her tears with her hanky. Abortion was unthinkable, and she couldn't bear the thought of carrying a baby to full term, and then never to see it again. 'Yet I couldn't take care of it, honey. It was the Depression and I was all on my own. If I'd stayed in Grass Valley with a baby I'd never have been allowed to hold my head up. Yet Edgar and I couldn't bear the thought of losing each other. We were very much in love, you must realize, it wasn't just a sordid affair. I was very honest with him: I told him I firmly believed it was his, but there was just a chance it wasn't, as I'd been

126

raped a couple of times on a trip to Mexico. Edgar had no doubts, however. He just *knew* it was his.'

So they decided they'd have to tell Annie. After the first shock, she was as good as gold about it. Lola had gone away for a few months, and then the Bolithos adopted her son. 'I named him Hector,' she said, 'after a Mexican friend who looked after me during my pregnancy – Hector's a very common name in Mexico.

'Hector doesn't know about it, sweetheart. Nobody knows. Oh he knows he's adopted but he thinks it was done through an agency. He doesn't like talking about it or even thinking about it, so don't ever bring it up, dear, will you? I guess he doesn't quite know where he belongs, and this trip has brought it home to him. I know I can trust you. I guess when Hec lost his mother he clung to me, and wanted me, and I couldn't see him hurt. I could never have told him about it because it would have totally destroyed his respect for his father, and it was terribly important, to me, for him to keep that. Naturally I loved Hector like my life, and I hated to think of him marrying someone and moving away, and perhaps I'd never see him again. Just old Lola, the auntie who'd raised him up! I could never have borne that, honey. Hector wanted to marry me and couldn't see any reasons why not. I knew I was too old to have another child – which is the only worry, isn't it? – so it seemed okay. Nothing matters so long as you're happy. And we've been happy. We've gotten along together. I don't quite know how, because we don't have much in common except I'm his wife and his mother. I just hope we can work it out, because I really love that guy.' She smiled at me under tear-stained lids. Simon's horn sounded three times. She whisked into her mac, and stood up. 'Don't think too badly of me, honey, huh?'

I blurted out: 'He told me you had a daughter. Tracy. He showed me her photo.'

Lola laughed. 'Oh shit! I wish he'd take things a bit more seriously. Tracy's our minister's daughter. Our god-child . . . 'Bye, honey.'

Before closing the door she winked at me and did a thumbs-up.

Over the next few days a mythology grew over what Lola had done, following her solo in the Sunday School. Tom's pals at the Trewellard Arms kept up a constant teasing banter about it whenever we were present. Apropos of nothing, after a silence, someone would say, '*Lola*!', with a kind of questioning astonishment at the name or the person or both. For some reason this caused snirts of laughter all round and beer up their noses. 'Some woman *she* was, ol' man!' 'She was a goer, *she* was!' And more gales of merriment. Sometimes she'd done a strip in the Meadery; sometimes she had donned overalls and helmet to go down with the night shift at Geevor to sing a song at the bottom of the shaft. Or not to sing, but to entertain them in other ways. I couldn't decide why they were teasing me, and Tom was no help either, joining in with the rest, though a shade uneasily; so I played along with it and turned the tables where I could. 'Tom fancied her, didn't you, Tom?' I said brightly; and Tom looked sheepish while his friends roared and pounded the tables with their tankards. It was many nights before they tired of it.

'*Lo*la!' ('Game old bird *she* was!'), heads thrown back, tears wiped with hairy forearms ('Handsome pair o' tits she had!'), heads shaken and eyes squeezed dry with too much painful laughter, dying away in painful gasps ('Jesus Christ! *Lo*la!'). Eyes so full of tears, they couldn't shut.

It rained steadily, day after day, but I felt happy. After the Hector hiatus, Tom and I struck up a more serious, steadfast relationship. We found we could talk to each other about important things, without being conscious of age. 'What do you think of death, Tom?' I asked him once. He puffed his cigarette for a moment, and then said he had once gone to pray with an old farmer who was dying of cancer. Before he left, he asked the old man if he would like him to say a prayer. 'Ess, if thee's a mind to,' he had said.

'So I kneeled down and started to pray. But before I had gone very far I heard this squelching noise. I carried on with my eyes closed, and the squelching went on. I opened my eyes – and what do 'ee think? Maister was there suckin' an orange! He died the next evenin'.'

Tom went to visit Hector, on a similar errand of mercy. I couldn't wait to find out what had been said. Had my name cropped up? What was said about me? What did Hector think of me now? If not me, what had they found to talk about, for two whole hours? 'Jesus Christ!' Tom exclaimed – whether in exasperation or as a statement of fact I couldn't discover.

With his work and his rugby, his preaching and his sick-visiting, I didn't see very much of Tom. But there was always the quiet hour when he came to my room to fetch his pyjamas. He would sit on my bed, light the last cigarette of the day, and chat. He was very understanding about the no-sex bit; I would have thought it wrong, as well as risky, with his parents lying next door; besides which, I was afraid, lest in the terribly intimate act I betrayed that I hadn't slept with him before. I couldn't, like Joanne, throw inhibitions to the wind, and he might have been disappointed. We confined ourselves to kisses, which were sweet.

The wounds inflicted on me by Hector gradually healed. Though I had so few clothes, and no money to buy new clothes, it was a long time before I risked wearing my royal-blue trouser-suit. But when he saw me in it, Tom's eyes popped in appreciation, and he said I looked 'handsome'. Then he was concerned because I shed a few tears.

I spent more time with his parents. Mr Polglaze took a week's holiday and borrowed a neighbour's car to show me more of Cornwall. We visited the museum of wreck treasure at the Admiral Benbow in Penzance, and the aquarium at Newlyn. They saw places and things they had never seen before, and said they were grateful to me. On a day when the north coast was black with rain we found a watery sun to the south, and after a picnic at Prussia Cove, an old smugglers' haunt, drove in a curve around Mount's Bay to the Lizard peninsula: Gunwalloe Cove, with its pretty church half-buried in sand dunes; Kynance Cove, where the sun broke through brilliantly and dazzled off immense contorted cliffs of many-coloured serpentine. The tones and spaces of Kynance were still with me when I washed down the plug hole the accumulated silt, the impregnating sand grains, of Gunwalloe.

One morning Arthur came into my bedroom and said, 'Would you like to go to Mexico?' When we arrived, it was a sand dune near Hayle, nicknamed Mexico by returning miners. Arthur threw back his head in laughter, at his little joke. It was pleasant bathing there, except for a slick of red tin on the water.

But when I – at last! – visited Land's End, I felt sad and depressed. There were only dazed tourists having their photos taken against artificial signposts marked *Land's End–Bolton*, or wherever they happened to come from. By the first-and-last Ladies I sat down and wept; and I couldn't explain why. I could only wonder if the two beautiful and stark coastlines began to grow aware, as they drew closer and even the weather became one, that time was running out for them. It looked like it; the tired horn burying itself in the blue virgin's lap. The moor flattened out into vast, bleak fields and airstrips and the cliffs lost their grandeur and ran down into the sea.

Sennen Cove, round the corner, was better. Here, one Sunday, Elsie and I watched a recording of 'Sunday Half Hour'. The setting sun flashed off Stanley Parkins's mop of white hair as he conducted the St Just Male Voice Choir and the Pendeen Band (including Arthur). Feebly, a thousand agnostic late-season tourists joined in.

It was a beautiful week with the Polglazes, running from place to place in the car, picnicking and paddling, laughing and getting wet. Never once did they give the impression – as they so easily might have done – of sizing me up as a prospective daughter-in-law. It was as though they already took it as a fact, and liked it. And I liked *them*, especially Mr Polglaze. Once, when his holiday was over, I strolled down to the house he was building near the tin mine. A figure in white dust, he straightened from the line of blocks when he saw me, and said, 'You've got a *lovely* pair of legs!' Said it with a genuineness and gentleness that made me glow.

He took out a cigarette and proudly explained how the house was going to be. With all his goodness and cheerfulness there was a sadness. A feeling, perhaps, that he ought to have made more of his life. He talked a lot about his war service in the navy, his wonderful times in Australia. He would have liked to settle in Sydney, but his sister had married an American serviceman and he hadn't liked to leave his mother all alone.

I said they had a lovely little home; and they must feel proud to have a fine son like Tom. He said of course they were; all the same, they would like to have had a daughter as well. He gave me a direct, hungry look that went through me; and I felt happy. But then I was plunged into depression because he said they very much wanted grandchildren. There weren't many of his family left. Apart from Tom, there were only his sister's children, in Santa Barbara, but they of course weren't Polglazes. He hoped Tom would settle down soon, he said – again looking at me poignantly. I was happy and gloomy for several days, wondering if an adopted grandson would be okay. Presumably yes, if Tom was happy and if they liked his wife.

Elsie treated me as a kind of grown-up daughter and friend. I spent a lot of time alone with her. She seemed never to stop working – and usually it was for others. Arthur called their house 'Trewellard Laundry and Bakers'. When she baked it seemed to be for half the village – 'a few yeast buns' for this arthritic old lady, 'a few sweet buns' for that poor old soul. There were even yeast buns for Hector – sent over by Tom or Arthur. Every Wednesday and Saturday there'd be an extra pasty for Mr Wearne, my fat asthmatic flasher. 'I do hate to see a man on his own,' she would say; and did her best to provide some home comfort. Twelve o'clock each Wednesday and Saturday, Mr Wearne would be wheezing on the doorstep with a cloth ready to carry away his hot pasty. 'Course he've got his *ways*,' she would say, 'but abm' we all?' Having decided I hadn't gossiped about him to the whole village, Mr Wearne became fond of me and offered me toffees.

Like all old men he liked to reminisce. He'd roll out magic names: Tolima, Orinoco, Magdalena; Lake Guatavita, with its sunken El Dorado. He had seen them all. Actually he wasn't as old as I had thought; probably no more than sixty. His weight and his wheezes made him seem old. He had cut out the Woodbines but was eating toffees to lessen the craving, which was making him fatter still. He groaned about it. I told him what a smashing voice he had, and if he dieted and got his breath back from cutting out the fags he'd be on 'Stars on Sunday' and have all the women running. He heaved with laughter and was pleased. Knowing my revulsion to creepy-crawlies, the barrel-like cripple entertained me with accounts of the creatures he'd encountered: the bushmaster, the bird-eating spider (he'd shared a room with one), the hairy scorpion (he'd trodden on many), the anaconda (he'd had a narrow shave with one), the gila monster, the tarantulas, even the black caiman crocodile that barked and snorted and roared when you approached. And having scared me to death, off he'd roll with his pasty, chuckling and wheezing.

I asked him once if he liked being a bachelor and he said he was used to it. Then one day he confided in me. (I don't know why so many people tell me their secrets.) He had lived for eight years with a woman in Mexico. Juanita Martinez, her name was. They'd had a little girl. 'Do 'ee know what we called her? ... Amy. After my mother.' Amy Martinez. But the mother had left him and disappeared, with Amy. And so he had come home. His puffy eyes were sad. Then he cheered up. 'Do 'ee know what the Mexicans used to call me? ... Francisco Wearne!' He coughed and spluttered his amusement. 'Ess! Francisco Wearne!'

'Nobody d'know what I just told you, my handsome,' he said, 'not even *she*.' He nodded through the window to where Elsie was hanging up washing. As if to say, if I tell anyone anything, it's usually her. I could understand that, as I too found it easy to talk to her. Elsie and I giggled and shed sentimental tears, two domestic women together, talking woman-talk. Mostly, of course, it was about Tom. ''Course I've *spoiled* him,' she'd say 'but there you are, what can you do?' I tried to suggest, delicately, I'd carry on the spoiling. She joked a lot about his nightly visits to me, to get his pyjamas, after she and Arthur had gone to bed; she was sure he gave me a cuddle! Smiling, protesting, I assured her it was *only* a cuddle.

18

All the tourists had gone, except me. In St Ives, on an Indian summer Saturday, while Tom was playing rugby, I sunbathed on an empty beach. The 'emmets', as Tom called them, had stowed away their tents, towed away their caravans, and I was left; I felt at home. It was in the same last hot spell that I lay on my bed naked, one afternoon, flat on my stomach, half-drowsing, and I heard Mr Polglaze come upstairs, after work, and go to the toilet. Then he must have pushed my door open, for I felt him stroking my hair, very gently. I could feel the trembling in his fingers, afraid to wake me. When I came down for tea, he was slumped in his chair, just raising a bleak exhausted smile for me ('It's a heller, you!'), while Elsie said he'd kill himself, working so hard in this heat. But soon he was talking to me, about what sort of day I'd had, with his usual mixture of courtesy, kindness and teasing.

The children who had haunted Auntie Elsie, expecting lemonade or money for iced lollies, had gone back to school. Elsie and Arthur inquired anxiously and tactfully if my job would be safe. I reassured them that it didn't matter. I was sick of tying shoelaces, wiping noses and washing dishes. If I wasn't a nuisance, I said, I could stay for a few more weeks, and would like to. That was grand, they said warmly.

A cold spell came, bringing spiders into the house. A hand I didn't recognize wrote in my notebook a quotation I didn't know: 'We ought even more to sympathize with the animal world, and wish for them and for ourselves, not that we should go to the Kingdom of God – the way might be too far for a spider – it would be much simpler if his Kingdom were to come here.' I liked the tenderness for spiders, at the same time as I loathed spiders. I thought it might have come from one of Tom's books, but he didn't know it. He made a note of it for his preaching.

September was a month of rich dreams. I dreamt often about Lola (Montez). I was with her in the half-buried church of Gunwalloe, only it was a Catholic church and it was in Prussia Cove instead. Lola started dancing on the gravestones, leaping effortlessly from one to another. I asked her wasn't it sacrilege and she said no, because they were all hers. There was Marie and Eliza and Rosanna and Dolores and Gilbert, and these were her three husbands, and this was her lover, the pirate John Carter, 'King of

Prussia', and these were the two children she had in Spain. She looked sad but went on dancing. The dead could only rest in peace if you danced on them, she said. (I think she said 'rust' in peace.)

I was in Rhodesia admiring my new gleaming-white deep freeze. But behind it was a curled-up bushmaster. Lola Montez appeared and said, life always had its surprises. There were things out of control, and that made life fantastic.

I was at the bottom of a mine shaft. All the way up, men were descending on a man-engine, stepping on, stepping off. Their lamps glowed like candles in the blackness, a vertical series of candles that went on for ever. They started to sing a carol, in deep harmony. It was the most wonderful sound I had ever heard, expressing joy and worship, hunger and the deaths of children, hope and despair, fellowship and solitude. I looked around for Lola in the darkness, and she was washing Mr Parkins's hair.

There was a performance of *The Winter's Tale*, overlooking the sea. The Queen was standing in her stony-stillness, youthful and beautiful, making my breath catch, yet 'not so much wrinkled, nothing So aged as this seems.' Music awoke her and she stepped into my embrace. 'Oh, you're warm!' I said. We lay on the cold ground, kissing. I knew she was a boy actor, so I put my hand up her skirt. To my surprise she was wearing suspenders, and all was smooth between her thighs. But then, under the suspenders she was wearing tights and there was a bulge. 'It's okay, I'm looking for my husband,' said the youth. We took off our clothes and I saw the youth had breasts and a vagina. She was taken aback when I laughed. She saw the funny side of it too and we both laughed hysterically. There were so many skins and tangles.

I was with Lola in an aquarium. Whatever fish tank we stood before, the creatures acknowledged Lola's presence. They nudged against the glass. She said, 'They all have their own music, honey. Something Mozart' (she pronounced the z as in 'zoo') 'couldn't get to.' I could see this in the timeless harmonic swayings of the sea horses, their tails hooked round the stems of coral; in the way the creatures glided through the water with the motion of old gentlemen in clubs, thoughtful old gentlemen, stooped and with hands clasped behind their backs. They were so like the two-dimensional cutouts on which my cardboard knights rode as a child; but I didn't want to hurt them.

I could not see the music, though, of the creatures that terrified me: the lobsters like grotesque First World War German tanks; the spider crabs that were simply inconceivably huge spiders. I clutched her arm as the spider crabs surged in a pack – they seemed to move together always – towards the corner, near where we stood, climbing on to and over the spotted dog fish resting on the sand. Why didn't it move away? I shuddered for it. Their sharp horny legs landed all over it; I feared it was going to be blinded. How awful to live in a fish tank with a dozen spider crabs.

Lola said, 'We're going to dance to the spider crabs' music. You wanna come?' Then I was inside the water, moving across sand, striking off a kind of trampoline, and gliding up into the dark corner. I could dance anywhere in this infinite and pleasantly limited universe. I felt how good it was to have just the right number of legs. And then Lola said, 'We're going to dance to the dog fish's music. You wanna come?' And I felt how good it was to be this streamlined shape, and how pleasant to be occasionally tickled by things passing across me. Then we passed from universe to universe, dancing always to the music of it. When we danced to the mackerel's music I knew what Lola had meant by saying 'those are never mackerel' to the Mousehole fishermen. A mackerel you could look at wasn't a mackerel, you had to be inside it to find it.

Lola said, 'Try it by yourself, honey.' I thought of the white horse in the midst of black cows in the field near the Men-an-Tol, and I became its midnight self, I danced to its still music. I realized that though we were all apart we were all, in a deeper sense, together, and it was *good*.

Somewhere was there a music made of all the musics? A music in which a dead or a crippled child was just a note struck from a black key, but indistinguishable from the white, just as vibrantly alive as all the rest?

And one night (without Lola Montez) I strolled down to the lighthouse to meet Tom from work. I watched the invisible sea for a while, then leaned my back to the wall and watched the lighthouse. The office block joining on to the lighthouse tower gave it, in the dark, the appearance of a church: a church that with benign intensity whirled its white beams to all seaward points. I grew dizzy at the thought of so much power and care and skill devoted *for ever* to the saving of a few lives. The four beautiful prisms, turning for ever on a half-ton of mercury; mains and emergency electric, and the gas burner if all else failed: and there was no way *all* could fail unless a maniac tore aside the daytime curtains and the sun flared through the burning glass.

A car, headlights blazing, screeched round the bend and pulled up outside the gates. I saw Mr Parkins get out, white hair fluffed around his peaked cap, and walk into the lighthouse. A few minutes later he came out again, went to his car, opened the door, turned

134

out the lights, and walked back in. The door opened again and in the stream of light I saw Tom. I loved him in his Trinity House uniform. (I'm a sucker for uniforms, and I envied Tom's aunt, swept away by an American Air Force major. In every war in history I'd have been the captain's doll.) Tom saw me and came to meet me. We kissed. We lay on the cliff grass and he fucked me crazily. We lay sleepily, naked. I was ready to drop into sleep, and I thought Tom already *was* asleep. But suddenly he took my breast between his hands, and sucked on my nipple so deep that he was drawing all the world's milk. And he was inside me again, but we were moving so gently it was still like sleep. I started to flutter there. Our skins were breaking up. There were no border guards. We crossed whenever and wherever we liked. I looked up at the white beams till I thought I could glimpse their prismatic colours. They spun above us like a fairground rocket, only soundless. I have never known a sound as beautiful as their silence. It was more beautiful even than the Cornish miners singing their carol on the man-engine rod. We spun, much more swiftly and slowly, with the earth through space.

Each afternoon now Mrs Polglaze would light a fire in the living room, and her husband would have his meal there. Since they had survived my Boeuf Stroganoff, Elsie agreed to let me try my hand at making a Cornish pasty – I was determined to learn. When Arthur's was taken out of the cooker, the pastry was too short and the pasty too long, overspilling the dinner plate. He ploughed through half of it manfully, while we waited for his verdict. 'I think I'll leave the rest,' he said; 'we're short of cement.' Then he twinkled at my discomfiture: 'Still, it's a start!' Tom's was being kept warm for him in the oven, but I suggested it should feed the birds instead.

It was Tom's first Harvest Festival service at his own little chapel, and he had a smart new grey suit for the occasion. I wore my green suit, and Elsie had bought me a hat to go with it and a new handbag. She had bought for herself a complete outfit, which I extravagantly admired. Arthur had been costing a house-extension at Marazion, and still wasn't back; he'd told us not to wait for him, as he would go straight to the chapel if he was late. Leaving Tom to sort out his notes, Elsie and I set off arm in arm, on a cool, dull evening. We were very early; it was one time of the year, she said, when you had to be early to be sure of a good seat.

The organ was playing something restful, as if the organist, Mr Webb, had had a big tea. After I had dipped my head, I had plenty of time to enjoy the sea of bright new hats, and the harvest gifts that filled every window ledge and cranny of the pleasant little church. Vegetables and fruit and sheaves of wheat, barley and oats mixed their colour and scent with the brittle sunlight coming and going, the fragrance of the polished pews, the warmth of packed bodies, the organ music; and during that waiting I felt again the brief experience of wholeness I had known in the coach ride with Lola. The feeling ended abruptly with two heavy sneezes (I had caught a cold from walking in the rain one night to meet Tom from work). Elsie offered me a wine gum and winked me to look at an absurd mauve and lemon creation in the pew in front: 'Look at she, 'minute!' she whispered. It gave me a pleasant attack of silent giggles, Elsie continuing to nudge me quietly and nod her head subtly towards the outrageous hat.

Tom followed the choir in from the vestry, and we stood for 'Come ye thankful people come'. There seemed a huge gap in the choir where Arthur should have been, and I felt Elsie's anxiety. The gap wasn't wholly filled by the expanse of Mr Wearne, who, catching my eye, gave me a wink. He was a St Just Methodist, but on these special occasions helped the village choir. We settled into our seats and our hands for Tom's flowing prayer ('We pray O Lord for all those who are sick and can't be with us tonight . . .'). I looked up at him through my fingers and admired him. As his Amen sounded there was a small commotion at the back of the chapel, and I looked over my shoulder. The back pew was crowding up to make room for Arthur, and beside him in the aisle was Hector in his wheelchair. He caught sight of me, lifted his hand to his face, twirled his fingers and mouthed a silent 'Hi!'

The singing had everything but Lola. Tom moved earnestly into his sermon. I'd bet him fifty pence he could not preach a sermon on my favourite text, 'If the salt have lost his savour, wherewith shall it be salted?' and he'd taken me on. I heard him begin: 'If the salt have lost his savour, wherewith shall it be salted? . . . If the *salt* have lost his savour, wherewith shall it be salted?' He moved around the pulpit in the grip of this agonizing dilemma, 'If the salt have lost his savour, *wherewith* shall it be salted?' I never found out the answer to his rhetorical question, because I was too entranced by his flushed face, lit by a beam of brighter sun through the window as evening fell: a kind of green sun of the chilly autumn evening; entranced by the pleading or threatening or triumphant arms, and by the motes of dust swirling in the sunbeams falling on the golden fruit. I was also uncomfortably aware of Hector's eyes boring into me from the back of the chapel.

'The day thou gavest, Lord, is ended', followed by a blessing and the sweetly sung Lord's Prayer ... and we were making our way slowly out. Arthur and Hector were in the cluster of men standing in the hedge opposite. Mr Wearne was drawing violently on a cigarette (he had relapsed) and wheezing that it had been a 'bleddy handsome service'. I gave Hector a hug, saying it was a lovely surprise. 'I made the bugger come,' said Arthur. 'I was passing the home on my way back and I thought, I'll get the bugger out of there!'

'He wouldn't take no for an answer.' Hector grinned.

Elsie, shaking hands and saying how pleased she was to meet him, asked him how he felt. Hector said he felt better in himself, but had an infection of the inner ear which made him stagger if he tried to walk. But on the whole he felt pretty good, so long as he rested. I was glad to see all the plasters were gone and there were no scars. He looked almost as good as new. Elsie enquired how dear Lola was, 'Dear of 'er.' And asked him if he didn't think it was time to go back with her to their lovely home. 'I don't think I could,' he said. 'They've slapped on a pretty steep bail.' He grinned at me lightly.

Tom joined us from the vestry, and held out his hand for his fifty pence. 'That was *good*, Tom!' I said fiddling with the clasp of my new handbag. He waved it away, smiling. 'Bleddy masterpiece, ol' man,' wheezed Mr Wearne.

Being unable to propel himself over the moors, Hector was obliged to let himself be one of the party going back to Arthur's house for a sing-song and some supper. I felt ill at ease with a stranger in our midst; someone who, while the fire was being stoked up, sat huddled under a rug, as though he was Scott on the last day, and who refused Elsie's sandwiches and buns because he'd been having trouble with his digestion. He looked as anxious to get away as I was for him to go. He raised only weak smiles at Arthur's best anecdotes, and looked wanly at a blank T V screen during the singing and playing. Mr Webb, the revived organist, was tickling the yellow ivories of the old piano.

I only half-attended, myself, to the Victorian ballads and songs from the shows. Crushed against Tom on the sofa (his nightly bed) I was listening more raptly to the duet our hands were making, where my fingers caressed his palm. He declined to fetch his accordion, and hardly spoke. Mr Wearne noticed his silence, and asked him if he was feeling all right. Tom said the service had taken more out of him than he had thought; and everyone agreed it had been a big ordeal for a young man. But I sensed in him tension

137

, and I felt it myself, never more urgently. ...... in our hands' touch. I hoped no one would see ...als flickering between us.

...... was fully prepared to make my own Harvest offering. ....ldn't be able to, because he was starting a week of night ... By the time we had taken Hector back to Penzance it would ... too late to linger on the return journey; and it was not to be rushed. But while we drove quietly back, I would surprise him by unzipping him, and force him to pull off the road. I would take his firm, tender cock in my mouth, that he loved so much, and this time I would amaze him even more by drinking his sperm. I was fat already, a little more weight wouldn't hurt. I would suggest he drive me out to the moor tomorrow, to Ding Dong, the old mine on the high lonely centre. And then – Ding Dong. While Hector, with infinite relief, was gathering himself to go, I slipped on my coat, saying it would be nice for Hector to have some company in the back of the van. Elsie advised me against going out because of my 'old cold', but I insisted I was dressed up warm. Tom had gone to the parking lot where the band wagon was kept: they said it would be more comfortable for Hector than Arthur's tiny dirty van. I steeled myself, too, to bring up the question of my sterilization. I hadn't told Tom yet, and I was dreading having to. But perhaps he was enough of a changeling himself – a man who could preach about gentle Jesus one day and fuck an old married lady the next – to accept the idea of adoption. He would if he loved me, and I was pretty sure he did.

However it wasn't to be – as Hector would say – because Tom had trouble starting the engine, and by the time Hector had been stowed in snugly it was too late for Tom to drive to Penzance and get back to the lighthouse in time. So his father got into the driving seat instead.

It was almost pitch-black in the back of the band wagon; we bumped along in silence. My mind was elsewhere; I had lost the chance of a quiet walk to the lighthouse with Tom, and I desperately wanted to talk to him. Tomorrow was too far away. Even then, he'd be sleeping, or at a rugby practice. He'd be sleeping in my room, so perhaps I could steal in and gently disturb him.

I thought I'd better be pleasant to Hector, since I'd never see him again. I addressed the darkness. 'So you've no idea when Lola is coming back, Hector?'

'No!' he said, with the startled sprightliness of a continuing dialogue. 'No! She's having a great time. The Johnsons have got a Labrador dog and two cats, so she's in her element. She gives the

138

dog a run every morning. In her last letter she said she was feeling a new woman, so I wrote back, "So am I, stay on another month!" It was a joke, of course.' He chuckled.

'Do you think you'll ever be close again, Hector?' I asked, picturing Lola and the Labrador hurtling up the M6. His face gleamed dully in the reflected light of a tuba. 'We'll only maybe get closer by drawing apart,' he said jovially. 'We're kind of somewhere on the east coast of Britain making for Land's End but from different angles!'

'That's very sad, Hector.'

'No, it's the only way we'll make it! There's a total eclipse of the sun at Land's End in the year two thousand. Did you know that?'

'No,' I said, 'I didn't.' I wondered if it was one of his little jokes.

'I guess that's when we'll meet up!'

'I'll come too, and we'll have chicken in the basket at the Meadery.'

'Swell! Why don't you do that?'

The engine was making an awful din, labouring uphill. I thought of the eclipse at Land's End, saw the moon's shadow stealing over the sun until they fused into blackness and blazing corona. Wouldn't it be wonderful if we could all meet up, under it – Lola and Hector, Tom and me, Arthur and Elsie, Daniel and Doll, Frank and Juanita, and all the wonderful Pendeen people? Tom preaching a sermon on 'the last shall be first and the first last'. Arthur blowing the Last Post followed by Reveille. One moment, sea and sky a warm inseparable blue; the next, Hector saying, It's Sirius! Lola leading the choir and band in 'Amazing Grace'. Not forgetting (who could ever forget?) all the children who had died here, a hundred years ago, before they had lived. 'Fifty per cent infant mortality,' Arthur had told Hector. 'Some *thing*, ol' man, wadn' it?' I saw them in yellow swimsuits. Not all the white sands of Sennen could hold them.

Hector's just-identifiable humming of 'Home Sweet Home' turned into a vast yawn. 'Gee, I'm sorry! It's all this excitement, I guess I'm not used to outings.'

'What do you find to do all day, Hector?'

'I've developed a technique of total recall. Mother passed on to me some of her secrets. I've chosen '59. Tracy was a sweet baby, Lola still a bombshell, Kennedy was still alive and so was Mother in a kind of way; I got academic tenure, and even discovered a dark nebula – Bolitho's Nebula – in Sagittarius: it was the last good work I did – at 27. I won the Grass Valley singles title in straight sets; and you could run your metal-detector over any skirt and get a reading. It's a beautiful enchantment. How did that verse of yours go, that I liked a lot – the one you wrote about your great-uncle? – 'Hearts with one object alone / Through summer and winter seem / Enchanted to a stone –'

From in front, we heard a shrill scream, stopping Hector and van dead.

19

'Christ, Hector, we've knocked someone down,' I said, my breast fluttering. We heard Arthur jump out, then nothing. We waited, not daring to breathe. The weird wind of the moor plucked at the metal box. The doors were wrenched open. 'The fan belt's broke,' Arthur said. 'Can I have your tights? Elsie'll get you a pair tomorrow.' Hector asked him about the scream, and he said it had been the belt slipping. He looked away delicately as I peeled off my tights; took them, and vanished. 'I'm sorry, Hector,' I said, 'but they're warmer and I've got a bad cold.' It was a ridiculous thing to say, and I was grateful he didn't bother to reply. It was cold with the door swinging, and Hector offered me his rug. I declined, and he didn't press the offer. Arthur came round again and reached in for a water can. 'It should last us,' he said, 'but we'll have to wait a bit for the engine to cool down. I'll shut the doors, keep the cold out.' He slammed the doors on us.

Hector took my hands and started to rub them, sympathizing with my cold. It was all his fault, he said; he was a terrible burden. He sounded so miserable I tried to cheer him up, reciting a limerick I'd composed about Lola Montez. I explained that she'd come from Limerick originally, so I thought she ought to have one. I recited –

<blockquote>
'Marie Gilbert said "Christ! if I grow up
A Limerick maid, I shall throw up;
   I'm no good in these stays,
   I'll be Lola Montez
And I'll tango and fuck till I blow up."'
</blockquote>

'That's beautiful,' said Hector. 'It's fantastic. I'd say that's the best thing you've read to us. Oh, I really love that. It's even better than the lighthouse poem. Oh boy! That's a humdinger!'

I squirmed. It was excessive. It wasn't *that* good. In fact I knew the first line was terribly clumsy; her name was a problem. But I didn't know if he was being sarcastic. He began stroking my hands,

140

leaning forward urgently, his eyes gleaming in the dark like a commando's. There was something he had to say, he said. He'd been thinking a lot. He struggled to find words as I coughed away. 'Here, have this,' he said, fumbling in his pocket and then pressing something cold and small into my palm. I had the horrorstruck feeling it was a ring, and he was going to propose to me. (I suppose I had it hazily in mind that his marriage to Lola was illegal.) I held up my palm and it was a Polo mint. 'It'll ease your throat,' he said. I thanked him, and put it in my mouth.

What he wanted to say, he continued, was – did I really want to visit California? I had spoken of it during the evening, after Arthur had said he planned a holiday, in a year or two, to visit his sister in Santa Barbara. Yes, truly, I said – very much. I was fascinated by what they'd told me about it. Then, said Hector, if I ever came he hoped I wouldn't be disappointed. I mustn't expect it to be in the United States. It was too far west for that. Many real Americans, from the East Coast, thought California was a part of Australia, and maybe they were right.

The engine revved, and we were away again, still climbing the moor. Hector yawned, and I said we would soon be in Penzance. Again we stopped, and the engine cut out. I swore, and Hector said, 'I guess we're here.'

The doors swung open. 'Make these yourself, did 'ee?' said Arthur – showing me the ripped tights. I said I couldn't understand it, they were expensive. I hopped out beside him. Steam billowed from the open bonnet.

'It's a bugger, you,' he said, standing helplessly over the engine. We had stopped in the middle of the moor. Through a hedge gap I saw the table-like blur of the Lanyon Quoit. The sky was covered; a bleak wind blew; I shivered and huddled into my thin coat. I spotted in the lights a hedgehog, motionless a few feet ahead of the van. It was directly in line with the wheel, and I edged it with my shoe into the ditch. It was an ill wind that blew no good to anyone, I thought. But who decided that little Cordelia Johnson should die and this hedgehog be saved, both by accident? Who did the draw?

'What are we going to do, Arthur?' I asked. He said he'd have to walk back to Madron, a mile or so away – there was a phone box there. He'd ring up Morley Treloar – he ran a garage and would bring a fan belt out to us. 'You get in and keep yourself as warm as you can,' he said. He shut the bonnet and strode off into the night. I jumped in by Hector and told him the bad news. 'It's a pity you're not wearing Lola's stockings, Hector. They'd have been strong enough, I'm sure.' I meant it as a light-hearted joke to keep up our

141

spirits, but I sensed his baleful glare, and apologized. I took out a cigarette, but he started coughing even before I lit it; so I put it away again.

Hector said he felt claustrophobic with the doors almost closed, so I pushed them open, and froze. He was just saying there was one other thing he felt he had to mention, and that was that these days you could have an operation to tighten the vaginal walls, when we saw headlights. They didn't swerve past but came right up to the doors, a fierce light – we both flinched back, thinking we were going to be hit. Then Arthur was peering in, saying he'd brought us a taxi. He had waved it down, and although the driver was off duty he had very kindly agreed to drive us into Penzance, since we had a sick man with us, and then take us back to Pendeen. It was a lot better than having me catch my death, waiting for an hour or more. He would drive out with Tom tomorrow to pick up the van.

Leaving Hector enthroned briefly on the road, creepier than the Bronze Age tomb, we shoved the big van on to the verge, and Arthur locked up. He climbed in the back of the taxi (an old-fashioned one with fold-up seats) and pulled Hector and chair while the driver pushed. When Hector was safely in, I sat in the front compartment with the driver. The engine purred healthily, and I was glad to be in a warm cab. I thanked the young man profusely and offered him a cigarette; we chatted over the low sounds of Radio 1. He had long hair sprouting under his cap, and I had recognized him at once as the scruffy young man who had left us stranded at the Men-an-Tol. I remarked, casually, that his present kindness was all the more commendable in view of his cavalier treatment of three holiday-makers – including a sick old lady – a few weeks back. He gave me a sideways stare, remembered me, and pretended not to. Pretended it wasn't him. He asked for directions to the home.

When we reached the sleepy house, he sprang quickly out to help with Hector. I found myself smiling at his embarrassment. Hector and I waved vague goodbyes as Arthur pushed him up the slope to the entrance. The young driver leapt back in, and I offered him another cigarette, cheerfully. He took it, grateful for my friendliness. And confessed. A couple of young hikers had given him the come-on. They'd wanted a lift to Zennor, and promised magical things if he took them there for nothing. One of them had lifted her sweater and flashed him her tits. He was really sorry, but the temptation had been too much. He figured we'd at least had a good ride around for nothing. When he got to Zennor, the buggers had run off! It served him right, I said, and he grinned ruefully.

'Bleddy handsome pair o' tits they was, too!' A door had opened on Arthur and Hector and swallowed them. I said he had made amends by this good deed, and I hoped he realized, now, that crime didn't pay. 'Youre bleddy right!' he said.

I added that he might be better advised, another time, to pay more heed to older women. Their tits might not be so hot, but they'd been brought up to keep their promises. 'Mind you,' he said, staring with twinkling eyes, 'yours aren't bad!' His mouth was not unlike Tom's, firm flesh with the prickle of a trim beard. I found it not unpleasant. His hand fondled me under my sweater. 'You can take it out,' I whispered, letting him lift my sweater and, after a struggle, free my breast from the cup. He sucked strongly. 'Bite me,' I told him. 'And the other.' He must have seen Arthur coming back, because he straightened suddenly. I slid my breasts back in, yanked down my sweater and hugged my coat round me.

By the time we had left the last traffic lights behind, I felt dreadful guilt. It was the old thing about feeling obligated to a benefactor. I could almost pretend I had helped along the good: his unkindness (to us) had been punished, but now his generosity had been rewarded. But I knew that was phoney. To have done such a thing with my future father-in-law only yards away. It was a sign, I felt, that abstinence was bad for me, bad for us both. I was confirmed in my decision that tomorrow should be 'ding dong' day.

But at Crows an Wra, the Witch's Cross, a poor silent huddle of hovels on the outskirts of the moor, I became apprehensive about Tom. I was sure something had happened to him. The worry escalated my guilt. He'd had an accident. He'd been knocked over by a car, on his way to the lighthouse, just at the moment the fan belt broke. Today was Tuesday. Tuesdays were always unlucky. I answered the driver's cheerful chatter curtly, and I could tell he thought I was angry with him. I didn't want him to think that, so I pressed his knee. At Pendeen, he waved aside Arthur's money. 'I reckon I owe her this!' he said, nodding at me, grinning.

Elsie was waiting up for us, in the living room, and straightway I knew I was right. She was too brightly smiling, yet too still; not sufficiently upset by our crisis on the moor. Normally she would have rushed to the kitchen to get us tea; tonight she just sat, and I could feel the strain of the bad news she didn't know how to break. It would come, I felt, after the first lull in the conversation, and so I chattered on too, not really wanting to hear it. Tom's father obviously had no sense that anything was wrong. But our voices died away, and I could feel her gathering the strength to speak.

'Now, you'd better sit down a minute, father,' she said; smiling still but with a kind of mistiness about the eyes and lips. Arthur sank down, suddenly pale. 'What's wrong?' he asked sharply. 'Well,' she said, 'it's Tom.' 'What about him?' he asked, in a deep, trembling voice. 'Well, he d'want to get married.' I closed my eyes and thanked God that he was all right; at that moment nothing else mattered, and it certainly didn't occur to me to think he might have asked *me* first. But I made a move to leave the room, because I didn't think it was my place to be there while I was discussed. 'No, sit down, Jo dear,' she said in her kind voice. 'You're like one of the family. I know Tom doesn't mind *you* knowing, because he and you are like *that*' – tying two of her fingers in a knot.

So I listened politely, smiling in the right places, asking intelligent questions, while Elsie told Arthur their boy wanted to marry Veronica Treloar; that he not only wanted to, but ought to, in the circumstances; that she wasn't a bad little maid; that of course it had been going on for a long time, and they'd never *really* finished with each other, only a trial separation; that he was afraid to tell his father to his face, and she had said, don't be silly; that 'what's to be will be'.

The night had cleared. All the stars were out, looking twice as many and twice as large as usual. Bal-maidens hammered unseen; the sea pounded unseen. The wind went bitterly through the holes of my sweater. The shock had cleared my cold as well as the sky.

I felt surprised that I felt only sad – not angry, not hysterical. Sad and embarrassed. I had overstayed my welcome. It seemed to me now that I had known all along he wasn't going to ask me to marry him. Since that day when I had cooled the relationship he had really done and said nothing that a young man wouldn't do with a mature lady-friend, a sentimental and pressing, reasonably attractive spinster aunt. I could even hear Lola saying, 'She needs all our lovingkindness, honey; she's a sick girl.' I had nothing to blame him for, except giving up his comfortable bed for two months, to sleep on a lumpy divan. I'd known, too, all along, he was more than passingly interested in Veronica Treloar, the morningsick beauty queen. I'd even teased him about her. Yet somehow, I was always convincing myself that what I wanted to happen would happen.

I would pack up and leave tomorrow. The only relief, the only amazing grace, was that when Elsie started to break the expected, unexpected news, I did not say, as I had thought of saying, 'I think Tom should have been here with me to tell you.'

I thought I'd better go back, and I headed up the lane away from

Botallack. I would say simply I couldn't sleep, and as it was a beautiful night I felt like a stroll to clear my chest. In the silent village, a shadow came round the corner towards me. I got my knee ready to jerk and my fingers to gouge. I saw it was a policeman, and had an impulse to turn and run. I was dressed in Joe's clothes and he would think I was Joe. But it was only the elderly constable who had called after Hector's crash. 'Hi!' I said, and he beamed as he came up close and recognized me. 'Better, are you?' he asked. 'I heard you been some poorly.' I said it was only a chill, and I was better. He nodded, turning and falling into step. 'Lovely night, isn't it?' he said, and I agreed. He didn't seem perturbed that a lady was wandering around Pendeen in the middle of the night.

He chatted to me pleasantly, softly – as if not to waken the sleepers in the houses. 'I've been trying to locate where you come from,' he said. 'You got a bit of Cornish in your background, haven't you?' I said I was flattered to think he thought so, but no. He was disappointed. 'I'm usually pretty good at picking up people's accents,' he said, 'and I would have said you had a bit of Cornish there somewhere. Not much, perhaps, but a touch.' I said it was probably because I'd been here for several weeks and, having been to drama school for a time, I picked up accents quickly. 'No,' he said. 'I heard it the first time I spoke to you. Don't matter.' But he sounded crestfallen that his proud skill had let him down. 'I did a voice identification course in London, couple o' years ago,' he said, as if still amazed at his venturesomeness.

'I'm London Irish.' I laughed uneasily. 'Ah!' he said. 'Yes, I picked up the bit of Irish! I ought to have known, anyway, from that handsome red hair!' I felt lifted by the compliment, and told him so; then turned the questioning to him. His name was Denzil and he lived alone since mother died. He wasn't looking forward to retiring, he would be lonely. But he had his garden and enjoyed a game of snooker at the Men's Institute. I saw into his quiet life. Maybe I should have gone with him to the Carnival, I thought; maybe it would have worked out. But here we were, striding along in the night, concerned for each other; and tomorrow I would be gone and I'd never see him again – not if the stars lasted a trillion years. Nor would I care, that was the terrible thing. It hurt me inside – to be saying to someone 'Are you a good snooker player, Denzil?' when I'd seen him only once before and would never see him again, nor wish to.

When I got in it was five o'clock by the grandfather clock in the hall; but Elsie was still up waiting for me, and it turned out to be only twenty-five past eleven. I had lost a couple of weeks, during which I had indeed been 'some poorly'. According to Mr Wearne, their worry over me had taken their minds off the shock of Tom's news. I agreed with him that Elsie and Arthur couldn't have done more for me if I was their own daughter; they had been as good as gold. Knowing Joe's ways, I realized it could not have been an easy fortnight.

At first they had thought a registry office would be best; but after talking it over with Tom and Veronica, and her parents, they decided on a proper white wedding, at the chapel. And not too rushed. Veronica was already one of the family, coming nearly every day to see Tom or his mother. She was a 'dear little maid' really; and her family were very respectable. Morley and Olga had been friends of the Polglazes since school days. Arthur was already saying to Veronica that he 'liked them well covered', with an appreciative laugh when she complained of getting fat. Elsie had started to knit a little jacket. I promised booties.

Veronica was reserved towards me at first. I didn't know what nasty things I had said to her. But no doubt Tom had told her it was my nerves, and not to take any notice. She warmed up, when I was friendly. I guessed I had been even nastier to Tom, too, and I apologized for anything I'd said amiss when I wasn't well. He said he deserved it, to some extent, because he could see I thought there was more than friendship between us. He should have said something, but he hadn't liked to hurt my feelings. 'A Cornishman never likes to hurt anybody, Tom!' I said; and when he saw I didn't mean it sarcastically, he blushed, and ruffled his old 'auntie's' hair.

Elsie was, even more than usual, all smiles and tears. She would miss her boy, even though he wouldn't be far away. They had been lucky enough to be offered one of the council flats by the recreation ground. And later, Arthur would build them a little home. He had planned to build a small bungalow at Cape Cornwall, for their retirement; but now he would build it for his son. Tom would be near – but he was gone. You gain a daughter but you lose a son. During one of Elsie's weepiest spells I offered to stay and keep her company for a few weeks after the wedding; but no, she said, it was wonderful of me to offer but she and Arthur had to get used to being on their own. She was disappointed, though, when I said that in any case I really ought to get back without any more delay. Surely, she said, I would stay for the wedding, which was very close now? No, I said, I'd better get back home. 'Well, home is

146

home, isn't it, dear?' she said; adding that Tom and Veronica would be disappointed.

I did see Denzil, my bashful policeman, again. On my last evening there was a social at the Sunday School. Mr Wearne and I were foxes caught in the box and made to marry. I was the last woman to sit on a lap in musical chairs, and was given a box of Malteasers. Black widows, even older than Lola, sat back against the walls, cackling at our antics. In the tea break there was post-man's knock. Veronica Treloar called Tom out to the dark damp porch, and Tom sent for me. I gave him a big hug (turning my mouth aside), and asked the grinning schoolboy postman for Mr Roberts. I heard applause and catcalls. 'See 'ee morra' night, Denzil!' somebody shouted. When the door clicked open and framed him in the light, he was red-faced, boyish in a tight suit with too-short sleeves. He was still bashfully grinning when I kissed him, and he kept his arms awkwardly by his sides. He didn't know who to send for; eventually his call came for Veronica, his niece. She trotted past me on her high heels. And Veronica, of course, sent for Mr Polglaze.

I shed a few tears the next morning when Elsie hugged me and loaded me up with a basket of pasties and buns to last a week. And broke down altogether when Arthur gently shook my hand, on the platform, and said, 'We'll miss you. Come back and see us.' I remember my last sight of him, slightly hunched in his shabby overcoat, his raised trilby as the train started, his kind lined face receding, the melancholy smile.

He had found me an empty compartment to spread myself out in. But at Redruth, I was swamped by seven burly clones of Tom, bulging out of their blazers. My Rousseau print was wrecked on the rack. I gathered they were at the end of a beery rugby tour. They had polished accents, and I recalled 'Draft that man a letter of sympathy'. But the Polglazes were strangers from another planet. Hector and Lola were closer; because somewhere out among the mine stacks, under the granite hill, they had spent a weekend with the Urens, a short, infinitely welcome break from their crazily-assumed burden. I was now fairly sure it had been a wife-swapping weekend. That was why Mr Uren had sounded so bad-tempered when I rang about Hector being no better. I had interrupted his coitus. As the train lay becalmed in the dusty, sleepy station, I leaned out to get a breath of air, and distinctly heard Lola's voice saying, 'You better answer that, honey. It could be Jo. She's a very sick girl.'

I tried to fantasize a gang rape, with seven brutal forwards and me as their hooker. But the fantasy wouldn't come. And not because they were cultured Oxford Greyhounds, discussing Buñuel. I felt too raped already, by the Bolithos and Polglazes. Like a police questioning where the tough guy punches you in the stomach and the nice guy gives you a cigarette: and he's the one who breaks you.

I took up the sweater I had started secretly for Tom, and had promised to Arthur for Christmas. As the train drew out, I remembered red-coated huntsmen on the granite hill, on Boxing Day mornings. The hill was Carn Brea. I had lived in this place for four years, as an evacuee during the war. I jumped as I recalled it, and my head swam. I thought I was going to faint. I had been happy in this little town. I cried when I had to leave. I was holding a new Christmas Annual instead of knitting. If I jumped off the moving train, I could find my way there easily. There was a cat which came running down the road to meet you if you whistled. That, at least, would not be likely to happen. But were the people still there who had been kind to me? I had had a reason for coming to Cornwall, but I had gone too far down.

20

The first snow fell, unseasonably early. London was as white all over as the icing sugar on the little piece of cake that came from Veronica and Tom Polglaze. There was a letter from Lola:

Dearest Jo,
I hope your keeping swell. I guess your Home sweet
Home like Hec and me, you cant beat it. Sure good to see
Grass Valley and all our beautifull Freinds. We had a
lovely trip across, the sea really peped Hector up. What a
wonderfull time we had together, maybe youll come this
way some day, bring Frank (Wearne), Elsie tells me you
are corresponding, well you could do a lot worse, honey.
I was surprised to see him, he'd lost a lot of weight. Youd
be more than welcome, honey. Hector sends love, he
seem a little better, touch wood, tho' some days better
than others, not gone back to work yet, luckily he's well
covered. They dont think its Multiple sclerosis, we have
to trust in the One above, what say you dear? I have'nt
been to good, lots of sickness (stomach), but Im okay so

148

long as I put my feet up, health is a wonderful blessing.
Did you get your eyes tested honey? Look after them,
our sight is very precious. I just had my front teeth
Crowned, Hector says its a big improvement but it sure is
expensive. He remind me to tell you we think youve still
got a mag of ours, no hurry dear but send it back
sometime, our minister wants to read it. Hector left
behind at the Home his lovely gold Watch, it belonged
to his Father, and its disapeared, he was very broken up.

What a surprise about Tom I just hope it was'nt on the
Rebound, I had to have a good talk with him, she seem a
nice Girl, I guess he was testing her out dear, with you,
and so are Olga and Morley, lovely people, they had us
visit them when I come down for Hec, and Elsie and
Arthur of course. Arthur picked me up from the Station
and drove me everywhere, could'nt do enough for me.
He said I had the best legs he's even seen on a woman! I
know he thinks a lot of you, dear. He's one of the best. I
feel Ive left lots of freinds behind, we play your Record a
lot dear, it bring back happy memories. Forgot to
mention I went to Paris with Beryl and her (*Freind*) for a
long weekend, good for Beryl but it would have been to
tiring for poor Hec. I've been keeping up my swiming, at
the public pool, good for the Figure (hah!), my coach use
to coach Esther Williams, she say I could go far but I
have'nt the time to put in. I auditioned for our light opera
company, their doing 7 brides for 7 brothers, just the
chorus-line, but I shall have to rest more as time goes on
so do'nt think I can manage it, a pity its wonderfull
music. Also doing some solo work, last week I
entertained about a hundred partialy disabled Veterans
(Topless!!) I never thought I'd have the nerve to face
them, and a nite or two ago more than a thousand old
college fraternity members, boy you can imagine how
shaky I felt. Then theres Xmas with this year a
coast-to-coast Hook-up. So I keep pretty busy. A busy
life is a happy one. Have you ever done any stage work.
We think youd make a wonderful little Actress, honey.

Hector has written down a place on a bit of paper for
me to tell you, where he wants to go next year. Its called
NEKROPOLIS, he heard about it on the lunch hour tv
show on vacation places. Its one of the Greek islands and
all the women there have stayed *Belted*!! Of course he'd

149

love that! Id love to visit Greece. Have you been there, dear? Its good to see him cheerfull again and taking an interest in life. I guess he's holding his own, pretty well, and thats a Blessing. Luckily Ive had Nursing experiance and we have a nice colored Neighbour, a big Girl, who gives me a hand lifting him in and out of the tub, because he's a weight as you know. Weve known her for years, I delivered her little son and helped her when she laid out her father, so what you give in this life you get back, what say you honey? Like you will, dear, for your wonderfull warm Heart, I feel years younger for having met you. Never a dull moment! I dont care where we go so long as we both have our health and strength, of course we could never hope to meet anyone like you again, that was a real Stroke of luck, wasn't it, because you can never be sure about those things. Well honey it's time to get Hector's supper (one of Elsie's *Recipes*) so no more for now, write soon and keep smiling.

lovingly

Lola

The weather turned unseasonably warm again; I was wearing my sleeveless dress; I roasted in a swimsuit in the park. It was the Indian summer to end all Indian summers. I worried a lot about Hector and Lola, trying to puzzle them out, when I probably should have been spending my time getting another job, stopping Dr Salmon from sticking an ice-pick in my brain, finding my childhood and where it all began. I found a magazine called *Experience*, hidden between Milton and Germaine Greer, and one of the contact ads caught my eye: 'Attractive mature American couple, cultivated, witty, highly-sexed, non-smokers, touring West Britain August, seek personable travelling companions, single, female, double, anything goes, expenses paid or subsidized. Like sexy undies. Sincere. Straight, no time-wasters or weirdos. Send frank letter, photo, all replies answered', and then a box number. There was a Social Security leaflet stuck in the page, like a bookmark. It had me convinced for a while of letters flowing between London and Grass Valley, culminating in a dramatic confrontation in the snack bar at Victoria Coach Station. My sister, enchanted by a touched-up ten-year-old colour photo of Hector in his beautiful garden against a backdrop of the Sierras, and comforted by the undraped photo of his eighty-year-old grandmother, had fallen for the bait of a cheap holiday. It explained Hector's sarcasm about having an up-to-date photo of myself; for Joanne would have sent one of the old *Penthouse* set.

But there were too many flaws. 'Cultivated' brought back Lola's uninhibited farts, the bathroom door wide open; 'highly-sexed' brought back Hector's desperate attempts to sustain an erection. Hector, also, would have mentioned his fetish specifically, I thought.

Then, on reading *The Dice Man*, I decided Hector was really Luke Rhinehart commanded by the dice to assume the role of hypochondriac tennis-playing professor of astronomy, hooked on garter belts and his mother – as opposed to being, say, a homosexual missionary. Lola was probably a failed pre-war Hollywood starlet hired for the occasion, and given her own dice-commands to determine her role. I phoned International Calls, for information, and they came up with the address on Lola's letter. Whatever part the dice might be playing, it was something more subtle.

Fierce winds scattered the leaves off the trees and I was almost blown off my feet, but I kept going. I wrote to the house in Redruth where I had lived, but a short note came back saying they were dead or had moved away. I was no more living my own life than was Mary when she became the daughter of her son. I was at the Planetarium, and discovered that Hector had lied to me about the stars over the Meadery; the ones he mentioned were winter not summer stars. I was shaken by this lie more than by any of the others.

I was visiting my son, at the home, and he seemed bright and happy. He was studying for his 'O' levels, and could type wonderfully well with his toes; and could also, by twisting his shoulders, use his hands to do a lot of things, without embarrassment. This time, when he called me 'Auntie', I was reminded of the children at Pendeen, who called anyone 'auntie' who gave them little gifts but didn't have the right to order them about or tell them off. About this time, Frank (Wearne) wrote that he had had news that his common-law wife, Juanita, was dead and his teenage daughter was in an orphanage in Mexico City.

Any hopes or expectations Dr Salmon had that the three faces of Eve were merging into one were sadly disappointed. More of us appeared – Jo Anne, Kate, and Catherine. Jo Anne seemed a religious nut, to quote Hector (I think she made a brief first appearance at Glastonbury), and kept gathering crucifixes and such. Kate got me into trouble by shoplifting at the Coop. Catherine, as far as I could see, was a recluse. She knew a lot about

151

us, and was writing this novel. I couldn't tell how many of us there were; there was no telling where the story would end. If I lived anywhere on this earth it was in the huddled, solitary flight of the Pleiades.

I surprised myself with some poems – to Daniel Lombard, Doll Pentreath, and Hector's stepmother (assuming Hector or Lola or both weren't spinning another line) . . .

The Reverend Daniel Lombard-Swan
sings on the waves so wild and bleak:
'My living is still further on,
still further on the cure I seek.'

—

With the doll she had mothered,
with mother and father,
with boys and maids,

beasts and birds,
curses and songs,
in her crazy old head,

herbs and flowers conferred
day and night-long
around her bed.

All that she loved
in their own tongue
came home and stayed,

and quietly moved
around, as a crone
muttered and prayed

in her simple words,
dying alone.
Cornish obeyed

her, slowly, like the herds
she had driven home.
But the sea bled

back to the whispered
moor-grass and moorstone
of her stone head.

Nothing was heard.
It was home,
where nothing is said.

—

I make for myself,
or someone makes for me,
a small clearing in my death.
I become a pool
reflecting itself. It is
childhood's pool, utterly clear.

I contemplate it. Who knows
how many years pass?
I look into it, it is full
of sunlight. Who knows
how many years pass?
A waterdrop,

perhaps it is a tear, breaks
the clear water. Circles
spread the pool into
the same pool that turns
into the same pool
and everything the same.
It is childhood's pool, utterly
clear, I am nothing

and I think of nothing.
Once a year I know
it is Good Friday and the pool
is lost. I am broken
into agonized fragments
for three days, then it clears
into the same pool again

and, for a time, something more,
though who it is I am
not certain. I return
to my childhood's pool,
utterly clear. A waterdrop,
perhaps it is a tear, breaks
the clear water, circles
spread the pool into

the same pool, childhood's
pool, I am being cared for
by someone who clearly loves me.

—

I missed my job in the school canteen. One meaningless, blank,
rainy day I turned out my old handbag. In that trashcan of lives I
came across an envelope, postmarked February, self-addressed in
Joan's childish script; and inside it a list of Cornish bed-and-
breakfast places. Poor Joan, trying to reach back to a lost wartime
paradise. She's a good kid. I think I'd get on with her. I found also
an airmail letter, postmarked June, scrawled over with Lola's
almost equally childish writing. I could hardly bring myself to read
it; I waited till I was in the consoling bath . . .

'Dear Joanne,' it said,
Were so thrilled everything's working out nicely and well
be meeting in a few weeks. How come we forgot to
mention your photo in our last, its great the hose and
garters look great on you, your like a film-star! We had
replies from a married couple and a few singles but did'nt
like the look, they sounded common, your the Tops!
Well have a lovely time together, youll see. Will write
again later.

Love from
Hector & Lola Bolitho.

For a week I raged at Joanne's malicious fun at my expense. She
could easily have told me; she let me make a fool of myself. Then I
thought the best thing to do was to get my own back. If and when
she broke through again she would find herself married, and she
wouldn't like it one bit.

I was pleased when Dr and Mrs Salmon agreed to be the wit-
nesses. But after all, I missed my wedding. The register is signed
Catherine MacDonagh.

I was sick or absent for all but the last day of our honeymoon
voyage. In awe, I stood in the chaste and silent room where the
dead poet had stored, for her sister to find, bundles of poems, tied
up in ribbons, and I heard the true ghost of her voice speak, quiet,
clear, assured, a reticent volcano: 'I dwell in Possibility – A fairer
House than Prose'. In the long days of the Greyhound bus I wrote a
letter to the world, tried not to open a packet of cigarettes, and
gathered notes and poems into order, while, outside, nature was
scattering hers. And by night, in my lover's embrace, the endless

ripe wheat of Illinois, the salt flats of Utah, the dry mountains of Nevada, and the astonishment of California, paradisal, lush and green, a spring in the fall, fruit groves and vineyards, palms and redwoods, and the amazing blue of the Pacific sea and sky.

We rested at the home of Joyce and Bill, Arthur's sister and brother-in-law, in Santa Barbara. They were wonderfully hospitable. Joyce and Frank hadn't set eyes on each other for over forty years, since she was a girl. Leaving most of our luggage there, we split our journey. I took a coach northwards towards the rugged land where the Cornish forebears of Hector and Lola had turned their native tin into gold. It was late fall. The distant peaks were snow-covered and a few flakes whirled past the windows of the centrally-heated coach. I thought of Hector sitting in front of me every Friday night, and saw him glide past me in the opposite lane, each Sunday, clutching a hot-water bottle to his stomach.

I worried about Frank's reunion with his olive-skinned Cornish-Mexican daughter. Since her mother's death a year ago, she had survived by scavenging in the Mexico City underworld, by thieving, drug-pushing and prostitution, before being taken into care. It so upset Frank he couldn't talk about it.

As we climbed higher into the foothills of the Sierras the coach laboured. We craned our heads to draw in every inch of the beautiful scenery. The trees were as Hector predicted, a riot of colours ... 'the reds and golds of plane trees, sycamores, maples and poplars mingling with the dark greens of the silver-tip firs and the digger pines....' There were the ruins of great dead mines. There was Pengelly's shoe store.

The light was fading. I found Hector sitting on the veranda of his house.

'Hi, Hector!' I said.

'Hi!' He smiled. 'What a wonderful surprise!'

Hector was in a cane chair and wrapped up deep in blankets. Dark glasses peered out from a wilderness of white hair and beard. He was thinner and smaller and still dentureless.

'How are you, Hector?' I said at length. He indicated that his hearing aid wasn't switched on, adjusted it, and I repeated the question.

'I keep pretty good.' He smiled.

Sensing my glance at the white stick hooked on his chair arm, he said genially, 'I'm getting about a bit now.'

He added, 'Lola is keen for me to get a dog. You know how she is about animals.'

'How *is* Lola?'

'Oh, she gets about wonderfully.'

'Is she here?'

'No.'

'Will she be back?'

He pondered. 'I can't say when. She's probably out doing good works somewhere.' He chuckled. 'She's a wonderful woman, you know. She looks after me wonderfully well. It's not easy. There are a lot of – pretty unpleasant chores.' His dark glasses stared at me blankly.

There was an awkward pause. We smiled at each other rather foolishly. I told him I was married now, and flashed my ring. 'You could have done a lot worse,' he said.

'I only wish Lola could have been here,' he said. 'She ought to rest more, but there's no telling her. They're all the same at that age, I guess. She's doing so much volunteer work. She may be in one of the bars downtown. Or the Church Youth Club. Or it may be her afternoon for the Pre-natal Clinic. I don't remember. She tries to get down there at least once a week. I'll be sure to tell her you visited.' There was another pause.

His fingers scraped the arm of his chair. Obviously he wasn't going to invite me in. His cordiality contained a dismissal. I looked at my watch. It was either six o'clock or half-past twelve. If I hurried I might catch the same coach back.

I still stood there, unsure what to do. 'She'll be real upset to have missed you,' he said encouragingly. 'Let's see – is it Saturday? She takes turns with our minister's wife and daughter arranging the church flowers. It might be her Saturday. But she'd have left by now, I guess. Most likely in some bar. She won't be back till the early hours.'

I said that, all the same, I'd like to see their little church I'd heard so much about.

'Surely!' he said, grasping it eagerly, and he gave me the directions.

I asked him if he had found what he was after.

'Not quite. I'm still working through *that*.' He chuckled, bringing his bony arm from under the blanket and pointing. I thought he meant the snowy mountain peak but when I looked I was surprised that the night had fallen so quickly and the sky was a white blaze of stars, Orion hunting.

'It's a pity you weren't here last week,' he said. 'You should have seen Lola in the can-can! They did Bach's *Orpheus in the Underworld*.'

156

As I walked down the drive Hector called after me genially, 'Come and see us again!'

I walked in the direction Hector had pointed, past the house of Lola Montez, 'surrounded by red bougainvillaea and blue morning glory and a prim fence'. The new Methodist Church of Grass Valley had white walls and a red slate roof shaped like a Spanish mission; but the names on some of the gravestones were Cornish. I peered into the dim interior. A girl was arranging flowers at the altar. I dipped my knee, and crossed myself.

The girl lit a candle. Long fair hair flowed down her back. Her green dress, dotted with silver flowers and stars, was gathered under her small bosom, and fell away in a curve that disguised her slimness; and she wore high heels and green stockings. There was a late-adolescent intensity and grace about her that I hoped for, for Frank's sake, in Amy Martinez. The girl, who was in profile, glanced in my direction and noticed me, and in her brief but generous and gentle smile, barely a tilting at the corners of her lips before she turned away again, I recognized Lola.